The Lynching Waltz

A Novel

by

Stephen L. Kanne

This book is a work of fiction; however, some events described in it were inspired by actual events. In addition, some persons described in this book are real persons or were inspired by real persons although their actions and/or dialogue are fictionalized (see the various Lists of Characters and also *Additional Comments by Author* at book's end). Except as noted in the previous sentence, any resemblance to actual persons, living or dead, is entirely coincidental.

Published by:
Fireside Publications
Oxford, Florida

Printed in the United States of America

First Edition: 2016
ISBN-13: 978-1-935517-33-7
ISBN-10: 1-935517-33-3
LCCN: 2015951134

Publisher's Cataloging-in-Publication Data is available upon request from Fireside Publications.

Visit http://firesidepubs.com to order additional copies of this book or to order other titles published by Fireside Publications.

The Lynching Waltz—the story of how a small community came to the defense of its black children in 1947 and unwittingly sowed the early seeds of the Civil Rights Movement.

Inspired by an actual racist incident of the author's youth, this is a remarkable story of how the good people of tiny Glencoe, Illinois, blunted a racist assault against its black children. Because all participants are gone and because what precisely occurred is unknown, the book has become a work of historical fiction.

Seen through the eyes of a black grandfather, retired federal judge James Lincoln Washburn Jr., and his twelve-year-old grandson, Jamie, the reader is carried away on a whirlwind journey of discovery which includes:

- a meeting with Bucky, the greatest baseball player of all time who never played;

- an encounter with large, oafish Bruno Steiner, a WWI hero who eventually becomes a great friend of Glencoe's children;

- a brutal, senseless racist atrocity perpetrated by the Ku Klux Klan;

- a Tuskegee aviator's perilous adventure in the flak-filled skies over Europe; and

- the tale of a brilliant slave who changes the lives of thousands.

With their journey of discovery now at an end, Judge Washburn and Jamie return to Glencoe where they witness the uplifting manner in which its citizens deal with racial injustice.

And, finally, in an Epilogue of both surprises and closure, the author promises a sequel on the shameful internment of Japanese Americans during WWII, yet another event of his youth.

I covered the civil rights movement as a newspaper reporter years ago. It was an exciting time and occasionally a dangerous time. I was beaten by white mobs on two occasions. I remember my editor—after I telephoned from the field to tell him of the latest beating—saying (safely from afar by phone) "they can't do that to us, you get right back there."

You can get back there yourself now, courtesy of Steve's magnificent book. You will travel back in history and meet a cast of memorable characters—each with his or her own story that will let the reader see how we got to where we are now—both the good and the bad—in race relations.

Oftentimes when a book attempts to send a message, things get overly preachy and self-righteous. Not here. This book lets the story carry its own weight, takes the reader back using a whole cast of characters who feel real, feel right. It's a series of well told tales that has importance not only for what it says but how it says it.

This is Steve's second book and it's spellbinding. His first book was a fine read but this second book is an important read.

Bill Husted,
Nationally Syndicated Columnist

As a retired research scientist, my reading tends toward nonfiction. Nonetheless, *The Lynching Waltz* piqued my interest for two reasons: first, its emphasis on American history; and second, the way in which it deals with racism—a problem now more than ever plaguing our society. I had previously read Steve Kanne's first novel, *The Furax Connection*, and was mesmerized by his writing. I must admit this also motivated me to pick up *Lynching*. And he didn't let me down. I was captivated by his characters and his five stories—all leading me into the sixth, a true tale of an ugly incident of his youth and how the citizens of his tiny community came together in dealing with its racist perpetrator. At book's end Mr. Kanne promises a sequel on the shameful internment of Japanese Americans during World War II. I only hope it will be as fascinating (and important) as I found *The Lynching Waltz* to be.

Gerald E. Adomian, Ph.D.

Stephen Kanne is a masterful storyteller as he weaves a tale against a background, rich with factual history of the early 1800's to the present day. As seen through the eyes of a young boy, *The Lynching Waltz* becomes a fascinating journey as the author pays homage to the many real people who created and irrevocably changed the course of our country's evolving history. The book's insight into the effect of racism is chilling in its authenticity, and compels the reader to try to make sense of those who would advocate and condone such atrocities.

The relationship of the key characters is beautiful and heartwarming, adding an extra dimension to the story as the characters travel from city to city, and back in time to an inspiring and touching conclusion. With the history of the United States as the stunning backdrop, this book is an insightful and thoroughly enjoyable read from cover to cover.

Karen Roubinov
Head Counselor
Long Beach Unified School District

In *The Lynching Waltz*, Steve Kanne masterfully weaves a tale of past and present in targeting the evils of racism. His blend of fictional characters and historic fact lends an authenticity to his novel that keeps the reader fully engaged. This book, while not always comfortable to read due to his vivid descriptions of horrendous abuse and mistreatment, allows the reader not only to see how far we have come in the battle against racial injustice, but also how far we still have to go. I feel that *Lynching* is an important work in that fight and will deservedly earn a place alongside other current pivotal literature of that genre. Highly recommended.

Larry M. Keil
CAPT, U.S. Public Health Service (Ret.)

In a democracy there is no room for racism. The battle against bigotry and ignorance is ongoing. Steve Kanne in his spellbinding historical novel, *The Lynching Waltz*, takes us on an odyssey through the past and into the present revealing to us all, once again, why racism should be eradicated. The author's indefatigable research reveals little known pieces of American history which led to monumental changes in human rights. The characters reflect the sacrifice and determination that one must have to seek freedom and justice. Kanne depicts true events with the small triumphs earned in the nostalgias, fatigues and horrors of a country struggling to grasp equality. *The Lynching Waltz* is able to mix real characters with individuals of imagination to create a gripping, and at times mysterious, voyage into the past. This is not easily done, but by the attempt, Kanne has succeeded in bringing an authenticity and rich fullness of believability to his work. I have read Steve Kanne's first novel, *The Furax Connection*, and enjoyed it immensely; this second novel shows the triumphs of a writer poised to become fully established. *The Lynching Waltz* is masterfully written and is a must read for anyone who is a student of our history and social reform. Bravo, a true accomplishment!

Burton E. Baldwin, Retired Educator
Recipient of Colorado Governor's Award for Excellence in Education
Recipient of 2013 Teacher of the Year Award from Colorado Association for Gifted and Talented

In my early years (prior to 1950) I often encountered racism, sometimes glossed over and other times right out there in the open. For example, seeing "Whites Only" signs at various business establishments and public facilities scattered across the country was not all that uncommon in those days. Fortunately, things have changed since then—much for the better. Today persons of color hold prominent positions in government, business and the professions, and a number are nationally-recognized educators, journalists, entertainers and athletes. Yet we still have a long way to go in erasing racism from our culture. In writing *The Lynching Waltz*, Steve Kanne has joined those trying to bring that about.

I discovered Mr. Kanne's writing some years ago when I read *The Furax Connection*. That novel took me back to my days in uniform during the Korean War and I was able to connect with a number of his characters who so closely resembled my army comrades. As a result, I decided to read *Lynching*, his latest novel. Once into it, I climbed aboard his journey of discovery and, like young Jamie Washburn, began to experience the evils of racism, sometimes at its very ugliest. Finally, arriving at Mr. Kanne's last stop, the true story of how a tiny community dealt with racism in a remarkable and surprising way, I knew the trip had been more than worthwhile.

I highly recommend *The Lynching Waltz*. Moving and uplifting. An important read for everyone.

Albert Efron
Fellow of American Institute of Architects

Author's Notes

The "N-Word" and Racial Stereotypes: This novel was inspired by an actual event that took place in 1947 in a tiny Midwest suburban community. It recounts how that community came together to thwart an attempt to have racism's evil views imposed on its residents.

Racists often use the N-word and other ugly expressions describing racial stereotypes, and, thus, I have my racist characters use these expressions in order to convey the full import of their nauseating views. Knowing my motives, I hope and trust that you will not find this offensive.

Finally, I further hope that once you reach book's end you will come away with the strong belief that pejoratives like the N-word, racial stereotypes, and racism in general have no place whatsoever in our nation (or, for that matter, anywhere else).

Special Thanks: I wish to thank the management of the Strater Hotel, Durango, Colorado, for graciously permitting me to use a photograph of its magnificent upright piano on the cover of this book.

Special Note Regarding Lists of Characters: A "List of Characters" is included with various sections of this book. Two letters and an asterisk are used in these Lists of Characters: "B" denotes black; "W" denotes white; and an asterisk denotes a real person. Also, some characters appear in several parts of the book and may only be mentioned in one of the Lists of Characters. Finally, a few characters have been omitted from any List of Characters for storyline purposes or because of their insignificance.

Dedicated to the late Eleanor Roosevelt

CONTENTS

Prologue

Prologue – List of Characters
["B" denotes black; "W" denotes white; * denotes a real person]

Judge James "Junior" Lincoln Washburn Jr. (Jamie's grandfather) B

Sarah Washburn (Jamie's grandmother) B

James "Jamie" Lincoln Washburn IV (twelve-year-old) B

7:58 a.m., Friday, July 25, 1969
Judge James L. Washburn Jr. Residence
Glencoe, Illinois

As twelve-year-olds are wont to do, James "Jamie" Lincoln Washburn IV was given to fantasizing. But this was no fantasy. Or was it? Here he was three feet off the floor hanging by a large rusty hook from the wall of his grandparents' basement. As he swayed from side-to-side, he looked down at the concrete slab below and saw an oval of sticky blood beginning to congeal. He'd heard about hideous forms of medieval torture. And for no reason he could think of, he was now one of its victims. Yet, strangely, he felt no pain, although admittedly hanging there was uncomfortable. He pushed back—back into inexplicable softness.

Still, he was puzzled. Why had they put him here? As he thought more about it, he realized that it had to be the work of his evil grandmother. She hated him even though to the world she professed to love him. Yes, it was all part of her grand plan—to get rid of him for good. Slowly. Painfully. He could only imagine her cackling while she thought about it.

And what of his stodgy old grandfather who always had his nose in a newspaper? Certainly not his style to torture his grandson. But then who had carried him into the basement? It had to have been his grandfather.

Suddenly Jamie began to cough and wheeze. He thought it must have been the puncture in his back made by that hook somehow letting the basement's foul air seep into his asthmatic lungs and ...

And then he heard his grandmother: "Jamie! James Lincoln Washburn the Fourth. Get yourself out of bed, get dressed, wash your face and brush your teeth.

i

We'll be having breakfast in fifteen minutes—and we aren't changing meal times for the likes of you! Now up and at 'em! Hear?"

"What time is it, Grandma?"

"Just about eight o'clock, so get goin'!"

With reluctance, Jamie got out of bed, took off his pajamas, and walked over to the large chair on which he'd draped his clothes the night before. Methodically, he began to dress before making his way into the adjacent guest bathroom.

———

Actually, he'd been hungrier than he thought. Yet his full stomach had done little to lessen his anxiety: Where was his mother going when she'd dropped him off here five days ago? For how long was he sentenced to stay with his grandparents? And, most important of all, what would he be doing while she was gone—because he was bored stiff?

As he sat alone at the breakfast room table, Jamie closed his eyes and thought of his father. How he missed him! He'd be home if his father were back. He was sure of that. But his father wasn't back. He'd been recalled to active duty by the Air Force and, as a military lawyer, was stationed in some far-off place called "Vietnam," wherever that was.

His father: So much taller than his bent-over grandfather and sometimes very scary. But most of the time pretty nice and easygoing. Not at all like his grandfather who was wound up tighter than a spring, always banging his fist on some hard surface and barking out commands. Probably like the way he banged his gavel in his courtroom before he retired. Now, though, Grandma was continually reminding him that even though he may have been a judge, those days were over. She was in

*charge of all gavel-banging in this house. And he'd better
stop making so much noise around here!*

Probably, Jamie thought, his grandfather must be
pretty unhappy, what with all that squabbling with his
grandmother.

And then he heard his grandfather call out:
"Jamie, if you've finished breakfast, come on into the
family room. Your grandmother and I—we need a little
company."

———

*Well, here he was again, slouched on that same old
overstuffed (and, he was certain, moldy and cockroach-
ridden) sofa in his grandparents' family room. What to
do? With nothing better in mind, he decided to challenge
the order of things and commit the unthinkable ... turn on
the TV and begin changing channels. He reached for the
remote and depressed the on-off button and then the
channel selector button.*

*While he was doing this, his grandfather, retired
federal district judge James "Junior" Lincoln Washburn
Jr., the first black to be appointed to the federal bench, sat
nearby in a large easy chair and appeared to be reading
the Chicago Tribune. In fact, he wasn't. He was studying
the look on his grandson's face which at the moment had
morphed into one of defiance. He had been expecting
something like this ever since the boy's mother had dumped
him off without instructions. Damn her! She had no
business leaving a twelve-year-old with two ancient relics.*

*As Jamie again depressed the channel selector, a
morning rerun of "American Bandstand" appeared on the
ancient TV's screen. Just what he wanted! Music.
Laughter. Dancing. There it was—everything he lacked in
this controlled, cloistered environment. His face morphed
once again, this time into pleasure as he watched teenagers
black, white, orange, yellow and green dance to the top ten.*

And, as Jamie's grandfather looked on in surprise (while at the same time making a mental note to have somebody come by and adjust the color on that damn TV set), he awaited the inevitable—the outburst from his wife which he knew would shortly be forthcoming.

"Jamie! Turn it off!"

"No!"

"Sarah..." Her husband tried to interject.

"Jamie! No dancing!"

"For God's sake, Sarah, let the boy be. A little dancin' never hurt..."

"Oh, and didn't it now?"

Junior sighed, as he always did when he knew his wife was right.

"That was a long time ago." He was well aware that blocking out the past would never make it go away ... or make it better ... or stop history from repeating itself.

"Jamie, what your grandmother's tryin' to say is that sometimes things happen for a reason. Just like you stoppin' on that dancin' show. You know we don't allow dancin' in this house. It's about time you understood why."

Junior sighed again as he studied his grandson. Now was the time. Soon he would walk him through that long dark passage which leads from boy to man just as he had done years ago with his own son.

———

"Didn't your parents ever teach you any history about our little Village of Glencoe? Or where you come from or who you are?"

Jamie looked down ... knowing if he said "No" he was in for a long-winded speech, but also knowing if he said "Yes" his grandfather would likely quiz him on how much he remembered. He could feel his stomach begin to churn.

"How 'bout Bruno Steiner, Amelia Polk, Isaiah Washburn or Christopher Wallace? Those names mean anythin' to you?"

Again Jamie remained silent.

Junior sighed yet a third time and shook his head. "Christopher Wallace ... . Well he's about as good a place to start as any." He looked at Sarah who was already heading for the kitchen.

"You mind packin' us a couple'a sandwiches? Jamie and I are about to go on one of them, what you call, 'road trips.' We'll be headin' on up to Northwestern tomorrow so's I can introduce him to Christopher Wallace. Then I'll be takin' him to meet the others."

"Where we gonna go, Grandpa?"

"Back in history, boy. To a time when a man could make a difference."

Christopher Wallace's Interview

Christopher Wallace's Interview – List of Characters
["B" denotes black; "W" denotes white; * denotes a real person]

Christopher "Chris" Wallace (a young boy) W
Maryanne Bowes Wallace (Chris' mother) W
William "Bill" Wallace (Chris' father) W
John "Champ" Champion (Blue Devils' owner) W
Bucky (Blue Devils' janitor/custodian) B

Christopher Wallace's Interview

Chapter 1

In the delivery room of the newly opened Van Diest Medical Center located in tiny, lily-white Webster City, Iowa, Christopher Wallace entered the world on a dreary Saturday afternoon in late March 1903. Transported from the hospital to the Wallace family home one week later, his first blurred sighting—like that of his older twin brothers several years before—was of an oversized framed photograph of his father, William Wallace, which hung on the otherwise barren wall of the home's master bedroom. In it William Wallace was pictured twenty years earlier deftly fielding a ground ball as a member of the Webster City Warriors. Christopher, known to his family as "Chris," would puzzle over that photograph until he was seven when, finally, his father took him aside and explained to him that he hadn't always been a banker, that in his youth he played semi-pro ball for the Warriors. Deepening his voice, he further intoned: "As their second baseman, I played for three years just a few notches below the majors—and, for sure, I would'a been called up if I hadn't injured my right knee so bad." Christopher, his eyes squinting in deep concentration, pictured his father batting in the winning run for the Warriors to the adoring cheers of local fans. A professional baseball player! Yes! That was what he would be someday. And given his extraordinary athletic ability, his dream would have become a reality but for the occurrence of two events: his mother's intervention and an unfortunate bicycle accident.

Christopher's mother, Maryann Bowes Wallace, was an attractive yet outspoken woman who wore so many hats that friends and family often lost count. In addition to being a wife and homemaker, she was an English teacher at Webster City High School, the founder and president of the

1

Webster City chapter of the National American Woman Suffrage Association, one of two reporters-at-large on the staff of the *Webster City Freeman*, and a member of the board of trustees of the local public library. People who knew her marveled at her ability to multitask, although this was a skill she had mastered years before as a student at Iowa State University—from which she graduated at the top of her class in 1893. While at the university she presided over the Government of Student Body, was a flutist in the university's orchestra, and, in her third year, was elected managing editor of the university's newspaper, *The Student* (later renamed the *Iowa State Daily*).

Given her many talents, it came as no surprise to anyone in the Wallace family that Maryann Bowes Wallace had planned an extracurricular course of studies for her three boys, to begin shortly after each had begun to talk. Sadly, however, she failed with the twins when they succumbed to their father's obsession and wound up spending almost all of their spare time on the baseball diamond.

And then, as if from an entirely different gene pool, Christopher appeared on the scene. From the beginning he was different. In contrast to his brothers' blue eyes and long handsome faces, his eyes were an extraordinarily intense dark brown and his unusually wide face was punctuated by abrupt square jowls; and, unlike his curly-haired blonde brethren, Christopher's hair was straight and black. Even his demeanor was different. While his brothers were often jovial, he was unusually serious, and he rarely smiled or laughed.

Being the third child to follow the identical route from womb to hospital room, Christopher's birth had not been a difficult one. In fact, years later Christopher overheard his mother confide to her sister, Ellen, that, "unlike the twins, why that Chris just slid on out." Because his arrival had been effortless and uncomplicated, and

2

because he was so different from the other two boys, Christopher became his mother's favorite and heir to her greatest passion: words. Whether spoken or written, Maryann Bowes Wallace was a lover of words. Thus it was that from age six she began to inculcate in Christopher a love for etymology. Stack upon stack of written materials would mysteriously appear in his bedroom which he knew he was expected to read. These included books, magazines, plays, essays, and speeches. And sometimes his mother would even insist that he read portions aloud.

"Communication, dear, is the universal key to everything of importance."

"But why, Mother?"

"Because, Chris, words are precursors to action. They dictate action. Whatever it is that you want will be set in motion by the words you use. Spoken words. Written words. You must expand your vocabulary. And then you must learn to use your words. Doing that, you will achieve whatever it is in life you desire."

"But what about Dad? Didn't he become a professional athlete because of his natural ability?"

"Yes, dear, that plus being told how to play baseball. Do you ever suppose he could have learned to play that game without instructions? And words, Chris, were used to convey those instructions to him. So even though he may have had innate ability, words transformed him into a gifted athlete—and later into a banker. Words gave him his skills. Words mold us all. Add to your word bank, Chris. Then draw upon it carefully and your life will be changed forever."

———

As if his mother's doggedness in forcing him to hone his verbal skills weren't enough to scuttle permanently all aspirations of becoming a baseball great, a bicycle accident in Christopher's sixth grade year did just

3

that. While coasting down a steep hill on his way to school with his hands behind his head and his baseball shoes dangling from the handlebars, one of the shoes became wedged in between the fork and spokes of the front wheel causing his bike to come to a sudden and unexpected stop. Christopher was catapulted some twenty feet forward landing face down in the middle of Seneca Street. His two front teeth were bent back into the roof of his mouth; he also suffered a broken nose and a compound fracture of his right arm just below the elbow. Dr. Orin Spiro, the family dentist, pried the teeth back into place, and the town GP, Dr. Whitman, taped a splint to his nose and put his arm in a cast. The teeth and nose healed perfectly, but when the cast was removed Christopher discovered that his right arm was half an inch shorter and that he could no longer throw a baseball. Unless he learned to play left-handed, his baseball career was over.

Strangely, however, Christopher didn't seem to care all that much. Even before the accident, his mother's persuasiveness had begun to steer him away from baseball and in an entirely different direction.

Christopher Wallace's Interview

Chapter 2

On April 6, 1917, almost two years after a German submarine sank the liner Lusitania sending one thousand one hundred ninety-eight innocents to their death, the United States declared war on Germany. Christopher's twin brothers, who had just turned eighteen, joined the U.S. Air Service. Christopher and his parents saw them off at the train station in Webster City. Shortly after their departure, Christopher's father received an offer from The First National Bank of Chicago to take charge of its personal banking group as a senior vice president. The position would require a move to Chicago, and it would also entail a great deal of traveling. But the salary was more than double his current salary—plus an excellent opportunity for advancement.

"How do you feel about the Windy City, Chris?" his father asked. "The White Sox and Cubs play there, you know."

Christopher was thrilled. He had never been to a major league game. Yes, moving to Chicago would be great.

His mother was also ecstatic. Teachers were in short supply in the Chicago area and she felt certain she could find a position more than comparable to her job at Webster City High. But more than that, she yearned to become affiliated with one of Chicago's large newspapers. And, from what she'd heard, home prices in Chicago were only slightly higher than those in Webster City.

In the end it was the salary increase that enticed the Wallaces. Two months later they had sold their Webster City home and were ensconced in an apartment in Oak Park, Illinois, a middle-income suburb eight and one-half miles west of Chicago's Loop, the downtown area where

The First National Bank was located. Christopher enrolled in Oak Park High School and within a few weeks he seemed to be adjusting. His mother immediately found a teaching job, but joining one of the Chicago papers was not as easy. That, she came to discover, would require more time—months in fact.

———

In the summer of 1918 Christopher's father scheduled a business trip to Kansas City. "So whaddya think, Maryann? Can Chris come along? It'd only be for a week."

Christopher's mother eyed her husband suspiciously wondering why he would want to take Chris with him. After all, this would be a first. "He's busy, Bill. I've got him running around Oak Park pretending to be a reporter. He wants to become one of the editors of his high school newspaper in the fall and I'm trying to teach him the ropes. Why should he go?"

"Oh, you know, just some time for the two of us to be together. That's about all." William Wallace hesitated. "Plus he'd be exposed to some great copy."

"Great copy?"

"Yep," William Wallace replied, "I'll be working with the Blue Devils' front office. Their owner wants to establish a credit line with the bank. Might give Chris a chance to see firsthand how the business side of a professional ball club functions. Not many kids his age get that kind of opportunity."

"Hmm. I suppose he'd like that. All right, Bill, I'll let him go. But on two conditions." She looked directly at her husband.

"First, only for a week. No longer. And, second, he'll have to agree to write up the trip. I'll want a feature length article."

"Only for a week, dear," her husband responded. "I

6

can't be gone longer than that. But you'll have to work out the 'writing up' part with Chris."

Christopher Wallace's Interview

Chapter 3

Ten days later, when she returned home from a long hard day, Maryann Bowes Wallace found a neatly typed stack of papers on her desk. Without so much as greeting her husband or son on their return, she quickly closed the door to the study and began to read:

An Unexpected Interview
By Christopher Wallace

Kansas City, Kansas. I was seated alone in the reception room of the Kansas City Blue Devils' executive offices nervously awaiting my interview with baseball luminary John Champion, the Blue Devils' owner. It was oppressively hot and humid—a typical Midwest July afternoon. I glanced over at the frosted glass door on which "John Champion, President" was painted in large black lettering. No signs of activity from within. I was beginning to wonder whether I'd been forgotten. Or maybe I'd gotten my times mixed up.

Just then a tall Negro with unusually wide shoulders, long sinewy arms, and large hands entered the room. He was dressed in a soiled gray sweatshirt tucked into brown work pants held up by a belt fashioned of clothesline. A tattered Blue Devils baseball cap covered his head, and his curly black hair bunched out from under it up over his ears and down the nape of his neck. He wore old baseball shoes, their cleats flattened by time— obvious hand-me-downs (maybe from a Blue Devils player). Their cracked leather gleamed from countless

8

coats of black shoe polish. In his right hand he held the handle of a push broom.

"You waitin' to see Champ?"

I nodded. "I've been here close to an hour. I'm supposed to interview him. Should I come back?"

"Nah. That's Champ's style. Likes to make 'em wait." He laughed. "What's your name, boy?"

"Christopher Wallace. People call me Chris."

"Chris, huh? Well okay Mr. Chris. You jes' follows me. Champ done told me to show you 'round. We won't be needin' my broom. Can't fungo with that." He chuckled as he rested the broom's handle against the wall. "C'mon now."

Then, as an afterthought, he said, "I'ze Bucky."

———

Bucky led me out the door and down the hall to a stairwell. We descended four flights of stairs. I was certain we were underground because Mr. Champion's offices were on the second floor.

"This way," Bucky said as he led me through a pair of double doors into a dark area.

"Hold on." Bucky flicked a switch, some lights came on and I saw we were at the entrance to a tunnel.

"We be there in a few minutes." Then he squinted. "What's that you're carryin'?"

"My notebook."

"Notebook, huh? So you be one of them writers?"

"That's what I'm trying to do. My mother works for a Chicago paper and I was hoping she'd get my interview in it."

"So that's it. What you writes you expects people to read?"

I nodded. "But it doesn't always turn out that way. It's up to my mother and her paper. Mostly, though, what I write will probably get in my high school paper."

"Pshaw." Bucky spat. "That ain't nothing. Not many people reads the high school paper, do they?"

I didn't reply. As we continued on down the tunnel, I was becoming increasingly uncomfortable. Who was this "Bucky" anyway? Was I really supposed to be following him?

"So how many reads it, boy—that high school paper of yours?"

"Oh, I don't know. I'd say there are close to two thousand students in my high school."

"So they all reads what you writes?"

"Maybe six, seven hundred."

"Shoot! That ain't nothing." Bucky spat again. "We's gonna talk about important things, you an' me. Then you's gonna write it up—an' I wants people to read it. Lottsa people. You think maybe you can get it in your momma's paper?"

"I'll try."

"You do more than that, boy. You gets it in there!" Bucky surprised me with his forcefulness. And I was beginning to become interested. What "important things"? Just then I saw a green glow. We were approaching the end of the tunnel.

———

Within a minute we walked out onto grass. We were standing midway between home plate and first base on the most beautiful baseball field I'd ever seen. Looking around I took in tiers of stands—seating for thousands of fans. We were at Blue Devils Field. I'd heard about it. But I never expected anything like this.

"Ain't this the cat's ass! The most beautiful sight in the world! I jes' loves it. Look at the symmetry, boy. The diamond. Not square. A sparklin' diamond." Licking his lips as he spoke, Bucky seemed to be spellbound.

"That there—the mound. Know how far it is from home plate?"

I shook my head.

"Exactly sixty feet, six inches."

I began making notes.

"Know why, boy?"

I shook my head a second time.

"Throwin' distance. Closer an' the batter don't see them balls comin' in too good so there be less hits; farther an' he gets too many. Champ set it all up."

I was busily writing.

"An' the bases, boy. Ninety feet apart. Closer means too many ground outs an' double plays; farther apart means too many hits." He smiled.

"It's a symphony, boy. *An' the most wonderful thing in all the world is bein' in that orchestra.*"

I was writing as fast as I could.

"To hear the crowd roarin' when you makes that special pitch or hits that homer. That's better than food, liquor, women, money. All that stuff."

Bucky walked over to home plate and moved a small portable backstop fashioned of wood and chain link fencing into place directly behind it.

"Now you stands behind that," he pointed, "an' watch you don't get hit. I'll go get me some balls. But jes' remember: the pitcher's like a wood carver. He carves a

11

path for that ball. Up, down; one side to the other; all which ways to fool them batters."

Bucky disappeared and then, a few moments later, reappeared with a canvas bag full of old baseballs. He walked to the pitcher's mound, poured the balls onto the ground and then, taking his hat off to wipe the sweat from his forehead, began pitching as I ducked behind the backstop.

———

"So, you wanna try, Chris?"

"No, sir," I said. I was gaining respect for Bucky. Fifteen consecutive pitches bore in at breakneck speed, each a strike. Yet each pitch was different. Some slid; others curved; some seemed to wobble up and down or from side to side.

"How many different pitches did you throw?"

Bucky laughed. "C'mon. I'll show you somethin' else." He gathered up the balls and walked to home plate. I noticed he was carrying a bat.

"No pitcher, so I'll jes' fungo." He pointed to left field. "Gotta get 'em up over the stands. Outta the park."

"But just hitting into the stands is a home run, Bucky."

"Yeah, but that's not the way I does it."

He began hitting balls. Each sailed up above the left field stands and out of sight.

"Now we does the same thing in center. That's even farther."

As Bucky spoke, I sensed that he was about as high as God would allow any human being to be—at least without crossing over into heaven.

12

Again, with continuing gusto, Bucky sent ball after ball over the center field bleachers. And he did the same thing in right field!

"Bucky, enough!" I cried. He glanced at me, a puzzled look on his face.

"Save it!" I continued.

Those two words, *"Save it."* I will forever damn myself for uttering them. When they left my lips the joy of the moment also left Bucky. Gone in an instant and forever. As if in confirmation, I saw his magical fungo bat slip to the ground, his shoulders slump and a look of sadness come over him.

And then I heard him repeat those two words: *"Save it!"* Followed by a question I will never forget: *"For what, boy—so's I can be in that orchestra?"*

———

Just before walking out onto Blue Devils Field Bucky told me we were going to be discussing some "important things." Now I sensed that the time had arrived.

———

"Come over here, boy. Forget that notebook. I wants to show you somethin'." Bucky held out his forearm.

"Take a look an' tells me what you sees."

"I, I ... I see your arm, Bucky," I stammered.

"No! What does you really sees?"

"A forearm. An elbow, a wrist."

"What else, boy? Tell me!" Bucky commanded.

"Skin, bones. Same as mine."

13

"Same as yours? That's shit, boy! Hold yours out against mine an' tells me!"

"Well, yours is black; mine's white. But otherwise they're the same."

"That's the difference, boy. I gots black paint under my skin; you gots white. An' that's the only damn difference, right?"

I nodded.

"An' that's why I can't be in that orchestra. Champ done told me so. An' like you, I didn't ask for no paint color when I was born, black or white. God jes' done give it to me."

Bucky again took off his hat, this time to wipe away a tear that had begun to roll down his cheek.

"I'ze the best there is, boy. I can pitch, hit ... everythin'. Wanna see me run bases?"

"No, I believe you."

"*Then why, boy, why? Why can't I play? Why can't I be in that orchestra? Why that damn paint make all the difference? Why?*"

"Maybe in a few years."

"Few years?" he scoffed. "Hell, I be thirty-two next year. That's almost too old."

"I'll do what I can. I'll get that article in the Chicago paper. Maybe when people read it they'll let you play."

"If'n I do, I'll dedicate that first home run to you, Chris."

"And I'll be there to see you hit it, Bucky. I promise."

——

In the train on my way back to Chicago the next day I thought about my unexpected interview. I knew that someday someone like Bucky, *with black paint under his skin*, would hit that first home run. More than anything else, I wanted to be there when he did. And Bucky would be there too. Maybe he'd be the hitter. Or maybe he'd just be seated next to me taking it all in. Or maybe he'd be there in spirit only. No matter, I knew that at that special moment in time Bucky would again be as high as God would allow any human being to be, even if by then he had crossed over into heaven.

Christopher Wallace's Interview

Chapter 4

When she had finished reading the article, Maryann Bowes Wallace sat at her desk for several minutes transfixed. Then, purposefully, she stood up, opened the door to the study and called out to her son: "Chris, we need to speak. Now!"

From the moment he had arrived back at his home, Chris had been on edge. He had no idea what his mother's reaction would be to his article. And now, from the tone of her voice, he knew he would shortly be realizing his worst fears. He was certain he had failed. Reluctantly, he entered the study.

"Sit down, young man, and ..."

"I'm sorry, Mother," he interrupted. "I know I shouldn't have written that." He nodded in the direction of the article. "It's just that ... I had to."

"Had to? I don't understand."

"It's what I learned on my trip with Dad. About what you've kept from me all these years: the horrors of racism. And that's not right, Mother. Because when you hide something like that what you're really doing is allowing it to spread.

"And so, when I wrote my article, what I was trying to do was show how racists destroyed the life of someone as gifted as Bucky. Maybe if people read what I've written, their attitudes will change. Maybe they'll begin to understand that a person with black skin is no different than a person with white skin—and that we all have feelings.

"Maybe ..." And then Chris paused. Had he said too much? He looked over at his mother who was staring at him intently.

"I know I'm trying to change things; but unless there's change, the Buckys of the world will never get a chance to play in that orchestra. And that's not right."

Now Chris had finished. Would there be repercussions? He looked at his mother who, surprisingly, remained silent for almost ten seconds.

In fact, Maryann Bowes Wallace was stunned by what she'd heard from her fifteen-year-old son. Looking at racism through his eyes seemed to open her own to its horrors.

"Chris," she said, her voice softening, "your article is extraordinarily important—and deeply moving. It cries out for readers. And, like you, I feel it must be read. Maybe if I can get it into my paper, that Bucky friend of yours will be able to play. I'll try my best." She thought for a moment.

"Has your father seen it?"

"No, ma'am."

"Well, it involves one of the bank's important clients so we'd better show it to him before I meet with my editor.

"One other thing, Chris: Over the years I've tried hard to help you expand your vistas. I think I've succeeded. But, at the same time, I've sheltered you from much of the world's ugliness. And I'm terribly sorry. I should have ..."

"It's all right, Mother. I'm blessed to have a teacher like you—and for that I'll always be grateful. Still, it's about time that I begin to learn from my own experiences."

"Like your chance interview with Bucky, Chris?"

"Yes, Mother, like my chance interview with Bucky."

4:06 p.m., Saturday, July 26, 1969
Northwestern University, Evanston, Illinois

As they exited the main entrance to the Writers' Museum at Northwestern University's Wallace School of Communications, Judge Washburn turned to his grandson. "Well, Jamie?"

Jamie was holding a pamphlet the guard had given him on the way out. It contained a history of the early life of Christopher Wallace—a history which he had just learned about from his grandfather—and the text of the famous Wallace article entitled "An Unexpected Interview."

"Was the article ever published in the Chicago papers, Grandpa? And was that the original in the glass case?"

"Never published, boy. Way too controversial for 1918. And I think what's in the glass case is the original, but I'm not sure. We could find out easy enough."

"How?"

"Your mother. She's been a docent here for years. And three years ago she was elected to the museum's board. She's been very active in helpin' to raise money. Come take a look."

The judge led his grandson back to the main doorway. Next to it, a large plaque was embedded in the building wall. It contained a number of lists of names of those who had given to the museum. Under the first category of donors, "Founders," appeared the name D. N. Washburn.

"I didn't know she had anything to do with this museum, Grandpa."

"There's lots of things you don't know, Jamie. Maybe that's why we're on our little journey of discovery. You're gonna wind up knowin' a whole lot more than when we started."

The old man smiled. "Any more questions, boy?"

Jamie shook his head.

"You disappoint me. Don't you want to know whether Christopher Wallace attended that baseball game? You know, the one he wrote about in his article where a black player hit that first home run?"

Jamie nodded.

"Well," the judge continued, "he almost did. He was at Ebbets Field in Brooklyn on April 15, 1947, when he saw the first black play in the major leagues."

"Jackie Robinson?"

"Right, boy. Christopher Wallace was there with his mother and Bucky. Christopher's father wasn't there. He'd died some years before."

"Did Jackie Robinson hit a home run, Grandpa?"

"Not that day. But he did in his third game. And before he retired he hit a whole lot of 'em—one hundred thirty-seven to be exact."

"What about Christopher Wallace, Grandpa?"

"What about him?"

"I mean, what became of him?"

"As you'd expect, he turned out to be one of the great advertisin' men of his time. He founded Wallace & Truscott, an international advertisin' and public relations firm. He gave millions to Northwestern. And he also made his mark in our little Village of Glencoe."

"Something about dancing? Right, Grandpa?"

Judge Washburn looked at his grandson with pride. That boy sure knew how to keep things in focus!

"Yep, somethin' about dancin'. But before we get into all that, there's somebody else I want you to meet." The old man looked at his watch. "Too late for that today. We'll do it in a few days. We better be gettin' on back to the house."

As they walked to the car, Judge Washburn noticed that his grandson was unusually quiet and that he shuffled

19

along instead of walking—and once or twice dejectedly kicked a stone out into the street.

"What's the matter?"

"Nothing. It's just that ..."

"It's just that ... what, Jamie?"

"Who is he—the one you want me to meet?"

"Name's Bruno Steiner."

"Well, couldn't we meet him tomorrow?"

The old man chuckled. "I guess we could at that. We'll leave in the mornin' right after breakfast."

Excerpt from Jamie's Notebook, Page 2

I don't know what Grandpa's got up his sleeve, but it's more than just getting us out of Grandma's hair. I personally think it's all about that dancing thing which somehow must be a pretty big family deal—mainly because dancing is against the law in my house and in Grandma and Grandpa's house. But I sure don't understand why Grandpa and I are on what he calls a "road trip." Not much of a road trip anyway if all we've done is drive up to Northwestern and back.

And Christopher Wallace is a real puzzle. I mean he's an important man and all that, but what does he have to do with dancing? I thought maybe Grandpa was going to tell me that he was a great dancer like, say, Arthur Murray. But after hearing all those things about Christopher Wallace, I don't even know if he can dance.

I now remember the one time I saw Christopher Wallace. I didn't talk to him. I just saw him. What impressed me most were his dark eyes which kind of stared out at you. He reminded me of a comic book character like Superman who has x-ray vision that can look inside you. Maybe that's how Christopher Wallace became so successful—looking inside people and figuring out what they were thinking.

Bruno Steiner's Loss

Bruno Steiner's Loss – List of Characters
["B" denotes black; "W" denotes white; * denotes a real person]

Corporal Bruno Steiner (army enlistee from the Chicago area) W

Captain Patrick Riley (commanding officer of Bruno's company) W

Sergeant Michael "Mac" McCrary (first sergeant of Bruno's company) W

Colonel David Davenport, M.D. (Rainbow Division physician) W

General Boatwright (Commandant of the Rainbow Division) W

Nurse Odile Nadow (Bruno's nurse from Ethiopia) B

Jean-Pierre (male nurse's aide) W

Joey Smythe (Bruno's army comrade) W

Patel Nadow (Odile's father) B

Gnesh Nadow (Odile's eldest brother) B

Karemi Nadow (Odile's mother) B

Tucker McConnell (Chicago attorney representing the Nadow family) W

Bruno Steiner's Loss

Chapter 1

The eighty-seven remaining members of Company B, First Battalion, 165th Regiment, 83rd Brigade, 42nd Infantry Division (the celebrated "Rainbow Division"), American Expeditionary Forces, were entrenched some three hundred yards west of the easterly edge of the Argonne Forest through which they had fought over the past ten days. Because the company had suffered so many casualties, it bore almost no resemblance to a functioning military unit. In fact, except for its sole surviving commissioned officer, the CO, Captain Patrick Riley, its First Sergeant, Michael "Mac" McCrary, and four others in leadership positions, the company was in dire need of officers and noncoms. It was for this reason that Private Bruno Steiner had been promoted to corporal the previous day.

———

As Corporal Steiner sat with the rest of the men in the trench that afternoon in the third week of October 1918, he tried to block out the moaning.

"They're not ours," Sergeant McCrary warned. "Stay in here!"

Bruno wondered how he knew that. What if they weren't German? What if they were American? Or French? Or British?

Sergeant McCrary could see that the moans were agitating the men. "Stay in here!" he bellowed again just as Bruno lifted himself up over the top of the trench's edge and began crawling toward the wounded man. As he did, he felt the "puff puff puff" of machine gun bullets overhead and heard grenades detonating around him. Intermittently the entire battlefield trembled from the impact of large

25

artillery shells. Consumed by fear, Bruno felt death closing in on him as he inched forward. And then a hand, sticky with blood, grasped his—the hand of a British soldier.

Bruno Steiner's Loss

Chapter 2

Dr. Davenport was at a loss as to what to do next. He had never seen a Negro officer before. His first reaction was to treat Corporal Steiner and then attend to the Negro—but the Negro's injuries were serious and he might not survive. In the end, he based his decision on the color of blood, not skin, and the British officer became his first priority.

———

"Goddamnit! Get that nigger out of this ward," General Boatwright raged.

"But, sir, the man's a brigadier. He outranks everyone here except you," his aide replied.

"Negroes don't serve alongside whites in the U.S. Army and that's where he is right now. Get him to an all-black unit."

"But sir, the doc said he's too seriously wounded to move."

"I'm not putting my ass on the line by letting a nigger sleep in the same room with whites. Cordon him off so there's no contact with any of our officers. And as soon as he can travel, send his black ass back to England.

"Now what about Steiner?"

"He's been sent to Chenonceau."

Bruno Steiner's Loss

Chapter 3

If the phoenix were a chateau it would be Chenonceau. Like the mythological bird of old, the stately residence had been torched and rebuilt, destroyed and reborn, cyclically, since it was first constructed in 1412. In 1535 it had been seized for unpaid debts to the Crown and later offered as a gift to Diane de Poitiers, mistress of Henry II. Obsessed with its beauty, she had its structure extended over the River Cher joining it to the opposite bank.

But Chenonceau's most unlikely reincarnation was its use as a military hospital ward for World War I wounded. And, oblivious to the beauty and history that surrounded him, this is where Corporal Bruno Steiner now lay—along with many others—on a mattress resting upon the magnificent black and white tiled flooring of the chateau's main interior bridge-gallery. If it hadn't been for the determination of his nurse, Odile Nadow, he might have slipped away, never regaining consciousness. But, like Bruno, she would have gladly sacrificed herself before giving up on the life of another.

———

"It's over, Corporal Bruno. The war! The armistice was signed a day ago. It's over!"

Corporal Bruno Steiner was having difficulty trying to piece together where he was and what he was hearing. He seemed to recall being transported somewhere—but where, he wasn't sure. And the voice that had just spoken to him: he had never heard it before It was a soft feminine voice with a British accent telling him something about an armistice. Yet all that he could assimilate were a series of words, nothing more. What he was hearing was obscured by incessant ringing in his ears and aching and throbbing in his head. He tried to swallow. Everything hurt and he kept his eyes shut, unwilling to open them.

"Corporal Bruno, wake up! I have your breakfast tray. Eat! It is a beautiful morning. Perhaps we can go out later."

And then he heard, "Do you need the urinal or a bedpan?"

Bruno finally opened his eyes. He glanced to one side and saw a stark gray limestone wall marred by dark rectangular outlines where framed objects once hung blocking out the sun's rays. Turning his head, he looked up, focusing on the person above him: the dark face of the woman who had been trying to minister to him. A classic face possessed of friendly brown eyes and an aquiline nose. She was smiling at him, her white teeth accented by her burnished complexion. He wanted to ask her who she was, but the ringing and aching prevented him from speaking. Trying as best he could, he sat up. He felt a tray placed on his lap followed by a spoon pressed to his lips.

"Please, Corporal Bruno! You haven't eaten in days. You must eat if you want to get well. Please!"

With effort, Bruno opened his mouth. In succession, he tasted soft-boiled egg, bread soaked in warm milk, and sugared tea.

And then he spoke for the first time since his arrival. "My ears ring; my head aches. It's hard to hear." He turned toward her. "Is it really true—that the war is over?"

"Yes, Corporal Bruno, the killing ended yesterday. That horrible war is finally over."

Bruno was stunned. He was having trouble comprehending an end to the carnage which he thought would go on forever.

"Who are you? And where am I?"

"I am your nurse, Odile Nadow. And you're in

France at Chateau Chenonceau. It once belonged to Henry II's favorite mistress. But now it's a military hospital."

"But you're Negro or African or …? And you're beautiful."

She smiled. "Yes, I'm African. But I was schooled in London."

She looked down at this hulk of a man she had been caring for since his arrival, waiting for the day he would open his eyes. She had overheard a medical officer, a captain, describe how he had been wounded: "He almost died of stupidity, for saving a damn Negro—and for what? If the war doesn't end soon, he'll be facing a court-martial!"

And it was at that moment she lost her heart to this oversized shell of a man lying limp and bloody on a stretcher. She had hoped, but never dreamed, that if he survived he might find her pleasing. But the reality was that she was African, a Negro … and he was white.

She looked at him now. So different than when he arrived. Still weak and undernourished, but alive.

"You know, Corporal Bruno, I believe I like you more when you're awake than when you're asleep—which is not what I say about most of my patients."

Bruno's heart skipped a beat. Never before had a woman said anything like that to him. Big as he was, back home in Waukegan, Illinois, he'd been the brunt of cruel ridicule—by girls most of all. They had given him the nickname "Tiny" because, as one of them told him, he was so big and clumsy. "Tiny! Tiny! Tiny!" they would chant, followed by their continual giggling. And when he could bear it no longer, he would turn and run away as fast as he could.

But this woman was different. Hadn't she said that *she liked him?*

As Bruno began to savor the moment, he heard one of the hospital orderlies call out: "Mademoiselle Odile!

Mademoiselle Odile! He is here. With his aide-de-camp, a captain."

"*Who* is here, Jean Pierre?"

"General Boatwright, Commandant of the Rainbow Division. He insists on seeing Corporal Bruno right away!"

"I will speak to him, Jean-Pierre."

Odile got up and exited the hospital dormitory room where Bruno and five others were recuperating. Outside in the waiting area she saw a major general and a captain, both wearing the patch of the Rainbow Division. "May I help you?" she asked.

With raised eyebrows, the aide looked over at General Boatwright.

"Girl," the general said, "go get us a nurse. We need to speak to Corporal Steiner."

"I am his nurse," Odile replied.

"Where we come from darkies empty bedpans. So get us a real nurse."

Odile could feel her blood pressure rising. She wheeled around and disappeared down the hallway. A few minutes later she returned with her supervisor.

"Yes, General?" the supervisor said.

"We need to see Corporal Steiner now. We've got some medals to give him. And we've both got busy schedules."

"I'm afraid that's impossible. Perhaps tomorrow or the next day. His nurse feels that he needs complete rest at the moment."

"His nurse!" General Boatwright scoffed, pointing to Odile. "I don't take orders from anyone—especially not from a damn nigger lady."

"I dare say you will, General. Nurse Nadow is an experienced registered nurse, a top graduate of one of London's finest medical academies; she's from a prominent Ethiopian family; and she is an honored guest of His Majesty. So unless you wish to create an international

31

incident, I suggest you leave at once. And by the way, do not ever refer to Nurse Nadow again in that derogatory manner! Do you understand?" The supervisor's face had turned red as she stared directly at General Boatwright.

Turning to his aide, the general said, "C'mon, Captain, we're not welcome here." As the two were about to leave, Corporal Bruno Steiner stumbled into the waiting area. "General," he said in a slurred voice. As he was attempting to salute, he slumped forward collapsing to the floor.

"Bruno!" Odile cried out. Realizing at once that she needed help getting him back to his bed, she rushed off in search of Jean-Pierre.

Speaking again to General Boatwright, this time in a raised voice, the supervisor rasped, "Leave at once, you bloody fool! Do not return—ever! And may God damn you for any injuries you've caused to our patient!"

Bruno Steiner's Loss

Chapter 4

"Well say, Bruno, you look swell. Better'n the last time I seen you when you was stretched out like a damn cadaver in front of our trench. Gee, I thought that explosion was gonna send you straight to hell. So, big guy, how you feelin'?"

As always, Joey Smythe from Bruno's company talked incessantly. Bruno smiled thinking how nice it was for him to visit.

"Joey, I thought you were going home?"

"I ain't. Cap Riley said we could take our discharges here in France if we wanted. So me and a couple of the boys decided to. We got a place in Etampes, not far from here. You can come live with us when they let you out—that is, if you wanna. When they discharge you they give you your back pay. Me, I got three hundred dollars. And pretty soon I'll get me some work, I hope. Plus I got this French mam'selle and we love it up pretty good just about every night." Joey winked.

"What do I have to do to get out in France?"

"You jes' give the captain a letter. I'll help you write it."

"How long do I have before I have to decide?"

"A week or two I'd say. Because I don't know where Captain Riley'll be after that. But maybe you just being here means you're discharged. I dunno."

"Will you come by again, Joey?"

"Sure, sure. Next time I'll bring my girl. A good looker—and she's got a friend or two. And Bruno ..." Now Joey began to speak in a whisper. "They all do it— regular like. It's nothing special. They just like it." He winked again at Bruno.

"Well Corporal Bruno, did you enjoy your visitor?" Odile asked.

"In a way, I guess. He told me I could get out of the Army here in France by giving my captain a letter. That's what he did."

Odile smiled. "It's not going to be quite that simple for you, I'm afraid. You're no longer assigned to your company. We have all your papers here. And there's an American doctor, Major Williamson, who comes by every so often to check on you. I think you'll have to work with him if you want to be discharged in France—if that's what you want.

"Is it, Bruno?" she asked, looking at him.

"I think so. Nothing for me in Waukegan. I have a brother back there—and my father. I hardly speak to my brother, and my father, well ..."

"Well, what?"

"He thinks I'm kinda big and stupid. And I guess he's right so ..."

"Bruno, no! You are not! You are a good man and you will find your way after you get well."

"I wish I knew what 'my way' was."

"Deep down you know, dear."

Bruno was stunned. Had he heard her correctly? *Dear*? "I, I ..." But he was unable to speak.

"Bruno, dearest Bruno, forget your father. Forget the past. Think of yourself. What do you want to do with your life?"

Bruno closed his eyes and thought for a moment. What did he really want? "I, I ... I want two things, Odile."

"Yes?"

"I want you and I want children."

"Me? And children? What are you trying to say?"

"It's ..." But Bruno could no longer speak. He had said too much.

Odile smiled. She came over to his bed, reached

under his blanket and embraced him. "I want you too, Bruno. I always have. And we shall have children, light brown ones." She smiled. "But we can't make them here in the chateau. We'll have to find another place—a place all to ourselves." Odile laid her head on Bruno's chest. She could feel his heart racing. She had been with men before, suave good-looking men. She had enjoyed them but never loved them. And here was this large, clumsy oafish man. Probably not all that bright; certainly not well educated. But kind—oh so kind! Perhaps this was why she had grown to love him.

———

In early summer eight weeks later Bruno and Odile were married in the Orleans town hall, a thirty-minute drive by carriage from Chateau Chenonceau. Orleans' mayor, Marcel Delatour, officiated. Jean-Pierre was a witness, Joey was best man, and Odile's supervisor was maid of honor. That same day Bruno received his papers discharging him from the Army in France.

Bruno Steiner's Loss

Chapter 5

Bruno had never ridden in a hansom cab before. Nor had he ever worn formal attire. "Just to meet my family, that's all," Odile had said when she purchased new clothing for him at that tiny expensive out-of-the-way shop in Paris.

"But why, Odile?"

"I'm afraid you're in for a surprise. But remember: I'm the same person you've always known."

Bruno understandably was confused. Traveling in a first class cabin on the boat from Le Havre to Dover confused him; the posh compartment on the train from Dover via London to Windermere further confused him; and now, wearing a morning coat and being driven in a hansom cab through rural back roads, totally befuddled him. As the hansom turned onto a long gravel driveway leading up to the Nadow family estate located in the midst of England's Lake District, Odile turned to her husband. "Not only do I have a large loving family, Bruno, but we live in a rather spacious home. It was wonderful growing up here. Why don't you close your eyes. I'll tell you when to open them. But brace yourself, my love."

Bruno closed his eyes. And as he did, he remembered that day back at Chenonceau when he had such difficulty opening them—and that, when he finally did, he saw Odile for the first time.

———

"All right, Bruno. Open your eyes. Then stand by me and I will introduce you to my family."

Bruno Steiner's Loss

Chapter 6

It took two weeks at Addis Manor for Bruno to get over the shocking discovery that he had married into extraordinary wealth. Having been raised in a tiny clapboard house in the blue collar community of Waukegan outside of Chicago, he now felt more uncomfortable than he had ever felt. Everything was foreign to him—having servants at his beck and call; being surrounded by the sumptuously furnished private quarters he and Odile occupied; and, most of all, for the first time in his life experiencing an intense sense of family. From the moment he arrived at Addis Manor, he had been unconditionally accepted by Odile's laughing, loving family members, particularly her five younger sisters who insisted on calling him "Uncle Bruno" despite the fact that he was their brother-in-law.

When he first met Odile's sisters—who ranged in age from three to thirteen—they had introduced him to their two favorite pastimes, birding and croquet. He, in turn, had showed them how to weave lanyards and bracelets fashioned from thin strips of leather he found in the estate's stables and how to play kick ball, pom pom pull away, and other games he learned while working at a children's day camp before entering the Army. But his greatest coup, the one that most captivated the sisters, was introducing them to fishing for perch from the family dock at nearby Lake Windermere, but only so long as he baited their hooks with worms.

———

As the summer wore on and fall approached, a subtle change began to occur in Odile. Bruno felt she wasn't entirely herself, that there was something different about her. Many mornings she would stay in bed until midday. And even though much of her appetite had disappeared, she was inexplicably gaining weight. Finally, Bruno could stand it no longer. "What *is* the matter?" he asked.

"Don't you know?" she replied. "Don't you *really* know?" Wearing a coquettish grin, she gently kissed him and then pressed a finger to his lips. "Our secret," she whispered. "We're going to add a little one to your entourage. Only this one will call you 'father,' not 'Uncle Bruno.'"

Bruno Steiner's Loss

Chapter 7

During the months that followed, Bruno grappled with the concept of fatherhood—that soon he would become a parent—and that Odile's parents would finally have a grandchild. He found it both startling and ironic that those wondrously intense acts of pleasure he and Odile shared would shortly bring them even greater pleasure in the form of their first child.

And then Bruno began to think of life after the baby's arrival. What would he be doing? He had at least one answer. Like Odile's parents, he and Odile would make more babies—*many more*. But beyond that, what? What did he really want to do with his life? Odile had asked him that very same question while he was recuperating at Chenonceau. And how had he answered? He remembered: *"I want you,"* he had said. *"And I want children."* But what had he meant? From the time he had spent at Addis Manor he now knew.

Over the past months while interacting with Odile's sisters, Bruno had come to realize how much he loved counseling children. And so he would form his own children's day camp—*Camp Odile*—like the one he worked at before joining the Army. He would teach many of the same things he had taught Odile's five sisters: arts and crafts, fishing, competitive sports, camping skills, and, above all, honesty, integrity and sound values. He must speak to Odile's father about this, for he would need capital to seed his venture.

Bruno Steiner's Loss

Chapter 8

In the manor's wood-paneled study Patel Nadow sat in a high back leather chair as he listened to Bruno. Finally, he asked, "Where will your campers come from?"

"Nearby homes and estates. From your children's friends and schoolmates. Maybe from the families of townspeople."

The old man nodded. "And where do you plan on building this camp, Bruno?"

"I was hoping you'd permit me to use your land adjacent to the Windermere family dock. I'll pay you rent."

"Of course. But that tract of land is only three acres. Where would you put an athletic field for a sport, say, like soccer? And wouldn't you need a large enclosed building—you know, one for use when it rained or during the winter and fall? And what about equipment—for camping, boating, archery, fishing? Where would all that be stored? And wouldn't you need a kitchen and dining hall to feed your campers?"

The old man looked over at Bruno. "Have you thought about these things? And what about counselors and the rest of your personnel? Even more important, do you have any idea what your costs will be?"

Bruno appeared puzzled. "I ... I ... I haven't really thought things through, I suppose," he stammered.

"I hadn't expected you to." Patel smiled paternally. "What you're proposing, Bruno, is a business. I like your idea, but what we need is a business plan. Something Gnesh can do. That's his training, you know." Gnesh Nadow was the eldest of Odile's two brothers. He was a chartered accountant and a graduate of the London School of Economics.

"Gnesh will tell us what is needed by way of land, facilities, personnel, and capital." The old man looked up and saw that Bruno appeared relieved.

Bruno Steiner's Loss

Chapter 9

Gnesh Nadow, the eldest of the family offspring, was a tiny slender unattractive man of thirty-four with two annoying nervous tics: he was constantly bobbing his large squat head up and down while, at the same time, his dark brown eyes darted from side to side. People who didn't know him well undoubtedly would have concluded that he was possessed of some strange hyperactive illness. In fact, he suffered from no such infirmity. Gnesh was a true genius, and his head and eye movements—like those of a scanning radar dish—were his way of absorbing facts, ideas, and concepts. Nothing escaped him. Thus, it was no surprise to his father when, ten days after first conferring with Bruno, Gnesh requested a meeting of the three to discuss the proposed business plan for what he now referred to as the "Lake District Community Center."

"So, Gnesh," Patel began, as he, Gnesh and Bruno sat together in the manor's study, "before we go into detail, explain in general terms how you envision this project unfolding."

Gnesh, head bobbing and eyes darting, began, speaking in a staccato which reminded Bruno of a rapidly firing machine gun.

"Brother Bruno here has a good idea, Father, but not sufficiently all-encompassing. I wish to expand upon it. But before I do, we must conduct further interviews."

"Further interviews?"

"Yes. I've already interviewed some forty-one Lake District residents. I told them we were thinking of developing a community center, and I asked them to tell me the kinds of facilities and services they would like us to have.

"So far they've come up with a list of thirty-two

items, including ..." Gnesh looked over at Bruno, "a day camp for children. They all seemed to be very high on Brother Bruno's idea, and they were all in agreement that the facility should operate year-round for use by both adults and children. Beyond that ..."

Gnesh withdrew several pieces of paper from a folder, handing one to his father and another to Bruno.

"Here's their list, Father. It might surprise you."

"A dining facility; a clinic; adult education; ballroom dancing; a swimming pool and a sauna; polo; a sports field; a child care center! My Lord, Gnesh, what else, for goodness sake?" Patel chuckled.

"I really don't know, Father. But I think I have to speak to more residents ... many more. Then what I'll do is prepare a business plan for a facility which offers the things most often requested—but with the ability to offer even more in the future."

———

After listening to Gnesh and then reading through the list, Bruno's head began to swirl. A community center for the entire Lake District! What was Gnesh talking about? All he'd hoped for was a small children's day camp. Admittedly, he would need a modest play field and a small building of sorts. But all these other things—a pool, a dining hall, a child care facility, a gymnasium, a ballroom, classrooms, dormitories, a meeting hall, a theater, a clinic! What had he started? Then his father-in-law began to speak.

"So you see, Bruno, it's just as I thought: you have planted a seed which I suspect will grow into a highly profitable enterprise—and one that will greatly benefit the residents of the Lake District."

He turned to Gnesh. "By all means, conduct as many interviews as you like. Once they're concluded and you've finalized your business plan, we'll review it. And when we do, I think we should have some of our friends from Quarles & Willson present." Quarles & Willson was an international firm of solicitors that had represented the Nadow family for many years.

"One more thing, Father," Gnesh said. "With your permission, I would like to instruct our local estate agent to look into acquiring options to purchase additional lands bounding our Windermere parcel. We need to do it before we begin construction since property nearby will only go up in value once word gets out."

"Excellent idea," Patel replied.

———

After Bruno had left the study, Gnesh began to speak. "Something else we must consider, Father: If Bruno and Odile choose to live in the United States, I fear their life will be most difficult. Racially-mixed marriages are not tolerated there, and children of such marriages suffer greatly."

"What are you trying to say, Gnesh?"

"That we must do everything we can to keep them here where they will fare far better. Perhaps not everywhere in Great Britain, but certainly here in the Lake District where our family is known and respected."

"I completely agree, Gnesh. And so we shall keep them here—by building Bruno his community center."

Bruno Steiner's Loss

Chapter 10

As the baby's birth approached, activity within the manor intensified at a frenetic pace—while, at the same time, all planning for the Lake District Community Center came to a temporary halt. This was a particularly happy time for Odile's parents who, contemplating the arrival of their first grandchild, were filled with excitement.

A large room in the quarters occupied by Bruno and Odile had been stripped bare and then repainted, recarpeted and refurnished—this time with a crib, a nurse's bed, a dresser, a bassinette, a large trunk full of infant's toys, and sundry other items of nursery furniture. In the closet Bruno spied two groups of baby clothing, one pink and the other baby blue. "But what if it's a girl; what do we do with the baby blue clothes?" he had asked Odile. "Then we'll just have to make a boy, won't we?" Odile had laughingly replied.

———

Several days later Odile introduced Bruno to a Mrs. Montgomery. "She and her sister are going to help with the delivery. They're qualified midwives."

———

Exactly two weeks later, at 3:40 a.m., Odile went into labor. When her contractions came within seconds of one another, Bruno was shooed from the room by Karemi, Odile's mother. She, along with the Montgomery sisters, now took charge while Bruno waited anxiously with his father-in-law in the study below. From time to time he would peer out through its partially open door and catch glimpses of servant girls scurrying up and down the stairs carrying various items including extra sheets and towels

45

and refilled hot water kettles.

By 8:00 a.m. Bruno had closed his eyes and fallen into a deep sleep only to be awakened by a piercing shriek followed by howling and wailing. He looked through the doorway and saw a servant girl covered in blood, her face buried in her hands, running down the stairs. He glanced over at Patel. "What is it?"

"Stay here, Bruno," Patel commanded. He got up and left the room.

———

Ten minutes later Patel, his wife, and Gnesh entered the study. Gnesh no longer bobbed his head, and his eyes had ceased darting from side to side. Instead, he stared sadly at Bruno who could see that he had been weeping. "I am so sorry, Brother Bruno. I ..." He stopped in mid-sentence.

"What is it?" Bruno asked. A sickening feeling had begun to come over him.

Patel, his arm around his wife's shoulders, reached out for Bruno. Stumbling forward, he wailed, "They are gone; they have left us."

"Gone? Left us? What are you saying? What happened?"

"The midwives called it a breach ... or something like that. They are both in heaven now, my son, and I ..." Patel began to sob.

Mrs. Montgomery entered the study. She was carrying a glass of water. "Here," she said, handing the glass and a small white pill to Bruno. "Take this. It will help. And I am so very sorry, Mr. Steiner."

"Sorry! Sorry! What have you done to my wife and child, you incompetent!" Bruno cried out. Grabbing her by the throat, he began to shake her uncontrollably until Patel, Gnesh, and one of the servant girls finally wrested the terrified woman from his grip.

"Please, Bruno," Patel said. "It wasn't Mrs. Montgomery's fault. She and her sister did the very best they could. It was the will of God."

But, as he collapsed to the floor, Bruno could no longer hear voices; they, along with all other sounds, were eclipsed by a high-pitched primal scream which came from his lips—a scream so woeful that it seemed to mark an end to every happiness he had ever known.

Bruno Steiner's Loss

Chapter 11

Following the death of his wife and child, Bruno became a virtual hermit cloistering himself in the quarters he and Odile had occupied, refusing to speak to anyone. When servants tried to deliver trays of food to him, he turned them away. Oftentimes sobbing could be heard coming from his bedroom.

This went on for three days until finally his father-in-law could bear it no longer. Ascending the stairs to the second floor where the quarters were located, Patel quietly opened the bedroom door. Inside he saw Bruno, head in hands, seated on the edge of the large four-poster bed he and Odile had shared.

"Forgive me for intruding, my son, but Karemi and I wanted you to know that all necessary arrangements have been made. Tomorrow Odile and the baby will be buried in the manor's cemetery. And at your mother-in-law's request, Odile will be holding the little one in her arms. We both implore you to be there—for the sake of our family.

"Here," Patel said, attempting to hand Bruno a dark blue suit, a white shirt, a tie and a pair of black shoes.

The words "for the sake of our family" seemed to awaken Bruno from his near-catatonic state. Realizing how kind and generous the Nadows had been to him and how much they also must be in pain, he knew he must honor their wishes. And when it was over, he also knew there would be time enough to grieve.

As respectfully as he could, he got up from the bed and walked over to his father-in-law—who by this time appeared to be trembling—and took the clothing from him. "Thank you, sir," he said.

———

Although he was present at the funeral, Bruno had no memory of the service other than sitting between two of the Nadow sisters—which ones, he couldn't recall. Afterward, it seemed as if the entire community had come by to pay their respects. But, again, Bruno had little memory of anything other than Patel handing him a folder containing papers which he had described as "travel information." Bruno also faintly recalled talking about his return to the United States.

Some hours after the service, Bruno's memory seemed to return and he remembered his father-in-law saying, "I respect your wish to return to Chicago. But I want you to know that you will forever be a part of our family. There will always be a place in our home and our hearts for you. We will await your return, and while you are away you will be deeply missed."

He also remembered that he and Patel had hugged and that the older man again had trembled.

"When Karemi and I go," Patel had said, "you will share in our wealth as if you were born to us. I have already made all the arrangements.

"We are old, Bruno. But if your mother-in-law's prayers are answered, we will bring Odile back through the birth of another daughter. We have had eight children, so why not another? Perhaps the Good Lord will indulge us one more time."

On hearing this, Bruno had smiled.

"Once you are aboard ship," his father-in-law had continued, "I would like you to review your travel papers. As you will see, Gnesh has made plans for you to meet with Tucker McConnell when you arrive in Chicago. He is a partner in the law firm that represents our family. He will make sure you stay in close touch with us and that our family wishes are carried out. Will you promise me that you will do that?"

"I promise, sir," Bruno had replied.

49

Bruno Steiner's Loss

Chapter 12

After spending more than a year in the bucolic surroundings of England's Lake District, the frenzied activity of Chicago's Loop—along with a cacophony of competing sounds—startled Bruno as he stood outside the LaSalle Street Station on that morning in 1920. Trying as best he could to get his bearings, he recalled the promise he'd made to his father-in-law. Reaching for the travel folder, he withdrew a sheet of paper with the attorney's name and address on it. As he read it over, a man in a dark suit approached.

"Pardon me, sir. Are you Mr. Steiner?"

Surprised, Bruno nodded.

"I'm here to help you with your bags, sir—and to escort you to Mr. McConnell's office. It's only a short walk from here."

"But how did you know ...?" Then Bruno remembered that Gnesh had made plans for him to meet with Mr. McConnell upon his arrival.

"I only have one bag."

"Allow me, sir," the man said, reaching for it. "And welcome back to Chicago, Mr. Steiner. Mr. McConnell tells me you're a war hero."

Bruno reddened. "Hero? No," he said, shaking his head. "I was just unlucky enough to be in the wrong place at the wrong time."

——

In the reception room of the offices of Quarles & Willson located on the eighth floor of the Home Insurance Building, one of Chicago's tallest skyscrapers, Bruno waited only briefly before a short stocky woman appeared.

"Mr. McConnell is tied up and asked that you make

50

yourself comfortable, sir. While you're waiting, may I offer you some coffee?"

"No thank you," Bruno replied. For some inexplicable reason, his head had begun to ache and he felt nervous and ill at ease. Coffee was the last thing he wanted.

Then he began to wonder: Maybe he should never have come back. Wouldn't he have been happier working on the new community center at this very moment? Or fishing for Windermere perch?

Just then a tall slender man entered the room. Smiling, he put his arm around Bruno's shoulders. "The man of many cables!" he quipped. "Come, let's head back to my den."

As they walked down a long corridor, he continued. "I've received five cables today from Patel Nadow. All about you. They wanted me to assure them that you arrived in one piece. I've sent a reply telling them you had. I hope I was right."

"I'm fine, Mr. McConnell. A bit confused, maybe. I have no idea where I'll be spending the night or what I'll be doing tomorrow."

"Not to worry, Bruno. Worrying's a big part of my job." Laughingly, he went on, "It is okay if I call you 'Bruno'?"

"Sure. And can I call you 'Tucker'?"

" 'Tuck,' " he replied.

"So come into my office and let's see where we're at."

———

Tucker McConnell, it turned out, was not simply one of the many attorneys who represented the Nadow interests. In a sense, he was also the family's Chicago surrogate. Early in his legal career he had made several trips to England, and, while there, had visited the Nadows at their home. He had even met Odile once, just before she enlisted in the Nursing Service.

In a series of lengthy cables from Patel he had learned in detail of Bruno's war injuries, of his marriage to Odile, and of the tragic death of his wife and child. He had also learned that Bruno was considered a full-fledged member of the Nadow family despite the fact that he'd never been formally adopted. He was, as Patel stated in one of his cables, "…deeply loved and revered by all of us here at Addis."

Tucker, a happily married family man with two small children, had on his own—and without any urging by Patel—decided to take Bruno under his wing. And so, on his first night back in the Chicago area, Bruno began an extended stay with the McConnell household. He was given his own private room and bath on the third floor of their overly-large Victorian home in Kenilworth, a tiny community on Chicago's North Shore. To his delight, Bruno soon discovered that Mrs. McConnell was a gifted "cuisinière" almost equal in talent to the revered "Cook" of Addis Manor.

———

At dinner one evening some four weeks later, Bruno proudly announced to the McConnells that he'd accepted a position with the Village of Glencoe Parks & Recreation Department. In summers, he told them, he'd be running a children's water safety course at Glencoe Beach; and in winters he'd be in charge of the ice skating program at one of the village's two rinks.

"And during the remainder of the year?" Tucker asked.

"Coaching sports and maybe teaching classes in arts and crafts."

"Wonderful, Bruno," Tucker said. "Just what you wanted. When do you start?"

"As soon as possible. When my first paycheck arrives, I'll begin looking for an apartment."

Tucker McConnell was silent for a moment. Finally, he said, "Let's you and I sit down after dinner, Bruno. I've got a few things to go over with you. Nadow family business."

———

"So we come to the end of your stay here," Tucker McConnell began as he and Bruno sat opposite one another in the library. "And, as I said, there's some Nadow family business to attend to."

Bruno looked puzzled.

"Bruno, I've been instructed to tell you that Patel Nadow and his wife have given you a lifetime annuity of sixty dollars a week. So, no matter what your work situation is, you've got a comfortable income for life."

Bruno was stunned. Sixty dollars a week—over three thousand dollars a year! And for life! A fortune! "Why, Tuck? Why?" he asked.

"I think you probably know that the Nadows consider you their son. In their own special way they've adopted you—I suppose because you were so good to their daughter and to their other children. Simply put, Bruno, they love you."

"But what do I do with all that money?"

"That, my friend, is entirely up to you. It's deposited monthly into our firm's trust account. Just call me and I'll send you a check. And there's already some seven hundred dollars in the account."

"For the moment, just hold on to it—unless I need some money when I rent an apartment. I'll let you know."

"One more thing, Bruno: please stay in close touch with us. My wife and I, and our two children, have grown very fond of you. And Glencoe is just a short distance from Kenilworth."

Jamie and his grandfather stood at the southeasterly corner of Glencoe's North Field which, in winter, became an ice skating rink. Both were staring at an engraved bronze plaque embedded in a large sculpted square of polished granite:

In Memory of Bruno Steiner
Honored Friend of Glencoe's Children
1897-1963

Jamie was holding on to the three-hole notebook in which he'd been making notes. After a few moments, he turned to his grandfather. "But Grandpa, what does he have to do with the story? Why have you spent so much time telling me about him?"

The old man smiled, for now he knew that Jamie had officially signed on to their road trip.

"You're askin' why Bruno is so important, Jamie, and I'm not gonna answer that question right now. But by the time we've finished our travels I promise you you'll have all the answers. And maybe some of 'em will surprise you. They sure surprised your daddy—'least I think they did.

"But I will say this: Bruno was different from the others—like when he had that need to save those wounded soldiers. Pretty unique. And he never married again— most likely because he knew he'd never find anyone he could love as much as Odile; and also probably because he felt he'd never meet up with someone who adored him like she did. Guess he wasn't about to settle for less. Don't suppose I would've. And to fill the void created by her loss, he devoted his life to children, needy ones most of all. That's what this plaque is all about."

54

Jamie began writing in his notebook.

"What about all his money, Grandpa? Did he keep it?"

"As you'd suspect, Bruno wasn't much into money—unless, of course, he could use it to help others. He didn't spend a whole lot on himself. When he first came to Glencoe he rented a one-bedroom furnished apartment in that red brick buildin' next to Doc Richman's office on Hazel. You've probably passed it a hundred times on your way to school. And that's where he stayed.

"I've heard tell that he cooked his own meals. Probably true because I'd run into him every now and then at the A&P.

"And for transportation he bought himself a used 1939 Chevy coupe which he drove until the day he died.

"Nope, boy, Bruno wasn't much into spendin' money on himself. But he sure was good to others, mostly children."

"How, Grandpa?"

"Well, with Tuck McConnell's help, he set up a foundation to benefit Glencoe's children, especially Negro children. That's where most of his money went—into that foundation. And the money was used for college tuition, medical bills, toys at Christmas, things like that. And sometimes when families were goin' through hard times, Bruno's foundation would help out. I remember when the Cook family got in trouble. Mr. Cook was laid off and the family had no money comin' in for almost a year. That's when Bruno stepped in. Usin' funds from his foundation, he saw to it that the Cooks had food on the table every night until Mr. Cook found another job.

"As I said, Jamie, Bruno was special."

———

As his grandfather spoke, Jamie was trying hard to find that common denominator: What did Bruno and

55

Christopher Wallace have in common? Both were white and both had ties to Glencoe. Bruno for sure had made Glencoe a better place, and probably Christopher Wallace also had —at least according to his grandfather.

"*I think I know,*" *Jamie said.*

"*Know what, boy?*"

"*Why you're taking me to meet all these people who aren't famous.*"

"*And why's that?*"

"*They're baby steps.*"

"*Baby steps. Yep, I'd say we've taken a few. But to where, Jamie? That's the question, isn't it?*" *The judge looked over at Jamie who remained silent.*

"*To answer that one, boy, you'd better ask yourself what Bruno and Christopher Wallace have to do with dancin'? Did you ask yourself that question?*"

"*No,*" *Jamie replied.* "*Does everyone you're introducing me to have something to do with dancing?*"

"*Maybe. Maybe not,*" *the judge chuckled.*

"*Anyway, there's not a whole lot more I'll be tellin' you about Bruno—at least not for now. So we'd better be gettin' on back. You'll be needin' a good night's sleep. Tomorrow we board the train.*"

"*Board the train? For where, Grandpa?*"

"*Greenville, Mississippi. Home of Amelia Polk. Your grandma knows all about it. Fact is, she's thrilled we'll finally be leavin' town. Told me she'd have both our bags packed. C'mon, let's head on over to the car.*"

"*But, wait, Grandpa. Who's Amelia Polk?*"

"*You'll meet her soon enough, boy. And from what I hear tell, that woman could sure play a mean piano.*"

Excerpt from Jamie's Notebook, Page 28

After I learned all those things about Bruno, I finally remembered who he was. He was at the North Field rink one winter day when I was about five. Mom dropped me off and it was the first time I went ice skating. I remember Mom telling me to go into the warming hut because she had to go somewhere. She told me to introduce myself to Bruno and that he would take care of me. I found that strange because Mom almost always insists on being with me. But not this time. And then I entered the hut, and there was Bruno. He was old and seemed kind of weak and clumsy. But very nice. He came over and asked me who I was. I told him. I remember that he put his big arm around my shoulders and told me to sit down and that he would help me get my skates on. He laced them up and tied the laces. And then he took my hand and we went out on the rink where everyone was skating. Bruno had shoes on, but he walked on the ice without slipping. Then he began teaching me how to skate and I started out. I wasn't very good at it, but he said that in time I'd get better—which I did. The nice thing about Bruno, though, was the good feeling I got just being with him. For some reason, he made me feel safe. Now that I know his story, I wonder why he didn't remarry and have a family of his own—because he obviously loved children. It seems to me that in a way his life was sad and lonely, except, of course, I think he probably considered all of Glencoe's children his children. If he did, then he had a pretty big family.

Amelia Polk's Lesson

Amelia Polk's Lesson – List of Characters
["B" denotes black; "W" denotes white; * denotes a real person]

Amelia Polk (young girl, later a teenager) W
Heather Polk (Amelia's mother) W
Jesse Colburn Polk (Amelia's father) W
Conrad Mertens (Amelia's piano teacher) W
Madame Marie Foucault (private school proprietor) W
Harlan Jefferson (pianist) B
Zachary Jefferson (pianist, son of Harlan Jefferson) B
Verne-Bob "Candy Man" Johnson (KKK Grand Titan,
    Greenville Dominion) W
Chauncey Miller (five-year-old) W

Amelia Polk's Lesson

Chapter 1

In 1899, at age three, Amelia Polk began her study of classical piano. Saturday mornings her father would walk her from her family's spacious Greenville, Mississippi, antebellum mansion overlooking Lake Ferguson, a channel of the nearby Mississippi River, to Conrad Mertens' house some five blocks away for her weekly lesson. By the time she was eight, Mr. Mertens came to realize that Amelia was not only extraordinarily talented, but that among all his students she alone possessed a special creative gift—the ability to compose. "Play me something of your own, Lia," he would say. And, in her quiet unassuming fashion, she would flex her tiny fingers, close her eyes, breath in deeply, and begin. What ushered forth was something both pleasing and indescribable. Most often, her works sounded to Mr. Mertens like some strange blend of Chopin and Liszt, but with a rhythm suggestive of Stephen Foster.

"How in Lord's name did you all come up with that, dear girl?" he would ask. In response, Amelia would blush and shake her head from side to side as if to say, "I wish I knew, but I just don't."

Shortly after her tenth birthday, Mr. Mertens met with Amelia's parents, Heather and Jesse Polk. "I can't teach her anything more—particularly since she plays better than I do. If you want her to progress, she's got to go to a big city like Birmingham or Nashville—or maybe New Orleans."

"How could we?" Heather Polk responded. "Papa here's got the cotton business. He cain't jes' portage it from one place to another."

"She's right, Mr. Mertens. I jes' cain't pick up and leave. The family business goes back two generations—to

61

Heather's grandpappy who founded it—and it's too damn good a livin' to close down. You sure there ain't another teacher 'round here?"

Mr. Mertens hesitated. "Well, actually, there is. Harlan Jefferson. You heard of him?"

Jesse Polk's eyes widened and his wife's jaw dropped as she seemed to recoil in revulsion. "You talkin' 'bout that fat nigger who plays in the red light houses?" she asked.

"I am. So happens he's the best pianist in these parts and he could teach Amelia a whole lot. But he's the only one in town who could. There just isn't anybody else. That's why I said she's got to go to a big city."

"Well," Jesse Polk interjected, turning to his wife, "what do you think of that Jefferson man, honey?"

"What do I think? You know damn well what I think, Jesse Colburn Polk! Ain't nothin' in this God-given world would 'llow our Amelia to have a nigger teacher. Jes' imagine her comin' home Saturdays stinkin' the way they do. And maybe while she's seated on that piano bench playing away that buck might try sticking his hand—or something else—up between her legs. You know how they is: always wantin' to poke away with their big sticks." She paused to catch her breath.

"What do I think? I think I'll take her to one of those cities. Or maybe she can study something else here in town. But no nigger teachers, not even women ones!"

"I agree. Jes' wanted to hear you out—that's all," Jesse Polk replied, trying to avoid further confrontation with his wife.

Then addressing Mr. Mertens, he continued. "And so far as the Polk family goes, Heather and I want to thank you kindly for coaxin' all that talent out of our little girl. We sure do appreciate it."

———

62

As with most things in life, the upshot of the Polks' meeting with Conrad Mertens was not entirely clear-cut. Rather than terminating Amelia's piano instruction altogether, her parents reduced her lessons to once a month. And to keep her occupied during the time that remained they enrolled her in the Greenville Dance and Etiquette Academy whose sole instructor, Madame Marie Foucault, was reputedly possessed of impeccable credentials and morals. They were thrilled that their daughter would soon be learning dance and society's dictates from this exemplary woman.

But had they looked into Madame Foucault's past, they would have discovered that her "credentials and morals" were of her own design and, upon closer inspection, were anything but impeccable. As evidenced by her rather extensive Parisian police record, in her early twenties she had been something of a hellion not only working as a nude dancer at Paris' famed Folies Bergère on weekends but also earning a handsome living as a common street walker on weeknights—a period during which she acquired a fascination for blacks and their music, something she would unwittingly pass on to her pupils years later.

———

After Amelia completed her second year at the academy during which time she was introduced to all forms of dance, Madame Foucault gave her a choice. She could continue on with either ballet or ballroom dancing, but not both (her instruction in etiquette would of course remain ongoing). Although Amelia enjoyed the disciplines of ballet, she much preferred dancing with a partner, a requirement of ballroom dancing; moreover, she loved improvisation, something which the rigidities of ballet did not permit.

"So what is eet to be, cherie?" Madame Foucault asked.

"I choose ballroom, Madame. I jes' love the foxtrot and the waltz—and those South American dances. And ..." she hesitated.

"And what, cherie?"

"Nothing, Madame." Amelia knew better than to tell of her desire to improvise—to create new dance steps and perhaps even new dances—although in her heart this was what she longed to do.

———

The ensuing years saw Amelia advance in her studies at the academy. Finally, three months shy of her eighteenth birthday Madame invited Amelia to join her and the other students in her salon located in the back of the academy's building for an early evening of socializing and music.

"Oh please may I go, Mother? Please!" Amelia begged.

"Well, what do you think, Jess?" her mother asked her husband.

"I see no harm in it. She's one fine lady, that Madame Foucault—and, like always, our Amelia might jes' pick up some more learnin'."

Amelia Polk's Lesson

Chapter 2

When Amelia entered Madame Marie Foucault's salon that Saturday evening a week later she was both stunned and mortified at what she saw, and she knew she must leave at once. Rather than finding a gathering of students, she was greeted by a mixed crowd of seedy unkempt people, some standing, others sitting—and still others stretched out on the floor. Most were barefoot, and a few, including one woman, wore nothing above the waist. Several were sound asleep. Those not half-naked were skimpily clad and almost everyone was smoking. This explained why Amelia was having such difficulty breathing—and seeing. But as she looked closely she was able to make out the figure of Madame, her hair down and dressed in a slip, sitting on the floor with her back against the wall. She held a glass of yellowish drink in one hand and a partially smoked cheroot in the other. A thin sickly looking man with long uncombed hair and a scraggly beard was seated next to her. One of his arms was casually draped over her shoulders and he looked as if he hadn't bathed in weeks—perhaps months. In the background Amelia heard the loud banging of unfamiliar piano music.

As she turned to leave, she saw that Madame had gotten up from the floor and was rushing over to her. "Ma petite cherie! A terrible mistake! You were expected tomorrow evening with zee other students. But please don't go! You are old enough! Please!" Without waiting for a response, Madame took Amelia firmly by the hand and led her to a table. On it were glasses filled with the same yellowish liquid Madame was drinking.

"Take one. Zis you weel like. Eet weel relax you. I promise. Eet is a licorice candy boisson. You like licorice, n'est pas?"

Resigned to staying at least for a short while so as not to offend Madame, Amelia lifted one of the glasses and took a sip. The smell was licorice, but the taste was bitter. She made a face, and put the glass back down on the table.

"No, no. Keep eet. Eet grows on you."

Amelia picked up the glass again as Madame tugged her to where the thin man was seated.

"Zis ees ma cher Henri. 'Ee and I are … well, you know … tres tres close." She giggled.

Without getting up, Henri proffered a hand to Amelia which she reluctantly grasped. And while she was shaking it, she was shocked to observe that Henri's fly was unbuttoned.

"But come, cherie. To zee piano. We meet zee Jeffersons."

Again, dragging her by the hand, Madame led her to an upright piano from which the strange, wonderful music was emanating. At the same time, Amelia saw the outline of a dark triangle between Madame's legs and what appeared to be the tiny bulges of her nipples. Horrified, she realized that Madame was wearing nothing under her slip—so entirely different from her customary attire when she taught.

At the piano Amelia saw two black men who closely resembled one another seated on the piano bench playing. Both were roundish in appearance, but one was larger and obviously older than the other. Their eyes were closed and their chubby heads were thrown back making it seem as if they were gazing up at the ceiling; at the same time their fingers danced across the keys. The larger and older of the two was seated on the left playing below middle C while the younger played above it. Occasionally the music required both to play in mid-keyboard and sometimes their hands would cross, but without ever touching. Amelia was amazed that they were able to do this, particularly with their eyes closed.

And the music? Fantastic! Infectious! Its melody and rhythm began to take hold of Amelia and she felt herself becoming a part of it. Instinctively her right foot began to tap to its beat. And then she experienced something which had never happened to her before: the music's notes began scrolling across her line of vision. She could see them! Hear them! Read them! Feel them! Not knowing how to react to this, or what to do, she began to drink from her now half-empty glass. Madame, who was standing next to her, smiled.

"Ah, so you see, cherie. Eet is as I told you, n'est pas? We all come to worship the mysterious yellow boisson."

"What are they playing, Madame?"

"That, cherie, they call 'ragtime.' "

Madame grasped the shoulder of the older man. "Harlan!" She gently shook him. "Zis ees Amelia. She plays what you call a 'mean piano.' "

Without missing a note, the older man half opened his eyes and looked back over his shoulder. He uttered one word: "Pleasure." But Amelia was too busy concentrating on the hand movements of the two players to reply. As her entire body began to sway to the music, she thought to herself that if she could play Rachmaninoff she could play this.

Then she heard Harlan's voice again. "This here's my boy, Zack." Zack, too, opened his eyes slightly as he looked back and nodded to Amelia.

It was at this moment that Madame did something which Amelia would later regret for the rest of her life: where the shoulders of the two men were almost touching, Madame inserted her hands and began to shove the two apart. "Move over, mes amis!" she commanded.

"I think the boss done wants us to 'llow this young lady to play with us," Harlan said.

Sensing concern in his father's voice, Zack nevertheless obediently slid over, making room for Amelia on the small piano bench.

Amelia hesitated for just a moment, for she fully understood that what she was about to do was wrong by any measure. Yet, overcome by an uncontrollable urge to become immersed in the music, she rebelliously seated herself between the two black men. Still watching their fingers fly across the keyboard, she began to play with them in perfect unison. And, as she did, she failed to notice Madame—who by this time was standing ten paces behind her—looking on in satisfaction.

Amelia Polk's Lesson

Chapter 3

Heather Polk had been uneasy ever since Amelia left for Madame Foucault's apartment earlier that evening. As a result, she just wouldn't stop carrying on over the fact that they allowed her to go in the first place. And now it was getting late and Amelia still wasn't home. Finally, Jesse Polk had had it with his wife's bellyaching.

"For Christ's sake, Heather! It's only half past midnight. Will you stop bein' such a worrywart. She's damn near eighteen, for God's sake! 'Member what we was doin' at that age? Some pretty heavy petting until two, maybe three, in the mornin' on that moth-eaten couch in your parents' basement if my memory serves me right?"

"We did no such thing! Only intimacies we've ever shared was after we was married. Long after—cuz you got so stinkin' drunk at our wedding you couldn't perform! And you haven't done much better since. That is, if my memory serves me right!"

"C'mon, Heather, let's stop bickerin'. I say we turn in. If she ain't home by 2:00 a.m. I'll hitch the horses to the buggy and go on over to the academy. Find out what's goin' on."

"Well, I'll be goin' too. So don't you be leavin' without me, you understand?"

Jesse Polk nodded.

———

At 2:30 a.m. Heather Polk shook her husband. "Wake up, Jess. She still ain't home. We'd better get on over there in a hurry."

———

69

Exactly forty-five minutes later Amelia's parents arrived in their buggy directly in front of the academy building's main entrance. They could hear piano music coming from within. Just then a disheveled looking couple pushed open the door and came stumbling out of the building. The woman was laughing in a high-pitched voice, while the man, holding a whiskey bottle to his lips, took a long pull. And then, raising the bottle to the sky, he cried out "To bed!" The woman leaned over in his direction and began nuzzling up against the side of his neck.

"Jesus!" Jesse Polk said to his wife in a whisper. "Did you see that? Looks like they just come out of some den of iniquity or other. Next thing you know he'll be jumping her right here in the street! And she—why she's like some bitch in heat!"

"I seen it. And I've had enough. I'm goin' in to fetch our daughter. You stay right here!"

———

Inside, things were far worse than Heather Polk had imagined. In only a slip, Madame Foucault—that so-called pillar of rectitude and propriety—had her hand inside some filthy man's pants and was ...

But Heather looked away. She couldn't bear to watch.

Where was Amelia? There! Christ! Squeezed in between two blacks on that piano bench. She looked more closely and saw those two pumping away, rubbing up against her, *pushing their asses and thighs right into hers.* And all three were drunk as skunks.

Heather continued to stare in amazement. Those black fingers! Whenever they left the keyboard they would lightly pass over Amelia's breasts. Those boys were helping themselves to a cheap feel! She was sure of it. And although she couldn't actually make it out, she knew that all Negroes had perpetual bulges in their pants, most as big as beer bottles! Lord God!

"Amelia," Heather Polk screamed. "Now! We're leaving. Get on over here!" But there was no reaction on Amelia's part.

"I said now!" Heather Polk screamed again, this time at the top of her voice. Still no response.

Heather Polk could stand it no longer. She rushed to the piano bench, grabbed Amelia by the hair from behind, and yanked with all her might. Taken by surprise, Amelia's hands flew up from the keyboard and she fell over backwards sliding to the floor as her mother, still holding on to her hair, began dragging her from the room.

———

The following evening, when things had simmered down slightly, the Polks had a chance to talk over the situation.

"We got ourselves two major problems," Heather Polk began. "First off, we gotta run that Madame Foucault out of town. Close down her academy. I'll handle that. When I spread the word 'bout what happened she'll be out of business." She thought for a moment.

"That brings us to our second problem—those two niggers. If I hadn't gotten there when I did, they'd a been ruttin' with our little girl right on the floor! Looked to me like both those boys was sportin' pokers 'bout the size of billy clubs—and probably twice as hard. They was rarin' to go."

"So what are you suggestin', Heather?" Jesse Polk asked.

"Well, seein' as those boys was takin' liberties with our little girl, I say it's time to bring in the candy man."

"Jesus, Heather! I think you've gone off your rocker. An hour ago I talked to Mertens about what happened. He swears those two boys are respectful as all

71

get out. He talked to them and they claim that Madame Foucault ordered them to 'llow Amelia to squeeze in between them on that bench, and that all they was doin' was playing away on the piano."

"That's horseshit, and you know it, Jesse Colburn Polk! Them boys was enjoyin' themselves to the hilt. What they was doin' was oilin' up our little girl for some heavy duty fornicatin'. I wish you could'a seen them rubbin' up against her the way they was. How'd you like it if she'd birthed a Negro baby? Would'a shamed both our families for good."

"I don't often lay down the law, Heather. But I'm doin' it this time: No candy man! You understand?"

"You was always a weakling, wasn't you, Jesse? Never could stick up for your rights. I should'a married a man with some backbone, not somebody as squeamish as you." Heather smirked: "Well, too late now, anyway. I already talked to the candy man."

"You did what?" Jesse screamed in a rage. How he sometimes despised his wife! How at this moment he wanted to take her by the throat and throttle the life out of her! But, sadly, he knew that she was right, that he lacked the courage to do this.

"I said I already talked to him. And he agrees with me one hundred percent. He told me he's gonna get goin' on this in the next day or two."

Amelia Polk's Lesson

Chapter 4

The "candy man" it turned out was tall, plump kindly Verne-Bob Johnson, a bachelor and owner of the popular Johnson's Candy Store located at the corner of Poplar and Main Streets in downtown Greenville. Despite its small size, the candy store was highly profitable, the result of Verne-Bob's business acumen, his effusive personality, and his cuddly Chester A. Arthur-like appearance. Verne-Bob's *modus operandi,* which he had perfected over the many years he'd owned the store, almost always followed the same script: When a customer entered he would hear his first name called out in a deep melodious voice by this balding rotund man almost six feet in height wearing a spotless white full-length shopkeeper's apron over a business suit and sporting an imposing mustache with its ends attached to bushy pork chop sideburns; followed by "Care to sample our special of the day?" Verne-Bob would then offer the customer a large tray filled with tiny pieces of the day's candy which might be anything from mint delights to dark chocolate fudgelets. And when the customer was a child under five, Verne-Bob would routinely ask a second question: "Say, there, little one, what's that a-growing out of your ear?" after which, by sleight of hand, he would extract a penny from the youngster's ear and hand it to him. The child's reaction was almost always the same—laughter of delight.

And so, after successfully operating his candy store for several decades, Verne-Bob had become wealthy. Part of that wealth was a large stash of cash which he kept hidden in the store's basement and from which, periodically, he would withdraw amounts to finance his two greatest passions: his maniacal hatred of all members of the Negro race and his fervent adoration of the Ku Klux Klan and all that it stood for.

Because Greenville was a small community, Verne-Bob's views did not go unnoticed. More than twenty years earlier he had been inducted into the KKK. After serving it faithfully for some eighteen years, he had been appointed Grand Titan of the Greenville Dominion. According to the Klan's precepts, in that capacity his word was law within the dominion and his judgments and decisions could not be questioned. As he told a close friend when he first assumed this high office, "My burdens are hellishly overwhelmin' and I feel them pressin' down on me every hour of every day. Truth is, I'm already havin' trouble sleepin'." In fact, the pressures which so plagued Verne-Bob were those imposed by the Klan's national charter which charged a Grand Titan with the weighty responsibilities "of keeping and maintaining all members of the Negro race residing within, or entering, his dominion under firm control and behaving in a civil manner" and "of doling out such penalties and punishments as he, in his sole judgment as Grand Titan, shall determine to be necessary or appropriate."

Thus, when, several hours before her acrimonious confrontation with her husband, Heather Polk had come to Verne-Bob seeking his counsel regarding what she considered to be the "shameful events" of the prior evening, he immediately understood that he was being consulted in his capacity as Grand Titan on an extremely important matter. He therefore ushered Heather into the store's back office where, after closing the door, the two could speak openly without fear of being overheard.

"What's goin' on, Heather?" he asked.

"Well, you all 'member our Amelia?"

"Sure do. Pretty little thing. She all right?"

"Not exactly, Verne-Bob. Somethin' terrible has happened and …" It was at this point that Heather broke down in tears—just exactly as she had planned to do while on her way to Verne-Bob's candy store.

"Sit on down, honey. Take some deep breaths. Try to pull yourself together. I do understand. And this here sounds serious."

"It is, Verne-Bob, and I do apologize. I'll be able to talk in minute or two."

"Take all the time you need, darlin'."

Finally, a minute or two later, Heather began to speak. "It's about Amelia. She went through some dreadful things last night." And then Heather told Verne-Bob in detail how her little girl had come within a hair's breadth of being raped by Harlan and Zachary Jefferson.

"This is damn serious. And I am so glad you came to see me. I don't even have to think this one over. I'd say this is definitely somethin' requirin' one of our little excursions."

"You mean to Saltair Field?" Heather said softly, trying as hard as she possibly could to conceal her excitement—for in some sick way she had always wanted to set in motion an event of such grandiose proportions.

"That's right. I'll be gettin' on this tomorrow or the next day. And you tell that little girl of yours I'm awful sorry 'bout what happened."

"I will, Verne-Bob. And I thank you kindly for sayin' that. Amelia thanks you too."

Verne-Bob was silent for a long moment. Then, shaking his head, he said in a low angry voice, almost in a whisper: "Them shit-eatin' niggers! I hate every damn one of 'em! No matter how hard I try, I can't get 'em to respect white folk, particularly women and girls."

Amelia Polk's Lesson

Chapter 5

At 7:30 a.m. on the following Sunday approximately three hundred twenty locals—men, women and children— were lined up on the Lake Ferguson ferry landing anxiously waiting to board the sternwheel steamer *Southern Belle* for its twenty-five minute voyage to Arkansas' Saltair Field located twelve miles to the south alongside the western edge of the Mississippi. The *Belle* was scheduled to leave on its first trip of the day ninety minutes later, but, to be on it and thus to be part of the first group to arrive at Saltair Field where they could lay claim to one of the better spots to view the day's festivities, most of those waiting had come to the landing at the crack of dawn. One couple, now at the front of the line, had arrived at 9:00 p.m. the night before. Restless children scurried in and about while a cacophony of loud background noises could be heard: from the crowd itself; from hawkers in straw hats shouting "candy, peanuts, popcorn, cracker jacks, sodie pop, beer, cee-gars, cigarettes, chawin' tabaccy and souven-eers"; and from an organ grinder's concertina. Suddenly, above the din, a woman began screaming. The organ grinder's monkey had broken loose from its tether and jumped up onto her shoulder where it was tugging at her pearl necklace. A man rushed up, grabbed the monkey by its neck and threw it at the organ grinder who, after placing his traumatized pet in its small cage, hurriedly packed up his organ and departed. As he disappeared from view, the crowd broke into applause.

Five-year-old Chauncey Miller, who had almost succeeded in consuming an entire box of cracker jacks, unexpectedly began tugging his father's coat sleeve. "They's comin', Daddy! I kin hear 'em!" Others apparently heard them too, for a hush fell over the crowd.

Far off in the distance the sound of a band playing "Dixie" was barely audible. Ever so slowly it grew louder and louder. And then there they were! The honorable members of the Order of the Ku Klux Klan, Greenville Dominion, swaying and marching to the beat of the South's national hymn.

"Sing, son!" Chauncey's father commanded, and little Chauncey, like the others, began to sing:

I wish I was in Dixie, Hooray! Hooray!

In Dixie's Land I'll take my stand

to live and die in Dixie.

Away, away, away down south in Dixie.

Away, away, away down south in Dixie.

"Keep singing, boy. And never forget who we are and what we stand for!"

As Chauncey and the others continued to sing, they watched the marchers parade by en route to the KKK barge one-half mile away, each, save the Grand Titan, adorned identically in a magnificent white silken robe and matching mask and white pointed hood. First came the bandsmen, in step as they played, their instruments swaying from side to side in unison; next, the eight honor bearers shouldering the two poles to which Harlan and Zachary Jefferson were tied hand and foot—each gagged, blindfolded and nude except for a loin cloth; followed by the Grand Titan whose costume was identical to all the others except for the addition of a large green and gold cross embroidered on its

77

front; alongside him marched a smaller Klansman who seemed to be having difficulty keeping up; and, finally, the remainder of the Greenville Klansmen, ninety strong, following along in step and cadence to the music.

"Here, Chauncey." His father placed a bag of stones in the small boy's hand. "Do what I done tol' you!"

Taking the bag, Chauncey ran as fast as his short legs would carry him, finally catching up to the two Negroes. "Dirty stinkin' niggers!" he cried out in his high-pitched voice as he began pelting them with stones. When some people in the crowd saw this, they began to cheer wildly.

Amelia Polk's Lesson

Chapter 6

Because they had come over on the *Belle's* third trip that morning, Amelia and her father were only able to find standing room near the back of Saltair Field. In front of them Amelia saw a sea of excited people—hundreds, perhaps thousands. She was confused. What were they all doing here?

In fact, unlike almost everyone else, Amelia had no idea why she was at Saltair Field that Sunday morning. All she remembered was being rousted out of bed by her father at 8:00 a.m. and told to get dressed. "We got to get on over to the Arkansas side," he had said. And when they'd finally arrived, here were all these people. What was going on? Where was her mother?

As Jesse Polk stood there next to his daughter, he suddenly realized what a damn fool he'd been to allow his wife to talk him into bringing her here! Now she'd see the results of her mother's evildoing firsthand. He had to get her away from here before she was scarred for life. He knew he didn't have much time. The insanity was about to begin.

"Amelia, honey," he said, nervously taking her by the arm, "I really think we should go back. We arrived too late; too many people in front of us blockin' our view. How 'bout if I take you over to Mertens' place for an extra session? I know you've been workin' hard on those keyboard exercises he gave you."

By now he was sweating profusely and Amelia realized that for some inexplicable reason her father had had a change of heart: he wanted her back home—not here at Saltair Field. And she still had no idea what was going on—or where her mother was. It was time to find out.

"I just want to see what's at the front, Daddy," she said as she pulled away from him and disappeared into the mass of people.

———

When Amelia arrived at the front of the crowd, she saw before her a gallows set atop a wide portable raised wooden platform. Two hooded Klansmen were standing on it chatting, one much taller than the other. The taller Klansman, with an embroidered cross on the front of his gown, was obviously candy man Verne-Bob Johnson, the Grand Titan. She had no idea who the shorter one was.

Off to her right there was a large circular pile of firewood neatly stacked to burn with maximum intensity. A ten-foot stake rose from its center.

"Hey, girlie!" a man called out in a happy voice. "Over here!"

Amelia turned around and saw a family of four seated on a large blanket. Next to it rested a half-open picnic basket.

"Hey, girlie, come join us. Sit yourself down," the man said. He was smiling.

Amelia saw that the four had moved over creating a corner spot for her on the blanket.

"C'mon, girlie!"

"Thank you kindly," Amelia said as she sat down.

"I'm Hersh Graves; this here is my wife, Anna; and our two sons, Bradley and Jacob."

"Nice to meet you all. I'm Amelia Polk."

"Jesus!" Hersh Graves said, his jaw dropping. "You're the one, ain't you?" Then, pointing to Amelia, he said to his wife in a lowered voice, "That there—she's the one, Mother!" He saw his wife's eyes widen.

"Gosh, I'm terrible sorry 'bout what happened to you, little lady. Them two boys who done that to you deserve everythin' they'll be gettin'. That's for darn sure!"

Amelia was puzzled: what in Lord's name was this man talking about? What two boys? And what had been done to her?

Amelia Polk's Lesson

Chapter 7

Some fifty yards behind the platform on which the gallows were erected a small group of Klansman had set up a portable cage into which they had thrown Harlan and Zachary Jefferson. Still wearing only loincloths, but with their gags and blindfolds removed, the two were lying on the bottom of the cage curled up trying to warm themselves—yet uncontrollably shaking with fear.

"Is they gonna kill us, Daddy?" Zachary asked.

Sadly his father nodded. "They calls this a lynchin', an' we's the ones they's gonna lynch. So listen closely, boy."

Zachary, whose eyes had been closed, looked at his father.

"You an' I—we's gonna go to our maker like men. No yellin', no screamin', no crying. None of that. You understand?"

"I do," Zachary replied.

"All right then: you still got that vial Conrad Mertens gave you?"

"Yes, Daddy."

"Well then, boy, pluck it out of you, break it open an' drink it. Now!"

"What's in it, Daddy?"

"Shut up, boy, an' do what I says. I already drank mine. It'll help you pass on over. An' once you does, you waits for me so we both enters heaven at exactly the same time. They gots a big piano up there we can play on. Won't be long now. An' don't you be worryin' 'bout any hurt when you passes on over. It only lasts a few seconds. An' then it be over. You understand?"

Zachary nodded. Reaching behind, he withdrew a tiny glass vial which he had secreted in his rectum.

Breaking it open, he swallowed its contents. Within seconds he began to feel relaxed and happy. Soon he knew he and his daddy would be playing ragtime together on that heavenly piano.

Amelia Polk's Lesson

Chapter 8

Grand Titan Verne-Bob Johnson looked at his pocket watch: 11:30 a.m. It was time. He beckoned to one of the Klansman standing behind the platform. The man nodded, handed Verne-Bob a megaphone and then began making his way toward the cage. Holding the megaphone at his side, Verne-Bob walked to the front of the platform where he raised his right hand for silence. When, almost half a minute later, the crowd quieted down, Verne-Bob raised the megaphone to his lips and began to speak.

"Mornin' folks. And welcome to our little correctional conclave. This will be our sixteenth, countin' from the time I was appointed Grand Titan. And, to tell the truth, I was hopin' the fifteenth would'a been our last, that it would'a taught our niggers a lesson: to keep their filthy hands off our women and girls. But niggers never seem to learn, do they?"

A murmur of concurrence could be heard coming from the crowd.

"Case you don't know, what happened is that the two bucks we'll be sendin' to hell today just couldn't restrain themselves. So I felt they had to be taught a lesson. And I've planned a harsh one. We'll have the youngest of these two boys swingin' from above. And we're gonna leave his body hangin' up there a-stinkin' away to serve as a reminder to all other niggers who might think of steppin' out of line." Verne-Bob glanced up at the horizontal beam forming a part of the scaffold. "The other ... well, we're gonna fry his black ass over there." Verne-Bob smiled as he pointed to the firewood. "And I jes' can't wait to hear him scream. How 'bout you?"

The crowd whistled, clapped and shouted.

"Now, about helpin' support your Klan: After the fire's done simmered down, we got small boxes for ash and bone. Dollar apiece. Jes' as soon as the fire starts, one of the Klansman will be comin' 'round to collect if you want a box. Good conclave souvenir, I might add."

———

On hearing this, Hersh Graves turned to his wife: "I'll be getting' three boxes, honey. Two for us and one for girlie here. That all right with you, young lady?"

Trying as best she could to be polite, Amelia nodded.

———

"And one more thing," Verne-Bob said as he put his arm over the shoulders of the shorter Klansman. "We got the mother of the girl who the two niggers was feelin' up. I'm givin' her the honor of springin' the trap and lightin' the fire. Only right: they did the fondlin' so she'll be doin' the dispatchin'." The shorter Klansman, now identified as a woman, waved to the crowd.

Verne-Bob turned. There, behind him, stood two Klansmen holding Harlan and Zachary Jefferson, their hands tied behind their backs. Both had heard Verne-Bob speak and now knew what awaited them. Zachary was so terrified he began to retch; and Harlan was shaking uncontrollably at the thought of being burned alive—made all the more horrible by the fact that the glass vial Conrad Mertens had given him had somehow slipped out of his rectum and disappeared. When he realized what he would have to endure, tears began to stream down his cheeks. Finally, his bowels gave way and liquid diarrhea began to seep out from under his loincloth and down both legs.

"Bring 'em on up," Verne-Bob commanded, and the two broken black musicians were dragged up onto the platform, both now quivering in fear. As they stood there, the shorter Klansman spat in Zachary's face. "I'm gonna jes' love this, little black boy!" she said. Then, excitedly, she began to jump up and down. "C'mon, let's see what you got. They say niggers is big. I don't believe it!" With that, she pulled off his loincloth revealing a shrunken penis. "Hah! Not so big after all!"

"Jesus, Heather!" Verne-Bob said. "Cover him up! They's kids out there!"

But Heather Polk wasn't listening. Instead, she rushed to the upright at the side of the platform where the hanging noose was tethered. Unfastening it, she carried it to the platform's center and jammed it over Zachary Jefferson's head, cinching it down onto his neck. Then, kicking him to the trap she ran back and fell against the large handle. There was a creaking sound as the trap sprung open and the boy's body fell through it.

"Good riddance, nigger boy!" Heather Polk screamed, again jumping up and down. "That'll teach you to keep your hands off of my little girl!"

When Zachary's body reached the end of the rope there was a loud snapping noise as his neck broke causing him to die instantly. Smiling, Heather Polk proudly removed her hood and then bowed to the crowd—who began cheering, whistling, and applauding.

———

Amelia now realized that it was her mother who had just murdered young Zachary Jefferson because of some crazy notion that he had molested her. "No!" she screamed as she ran toward the platform.

"Stop!" she screamed, hauling herself up onto it. "They didn't do anything to me. We were just playing the piano together. That's all!" Extending both hands, she ran at her mother shoving her backwards. "Stop! No! No! Leave him alone! Stop!"

86

When Heather regained her balance, she screamed to Verne-Bob: "Our little girl's in a state of denial. Get her out of here! She'll ruin everything. Now!"

Verne-Bob nodded and beckoned to one of the Klansman who came up onto the platform and carried a biting, scratching Amelia down off it.

"Sorry for that interruption, folks," Verne-Bob said through his megaphone. He again motioned to the same Klansman who grabbed Harlan Jefferson by the arm and yanked him toward the stake.

"You wanna tie him up, Verne-Bob?" the Klansman asked.

"No, you go 'head. I'll just let Heather here start the fire."

——

Strangely, while all this was going on, Verne-Bob was having serious regrets. From his many visits to Madame Foucoult's, it finally dawned on him that his victims were those two piano players whose music he loved—and whose music he would never hear again. And Heather Polk's story about those two well-behaved respectful blacks molesting her daughter? A load o' crap! Yet there was no turning back, for today's events had gone too far. And, anyway, this wasn't about truth; this was about keeping niggers in their place. Besides, the last KKK conclave had been more than a year ago. So it was time. Too bad, though, it had to be those two boys.

——

Jesse Polk had finally made his way to the front of the crowd. Spying his weeping daughter behind the platform, he walked over to her.

"Time to go, Lia," he said. "You've already seen too much."

87

"But why, Daddy? What did they do? And why is Momma murderin' them?"

"C'mon," he said. "Our boat's leavin' in a few minutes."

As they neared the wharf, they heard a series of horrifying screams lasting several minutes: the last sounds uttered by Harlan Jefferson.

———

When, finally, Amelia and her father arrived back at the Polk family home Amelia ran up to her room, locked the door, and threw herself face down on the bed. Silently she began to cry uncontrollably, for she knew that two innocents—two extraordinary talents—had been murdered by her mother.

Sometime later there was a knock on her door. "Amelia, honey, please let me in."

"Go away, Daddy."

"No, Amelia, we've got to talk before your mother gets back. Please!"

Reluctantly, Amelia got up from her bed and unlocked the door.

"Honey, I'm so ashamed of your mother. Those two boys …"

"They were great talents, Daddy."

"I know. Let's sit down. We gotta talk."

"About what, Daddy?"

"Your future, Amelia. You've got to leave Greenville. You've got to go." Jesse Polk handed her an envelope. "Here. It's all the cash I could lay my hands on. Take it. Conrad Mertens is downstairs. He'll take you to the train station. He's got friends in Chicago. He'll tell you all about them. But you've got to leave. I don't want you around your mother or the kind of things that happened today. You understand?"

Amelia nodded.

"And one more thing, Amelia—a lesson you must never forget. Don't ever allow the races to mix. It only leads to hatred and murder. The Jeffersons was decent men, and they bein' black didn't amount to nothin' bad. But when they was mixed up with whites ... well, you saw what happened. So promise me, Amelia: you'll never allow blacks and whites to mix."

"I promise, Daddy."

"All right, then. Let's go on downstairs."

———

"Where's that daughter of mine?" Heather Polk asked shortly after returning.

"She'll be back. She went over to Mertens' place."

Heather Polk nodded approvingly. "I did good today, didn't I, Jesse?"

"You did, dear. C'mon over and let me hug you." Jesse Polk extended his arms as his wife melted into them.

"I'm so proud of you," Jesse Polk said as he reached up and caressed the back of his wife's neck. "You're so special." And then, placing his hands gently around her throat, he began choking her with a rage repressed by his many years of shameful cowardice.

"Jesse, please ..." was all Heather Polk was able to utter in a shocked gasping voice before slipping into unconsciousness.

———

Jesse Polk looked down at his wife's lifeless body. Satisfied, he slowly walked up the ornate staircase. Several minutes later the sound of a gunshot could be heard reverberating throughout the second floor of the Polk family home.

3:00 p.m., Wednesday, July 30, 1969
Jefferson Memorial Library
Greenville, Mississippi

Like father, like son, Judge Junior Washburn mused as he watched tears streaming down the cheeks of his grandson. The two were standing in front of the main entrance to Greenville's Harlan and Zachary Jefferson Memorial Library. The judge recalled how Christopher Wallace had talked him into bringing Jamie's father, James, to this same place in August 1947, just a few weeks before that dancing thing came to a head. James, all six feet four inches of him—and a hardened air combat veteran to boot—had broken down and cried in similar fashion. After that, the judge realized how important it was that his son—and now his grandson—know all about the cold-blooded murders of the Jeffersons. True, Greenville had tried to make amends—this library, for example. But, still, those murders must never be forgotten.

"Come here, Jamie," the judge said. "You need some lovin'. I 'spect that's what old grandfathers are for."

"You're not old," Jamie said, embracing the judge.

"Sometimes we just need one another, boy. And I guess this is one of those times."

"I love you, Grandpa."

"And I love you too, Jamie. I just felt that I had to bring you here so's I could show you the old Polk home and the academy buildin'—and then take you down river to Saltair Field. Seein' those places made it a whole lot easier for me to tell you all about Amelia Polk and the Jeffersons. And that's important. All part of our journey of discovery.

"Fact is, I took the same trip with your daddy years ago. Just like you, he cried."

"Dad cried?"

"Yep. And when Christopher Wallace took me

90

down here almost thirty years ago and told me about the Jeffersons, I cried too. I guess that's when I decided that even if I couldn't change the past, maybe in some small way I could use its rubble to repave the future."

"Is that when you decided to become a judge?"

"Don't know for sure. Maybe."

"And have you changed things, Grandpa?"

"Don't know as I did all that much changin' as a judge. But later on ..." The old man stopped in mid-sentence, not wanting to continue.

"Somethin' you should know about us, boy: We Washburns are sentimental—and we place a whole lot of store in history, because knowin' history makes for knowin' how to change the future. What you learned today is history, Jamie, important history. Plus, the Jeffersons' lynchin's weren't the only ones. There were hundreds of others."

"But why, Grandpa? Why?"

"Figured you'd be askin' that. Your daddy asked me the same question. And after he came down here he even took a summer course on racial bigotry. Taught by one of his university contemporaries, Gordon Arles. Arles' book, Explaining Racial Prejudice, *was considered the last word on the subject at the time. I read it; so did your daddy. Still, neither one of us has the answers. What fuels man's inhumanity to man escapes all logic and reason. Maybe it's greed; or fear; or a hunger for power. Who knows? It was present back when the Jeffersons were murdered; it existed durin' the last war when millions were exterminated; and it still exists today. Wish I had those answers, boy. I just don't."*

The judge saw that his grandson was no longer crying.

"C'mon, let's go inside the library. I want you to hear some of that Jefferson ragtime."

"Really, Grandpa?"

91

"Yep. *Mertens could play it. He recorded it years back—just before he died. The library's gonna be playin' some of it in their auditorium beginnin' in a few minutes. We'll listen to it; and then I want to go to the bookstore. There's an important book they sell in there, 'Saltair Sadness.' And they've also got a tape recordin' of some Jefferson ragtime. I'm gonna buy you both.*

"The book's important, Jamie. *All about the Jeffersons' murders. For you to keep so's you can tell your children and grandchildren what you learned today.*

"And the tape recordin's special—somethin' to remind you of our trip down here."

"I'll keep them both forever, Grandpa."

"Knew you would, boy."

———

Several hours later Jamie was seated on a wooden bench in the Greenville train station writing in his notebook. His grandfather had just returned after buying a newspaper and some candy at the newsstand.

"I'll be glad to be getting home, Grandpa."

"Home? *Who said anythin' about home? We're not done travelin'. Not by a long shot. We gotta go on down to Tuskegee, Alabama, to learn more about that Glencoe dancin' puzzle.*"

"Tuskegee? *What's there, Grandpa?*"

"Didn't *your daddy ever tell you anythin' about Tuskegee, Jamie?*"

"No."

"That *son of mine! Never says a word, does he? Well Tuskegee is all about your daddy. And that's where we'll be headin' next. Train leaves in about an hour.*"

Excerpt from Jamie's Notebook, Page 55

About two hours before we arrive in Tuskegee:

I was pretty miserable when I crawled into the upper berth last night. I shouldn't have done it, I guess, but just before getting into bed I took a look at that eight-track tape Grandpa bought for me. It had a photo on it of a Negro dangling by his neck from a scaffold. I wonder if he was Zachary Jefferson? I'll have to ask Grandpa. But the whole thing did more than upset me—it sickened me. I guess back then people considered lynchings to be common events—maybe something like a community social or a town dance. Probably some were even set to music. I can just imagine Negroes being hanged or burned at the stake while the local band played on.

Before we went to bed last night Grandpa told me we'd be having breakfast in the dining car, which is where we ate dinner last night. Good food but a strange place: everyone who works in there is black except the headwaiter. And all the passengers I've seen on the train so far are white—except Grandpa and me.

James Washburn's Promises

James Washburn's Promises – List of Characters
["B" denotes black; "W" denotes white; * denotes a real person]

James Lincoln Washburn III (Jamie's father, military officer/attorney) B

Captain Benton B. Donald Jr. (later colonel and eventually general) B

Franklin Roosevelt (thirty-second US president) W*

Anna Eleanor "Babs" Roosevelt (wife of Franklin Roosevelt, First Lady) W*

Jared (secret service agent assigned to First Lady) W

Charles "Skip" Taylor (flight instructor, Tuskegee Institute) B

Phillip Kelsey (military officer, instructed Tuskegees in air tactics) W

Daniel "Danny" Hawthorne Ehrenreich (student at Boston's Latin School and MIT, later pilot-in-command of B-17 *Sluggo's Awakening*) W

Bailey Shirk (Boston's Latin School teacher) W

Wit Welch (*Bay State Skyriders* salesperson) W

Noah Wilson (B-17's navigator) W

Francis "Frank" Bennett (B-17's co-pilot) W

"Shorty" (B-17's ball turret gunner, oldest crew member) W

Stanley Hope (B-17's left waist gunner) W

Margaret Carlton (Central School teacher) W

Warren Richman, M.D. (Glencoe physician) W

James Washburn's Promises

Chapter 1

From all outward appearances First Lady Eleanor Roosevelt and her husband, President Franklin Roosevelt, were certainly an odd couple: she, with a small round head, recessed chin, crooked buck teeth, and an elongated torso which she held erect making her appear far taller than he; and he, round-shouldered and weary, his enormous partially balding head held back at an ungainly angle punctuated by the silver cigarette holder clenched between his teeth, the glowing tip of its cigarette pointing skyward. Similarly, their apparel contrasted. She, oblivious to fashion, wore no makeup and had on a slightly wrinkled black shapeless ankle-length dress along with a strange pointed black hat pinned to her knotted bun; and he, since his Harvard undergraduate days scrupulously conscious of attire, dressed in a neatly pressed seersucker suit, a fresh white shirt, and a colorful striped repp tie.

The two sat outside on the White House veranda at a small round rattan table with a glass top on which their drinks rested. She drank tea with lemon while he was on his third martini. It was approaching 5:00 p.m. and the cool crisp autumn air seemed to please them both. Raising his glass, he sipped the ice-cold gin before glancing out over the wide expanse of lawn, beyond the flowers—beyond even the wrought iron fence behind which tall shrubs grew ensuring privacy—to where he could follow the sun, now a large orange ball on its downward course toward the horizon. He sighed and thought of her. Without looking, he knew her eyes were closed and that her mind was racing.

She had asked to join him this afternoon, a rare occurrence these days. She wanted something. Whatever it was, he was sure it would surprise him. He knew her so well. After all, they had been married for decades. And now he began to think of their early years.

Oh the times they had! The drinking; the partying; the lovemaking; the parenting; and, best of all, the children. But those were all in the past. Lovemaking for him, a strange activity given his paralysis, he now reserved for others; and martinis had become his solitary afternoon respite. How sad that they were no longer soul mates and lovers, something they both understood. Instead, she had assumed a new role, that of his eyes and ears.

Still clenching the cigarette holder between his teeth, he smiled broadly, his way of bracing himself for what was certain to be a request from her of such outlandish proportions that any other person would reject it out of hand—a request he knew he must grant. He owed her that much. He sipped his martini once again. And then, finally, he asked the question she had been anticipating for well over half an hour: "Well, Babs, what is it?"

James Washburn's Promises

Chapter 2

The sweltering hangar reeked of degreaser and fuel as the two secret service agents tasked to guard the First Lady looked on in horror. They now realized that within a few minutes she would be placing her life on the line. "Ma'am, please!" the older of the two said. "We can't let you do this!"

Eleanor Roosevelt smiled at him dismissively as she finished buttoning up the front of the flight suit Charles "Skip" Taylor insisted she put on. "Now, Jared … you and Roy go get something to eat. I'll be fine. Skip here will see to everything, won't you?" She looked over at the lanky Negro also wearing a flight suit.

"Not a thing to worry 'bout, Mrs. R.," he replied. "I'll have you flying my little play toy in no time." He affectionately patted the fading yellow fabric which covered the fuselage of his tiny two-seater aircraft.

"You see," Mrs. Roosevelt said as she continued addressing the two agents, "I really will be fine. So please go get some lunch."

"Yes, ma'am," Jared replied. It was always the same with her. He knew that once she'd made up her mind there was no changing it. Maybe that was why he'd grown to hate his job. Whenever he was assigned to travel with her he was plagued by those damn headaches—probably brought on by worries that if something happened to her his pension would go up in smoke.

———

Eleanor Roosevelt stood alone in the rundown hangar which abutted Moton Field, a small airfield named after the second president of nearby Tuskegee Institute. For some reason—she wasn't quite sure what it was—Skip

99

Taylor had disappeared for the moment. She had concluded that he was indeed an unusual man. He'd been flying since he was a teenager. Some years back, at the request of Tuskegee's current president, Frederick Douglass Patterson, Skip had inaugurated a Civilian Pilot Training Program for the Institute's all-Negro student body. Over those years, he'd taught a respectable number of Negro youngsters to fly, so many in fact that some time ago he'd lost count.

While she awaited Skip's return, Eleanor Roosevelt's thoughts drifted back to what she and her husband had discussed on the White House veranda several months before. How she had misjudged him! He had wanted this as much as she. She smiled as she recalled their conversation:

"The American Negro, Franklin, is not being treated as a citizen—at least not in the true sense. Just think of the dreadful discrimination he's forced to endure. And that, my dear, is your government's fault." She *chuckled now remembering the way she'd emphasized the words "your government's fault." It was all part of her prearranged grand plan to add a modicum of guilt to the pot.*

"Another thing, Franklin. That despicable Army War College study stating that Negroes aren't intelligent enough to fly airplanes. Poppycock!"

She recalled looking for a reaction from him, but there was none. Was he even listening?

"And those three senators: Harry Schwartz and Styles Bridges—and that pushy little man from Missouri. What's his name?"

"Truman, Babs," the president had replied.

Aha! He was listening!

"Yes, Truman. Well, those three have been pressuring me to have you authorize the formation of a Negro pursuit squadron and build an airfield for it."

100

Still no reaction. Puzzling.

"You'll always need the Negro vote, Franklin. A Negro pursuit squadron might help."

Nothing.

"You were the first person to say that your margin of victory in the '36 election would have improved if more Negroes had voted for you. Well, the 1940 election is coming up in a little over a month and ..."

She remembered that at this point her husband had begun to laugh aloud.

"Enough, Babs. I completely agree with you. For some time now I've been meaning to authorize a Negro flying unit and have an airfield built for them. That's what you want, isn't it?"

"Precisely."

Thank God, he had been listening!

"Well, consider it done. I'll have Harry Hopkins get to work on it immediately. I suspect we'll have this thing approved early next year—that is, assuming I'm reelected. And if I am, I'll authorize construction of that airfield. But before I permit the program to get underway, I'll have to have something to rebut that damn War College study—and that, Babs, is where you come in: when you can tell me, based on your own observations, that you're convinced that Negroes can fly airplanes, I'll see to it that flight training begins. Do we understand one another?"

Eleanor Roosevelt remembered leaning over and kissing her husband on the cheek.

"One more thing, Babs: whatever you do, I don't want you setting foot in any cockpit. You're way too important to me to be doing something as foolish as that."

"I wouldn't dream of it, my dear," she remembered replying.

———

101

Skip Taylor reappeared. He was holding a leather flying helmet and a pair of goggles. "Better put these on, Mrs. R. It's gonna be cold and windy up there."

James Washburn's Promises

Chapter 3

"Heavens to Betsy!" Eleanor Roosevelt thought, removing her helmet and goggles. "My cheeks are red as beets!" She smiled as she viewed her face in the mirror of the washroom just down the hall from Skip Taylor's office at Tuskegee Institute. She also felt slightly tipsy—as if, like her husband, she had just finished her third martini. No wonder: rarely had she been so invigorated and elated. She thought of poor Jared who must have turned green when Skip's plane had come barreling in upside down along the length of the runway. At the time it seemed to her as if they were only a few feet above its concrete surface, but later Skip had assured her there was at least twenty feet of clearance between the tip of the plane's vertical stabilizer and the ground.

Her biggest thrill, though, was when Skip had let her execute a takeoff without his help—and she had done it perfectly: advancing the throttle to full power and then, when his tiny airplane was rolling down the runway at sixty knots, gently pulling back on the stick causing it to leave the ground and rotate skyward! Damn, if Franklin would only let me take flying lessons. But of course she knew he wouldn't. Well, she'd better get back to Skip's office. He'd told her there were some people he wanted her to meet.

———

"Mrs. R., I'd like to introduce you to Captain Benton B. Donald Jr. and James Washburn. They're both on the faculty here at the institute, and I've given them primary flight instruction. I'd say they fly about as well as I do."

"Now, Skip, I really find that hard to believe," the First Lady said as she shook hands first with Captain Donald and then with James Washburn.

"You know," she continued, "I do believe we've met, Captain—that is, if your father is Brigadier General Benton B. Donald."

"We did meet briefly last year, ma'am, when my father received his star."

"Of course. And if my memory serves me, your father mentioned that you were going to follow in his footsteps."

"Correct, ma'am. I graduated from the Point."

Mrs. Roosevelt was silent for a long moment. "I suspect you had some difficult times there, didn't you?"

Captain Donald appeared uncomfortable. He looked over at Skip.

"He did well at West Point, Mrs. R. Finished twenty-seventh out of a class of three hundred twelve. So I'd say he didn't find the curriculum all that difficult."

"Skip, you know perfectly well that's not what I mean. I'm talking about the way he was treated." Turning to Captain Donald, she continued. "Would you like to tell me about that, Captain?"

"With all respect, ma'am, no. That's in the past. What I want to do is begin basic flight instruction at TAAF—and we need your husband's okay to get the program started."

"TAAF?"

"Tuskegee Army Air Field, ma'am. The one that was completed two months ago."

"Ah, yes. The new airfield. Well, all right, we'll forget about your West Point experience, Captain. But I must say that unless you tell me about the problems you encountered when you were a cadet, I can't get them fixed."

"Understood, ma'am."

"And you, Mr. Washburn. I'm not letting you off the hook either. How is that ornery father of yours?"

A look of surprise came over James' face. "You know my father, ma'am?"

"He's probably the best trial lawyer west of Washington, D.C. And you look just like him, except that you're about a foot taller. Some years back I was asked to speak at an American Bar Association convention, and that's where we met. We've been friends ever since. I'm surprised he hasn't mentioned me. In fact, shortly after we met I had him represent a relative of mine in a rather nasty lawsuit. Needless to say, your father crushed opposing counsel—much to the delight of my relative and the president. So I have nothing but the utmost respect for him and his legal ability. If you're half the man he is, you'll set the world on fire in whatever it is you choose to do—that is, if you've decided."

"I'm sure my father's ears are burning, Mrs. Roosevelt. And I'm not surprised he hasn't told me about you. He's extraordinarily tight-lipped except when it comes to my future—and then he won't keep quiet. At his insistence, I did go to law school. But after I finished—and over his strenuous objections—I decided to come down here and teach for a while. That's when Captain Donald and I became friends and Skip introduced me to flying. And now I'm hooked."

"Hooked?"

"On flying, ma'am. You saw how it was today. When Skip sinks his talons into you, well … flying just gets into your blood. As soon as the president gives his okay and flight training begins, I'm going to enlist. With my law degree and my civilian pilot training, Captain Donald has assured me I'll be able to go directly into the Army Air Corps as a cadet and receive flight training here at TAAF as a member of the 99th Pursuit Squadron."

"The 99th Pursuit Squadron?"

"That's the all-Negro unit we're hoping your husband will authorize."

"Consider it a *fait accompli*. I'll make certain of that." Mrs. Roosevelt smiled.

"And by the way, Mr. Washburn, I'm curious to know how your father has taken to all this?"

"Not well, Mrs. Roosevelt. But at the same time he knows—we all know—that there's a war coming on and that we'll be fighting alongside Great Britain in a matter of months."

"Really? And how can you be so sure of that?"

"It was a dead giveaway, ma'am, when your husband concocted that spurious Lend Lease program."

"My, young man, you don't mince words, do you?" Eleanor Roosevelt chuckled. "Well rest assured I won't mention to the president that Junior Washburn's son considers the Lend Lease program a sham. If he heard that, I'm afraid you'd be spending the duration of the war on KP rather than in the cockpit of an airplane."

"Sorry, ma'am, but we here at the institute ..."

"James, for Christ's sake, enough!" Captain Donald cut in. "Mrs. Roosevelt didn't come all the way down here to get our take on world affairs; she came to see if Negroes could fly airplanes. Skip's convinced her of that. And now he's decided to introduce her to two future Army aviators. That's all!" Captain Donald saw that Skip was nodding. "So clam up!"

"Yes, sir," James replied.

Captain Donald continued to glare at him for several seconds before addressing Mrs. Roosevelt. "Ma'am, I take it you'd like to see TAAF before you leave?"

"I would indeed, Captain."

"Well, if you like, I'd be glad to drive you over there and give you a Cook's tour. Some of the instructors and staff are there right now waiting for the program to begin."

"I accept your kind offer, Captain. And the instructors and staff you refer to: are they Negro or white?"

"The enlisted people are Negro, ma'am. They're the squadron support staff and they were trained earlier in the year at Chanute Field in Illinois. But the CO, Executive Officer and flight instructors are all white."

"And spit and polish regular Army, I suppose?"

"Exactly, ma'am."

"Well you understand that once the program gets underway things aren't going to be easy for you. I'm sure those instructors are aware of the Army's 1925 War College study which concluded that Negroes aren't bright enough to fly airplanes. If my instincts are correct, they're going to go out of their way to confirm the study's findings. So you'd better be prepared for some difficult times ahead."

"Believe me when I tell you, Mrs. Roosevelt: I know how to deal with that."

"I'm sure you do. I just hope the cadets who join you in the program are able to do the same."

"I'll make sure they are, ma'am."

Mrs. Roosevelt saw that James Washburn had been listening intently to the conversation. She continued: "One more thing, Captain. When war comes—just as Mr. Washburn here says it will—the 99th Pursuit Squadron will have two missions, one assigned by the Army Air Corps and the other by me."

"Pardon, ma'am?"

"The Army Air Corps, Captain, will assign you your military mission. And right now I'm assigning a second mission—to you, to James, and to the other members of the Tuskegee airmen. You are to fight on against the evils of racial intolerance which are festering within our nation. That battle may span decades, Captain, but win it you must. If you do not, our nation will be torn asunder."

Then, narrowing her eyes as she bore in on Captain Donald, she continued with a forcefulness he found

107

surprising: "And Captain, when your unit is operational, I want it to become the finest pursuit squadron in the United States Army Air Force. I want its record to be so outstanding that it will be honored throughout the land. Do that and you will go a long way in demonstrating that Negroes are Americans in the truest and most complete sense—and that they deserve to be treated as equals. May I count on you to do that?"

Captain Benton B. Donald Jr. swallowed hard, realizing that he had just received a direct order from the nation's First Lady.

"Yes, ma'am," he replied as he drew himself up to attention and saluted.

———

In the president's office several weeks later President Roosevelt met with Harry Hopkins, one of his closest advisors. "Can you update me on the status of that all-Negro squadron, Harry?"

"It's been approved by the War Department, Mr. President."

"Excellent," the president replied.

James Washburn's Promises

Chapter 4

Where had the time gone since he had begun flight training more than three years ago? James was having difficulty constructing a timeline, perhaps because during those intervening years his hopes would soar one day only to be dashed the next.

James remembered feeling more jubilant than he'd ever felt that sunny cool afternoon in late March 1942 when he'd received his silver pilot's wings and his commission in the United States Army Air Force as a second lieutenant. His months of hard work and training—of overcoming the persistent attempts by his white instructors to prove to him, to themselves, and to the world, that Negroes were incapable of flying airplanes—had finally paid off. Yet when they'd gone into town that evening to celebrate, he also recalled the rage which had welled up within him when one of the locals spit in his face. He wanted to kill that damn cracker, but, thanks to Captain Donald who had grabbed hold of him and shepherded him back to TAAF, he hadn't.

Still, there was more frustration: for over a year after his graduation their unit, the 99th Fighter Squadron, had sat on its hands at TAAF because their CO, Major Ronald Langston, stubbornly refused to believe that, no matter what their training, Negroes would ever be able to cut it as pilots.

And then his elation when Major Neal Peterson replaced Langston and prevailed upon the powers that be to allow them to go into combat, culminating on that unforgettable day when they finally received their orders to North Africa.

James remembered their ocean crossing on the *USS Mariposa*, his seasickness, and how Ben Donald, by then a lieutenant colonel, had taken command of the troops on board—the first time in history a black army officer had ever commanded white soldiers.

At the ancient North African city of Tunis, their final destination, came yet another concern: when the 99th became a part of the 21st Fighter Group and James and the others realized they were going to be sent out on their first mission without any training in combat flying; followed by his relief upon meeting Lieutenant Colonel Phillip Kelsey, an ex-Flying Tiger, who moved in with them and, in a week's time, taught them everything he knew about flying the P-40L Warhawk in combat.

Then came their first combat assignment, a low level strafing attack of enemy fortifications on the island of Pantelleria on June 2, 1943. Once it was captured by the Allies, this tiny volcanic speck located in the Strait of Sicily would serve as an important Allied air base in *Operation Corkscrew*, the upcoming invasion of Sicily. Although they acquitted themselves with distinction, once again racism reared its ugly head in the person of the 21st CO, Colonel Paul Munro, who claimed that they were the poorest performing squadron in the group and should be decommissioned. Only through the extraordinary efforts of Ben Donald were Munro's attempts to have the 99th disbanded finally derailed. But, still, to James it seemed racism just wouldn't go away.

———

In every human experience there comes a turning point. For James and the others it was the moment Munro lost his battle to scuttle the 99th. From that time on, things began to go their way. In October they were detached from Munro's 21st FG and reassigned to the 83rd Fighter Group commanded by Colonel Ezra Kling Jr. Their new group's mission: to support the invasion of Italy. Kling, who turned out to be as color blind as Neal Peterson and Phil

110

Kelsey, viewed the 99th simply as an addition to his team. He intentionally created mixed squadrons of whites and blacks so that James and the others could learn from seasoned combat fliers. Once treated with decency and respect, their confidence soared and their performance improved.

In March 1944 the 99th began a series of aircraft upgrades, transitioning first from the P-40 Warhawk to the much smaller but more advanced P-39 Bell Airacobra; next, a few months later, to Republic's daunting P-47 Thunderbolt, the largest, heaviest, most powerful and most expensive fighter of its time; and, finally, in July 1944, to the wondrous P-51C Mustang, by all accounts the finest fighter of World War II. Accompanying the arrival of the Mustang came more changes for the 99th, all to the good.

As the war progressed in a northerly direction up the Italian peninsula, the 99th, which by now had been awarded two Distinguished Unit Citations, joined three other squadrons made up of recent Tuskegee graduates, the 100th, the 301st, and the 302nd, to form the 332nd Fighter Group, an all-black unit commanded by Colonel Benton Donald, newly appointed to full colonel.

For James, this was truly the high point of his years in the service. Stationed on Italy's Adriatic coast at Ramitelli Air Field, the 332nd would soon begin bomber escort duty, but not before the spinners and vertical stabilizers of its Mustangs were painted an outlandish bright red as if to announce to the world that, yes, Negroes could fly airplanes! And soon the reputation of the 332nd would spread. To the enemy aviators of Nazi Germany's *Luftwaffe* they would be known as the dreaded *Schwarze Vogelmenschen* or "black birdmen"; and to allied bomber crews they would simply be the *Red Tails* or, perhaps more appropriately, the beloved *Red Tail Angels*.

Chapter 5

James thought of his first escort mission months before. That had been a time when he considered piloting a fighter fun, even romantic. But that had been short-lived. Now it was hard, strenuous work, well thought out ahead of time, and subject to that one all-important constraint imposed by Colonel Donald:

"Gentlemen, we have all graduated. First from the P-40 to the Bell Airacobra; then on to the P-47; and now to the Mustang which we all know can outrun and outmaneuver the best the Jerries have to offer.

"But I'm not gonna let you use it to rack up kills— that is, unless it's part of our mission. Which is ..." he paused, lowering his voice so they all had to listen carefully, *"to shepherd our bombers to their target zone and then back home.*

"I realize we can't control flak, but we sure as hell can keep those Me 109s and Focke-Wulf 190s away from our bombers.

"Bottom line: No Red Tail will permit any German fighter to bring down even one of our bombers. Not a single damn one of 'em! Never, ever! Not so long as this group is operational! Not so long as I am in command! Understood?" He looked around the room. No one said a word.

Then he continued. *"Be assured that I will court-martial any man who takes off on a shooting spree and abandons his bombers."*

James Washburn's Promises

Chapter 6

March 24, 1945: a date James would always remember.

Aloft in the cockpit of his P-51C Mustang, James was soothed by the loud throbbing of its powerful Packard Merlin engine. "Do not ever forget that we have achieved a surreal oneness, your soul and I," the engine's humming seemed to say to him. "I know that," James thought. "That's why I've given you a very special name: *My Promises.*"

My Promises. The name transported James back in time to two sacred promises, one made a very long time ago:

The first he'd made the morning after graduation day when he'd almost clobbered that racist for spitting on him. Ben Donald had taken them all aside that morning and, drawing upon his West Point experience, had told them to ignore racial slurs and insults and instead —and to quote Ben—"just get on with it." Then Ben had made them all promise to become the best damn pilots in the Army Air Force and to demonstrate to themselves, to each other, to America, and to the world that Negroes could fly airplanes. And thus far under Ben's leadership they had kept that promise: The Red Tails' record as bomber escorts was one of the best in history.   The first promise remained unbroken.

And the second promise? A very personal one. James smiled as he recalled that freezing morning in January when, as a second grader, he had been on his way to school. Slipping and sliding north on the sidewalk along the east side of Vernon Avenue, Glencoe's main thoroughfare, he came to its intersection with Hazel Street. It was here that he was to cross over to the west side of

113

Vernon and continue on up Hazel to Central School. He stopped, looked in both directions and then began to cross. Out of nowhere, a car slammed into him. As he fell to the street's icy surface, he felt a searing pain in his left thigh.

"How do you feel, son?" James had been unconscious. But now as he looked up he saw a tall man in a white coat looking down at him. A stethoscope hung from the man's neck, and he held James' wrist apparently taking his pulse. It was Dr. Richman, the man who hit him.

"You had a close call there. Your parents are on the way. I've also called Miss Carlton. She said she'll be by as soon as possible." Miss Margaret Carlton was his second grade teacher.

James closed his eyes and drifted back into unconsciousness. He awoke to the sound of voices hovering over him.

"My fault," Dr. Richman said. "The street was covered with ice and I skidded into the intersection. Good thing it happened just a few feet from my office."

"But we must pay you," he heard his father say.

"Nonsense. Pay me for running into your boy? I couldn't accept a penny from you."

"But he was out in the middle of street, wasn't he?" his father continued.

"Just an unfortunate accident. The x-rays don't show any breaks. He'll just be sore as hell for a week or two."

It was at this point that Miss Carlton cleared her throat. "James is the one who must pay for this." She hesitated for a moment before emphatically adding with finality: "And he must pay dearly!"

"James must pay?" his father asked, perplexed. Dr. Richman also seemed confused.

"That's right. I want James to pay," Miss Carlton repeated. "A valuable lesson learned is quickly forgotten unless there's repayment." Then reaching out, she grasped

the tiny boy's shoulders and gently shook him. His eyes opened.

"Have you been listening?"

"What?"

"I see you haven't been. Well, then, listen now: James, you were in the middle of the street. You didn't do anything wrong. And Dr. Richman's car hit a patch of ice and skidded into you. And he didn't do anything wrong. What happened is something we call an 'accident.' You do understand that, don't you?"

"Yes, ma'am."

"And you could have been killed."

"I know, ma'am."

"Of course you know that. And the only reason you weren't was because the Almighty intervened. He spared you."

James nodded.

"And for that you owe him your thanks—and something even more important, James: you owe him repayment of a very large debt."

"I don't understand."

"You will, young man. You will. You will carry this debt with you until the right moment arrives. And when it does, you must make repayment in full. You owe it to the Almighty." Miss Carlton looked down at James and saw that he was listening.

"Now will you promise to do that?"

"Yes, but …" James hesitated, "when will I know it's time for repayment?"

"Trust me, James: you will know. It may not be for many years, but you will know." James saw that his parents and Dr. Richman were nodding approvingly.

———

James glanced down over his right shoulder. There, two thousand feet below, Ramitelli Airfield was beginning to fade from view. He looked at his watch: exactly thirty-three minutes before their scheduled rendezvous with the B-17s they had been assigned to escort back from the target area.

"Keep your eyes peeled," James commanded, as he spoke over the radio to the three other members of Able Flight who were spaced roughly two thousand feet apart in a loose diamond-shaped tactical spread with James in the lead—a formation designed for maximum scanning of the skies in search of enemy fighters.

With red tails gleaming in the morning Italian sun, the four P-51s making up Able Flight flew ahead of the squadron's three other flights. Once again Able was on its way to do the job it had done so often in the past: make damn sure its charges, a formation of twelve B-17s, returned home safely from their target area—undamaged and without a single casualty. To the members of Able Flight this would be a cakewalk—*or so they thought.*

James Washburn's Promises

Chapter 7

In early 1939 Ernie Bushmiller's comic strip, *Nancy*, had a large and loyal following. Whenever Danny Ehrenreich first opened the paper his attention was always drawn to it, perhaps because he identified with Nancy's inseparable sluggish companion from the wrong side of the tracks aptly named "Sluggo." Like Sluggo, Danny's favorite pastime—at least while a teenager—was napping. Once in U.S. history class at Boston's famed Latin School while Mr. Bailey Shirk, his teacher, was holding forth on the Articles of Confederation, Danny fell into a deep sleep, so deep in fact that he began to snore just as old Shirk started explaining why the Articles were no damn good and needed to be replaced by a constitution. "Ehrenreich!" he remembered Bailey screaming at him, "pick your head up, man! For God's sake start listening and learning or you'll never amount to anything!"

Among the Latin School faculty Bailey Shirk had a reputation for prescience. Yet in the case of Danny Ehrenreich he was dead wrong. Surprisingly (at least to Bailey Shirk), Danny graduated close to the top of his class at Latin before matriculating at MIT where he excelled. There his professors identified him as some kind of a whiz kid, someone who absorbed and understood just about anything and everything presented in class. In fact, while at MIT Danny seemed to be so energized and full of questions—just the opposite of his sluggishness in high school—that one of his classmates accused him of being hyperkinetic. Danny, however, suffered neither from overly active behavior nor from narcolepsy. In high school he had been bored; at MIT he was alive. Somehow, he knew that eventually he would become a professor of engineering, though in what field he wasn't sure. To his parents delight, Danny's life had finally settled in. His future was beginning to unfold in what his father considered "an orderly fashion," never again to be as out of kilter as it had been at Latin. Finally, Danny was on the road to amounting to something.

And that in fact would have been the way things played out except for Danny's chance encounter with fast-talking Wit Welch.

Wit's first job—and the highlight of his career—had been as a barker with a rundown carnival. By the time Wit met Danny, he had sunk to the bottom of the barrel as director of marketing for Bay State Skyriders, a shaky flight training school headquartered in Summerville, exactly seven nautical miles from the MIT campus. For nearly a year Bay State had teetered on the brink of insolvency and Wit had been hired on to use his carnival salesmanship skills to turn it around.

And so, while school was in session, he made a point of visiting every high school and every institution of higher learning in the Boston area at least twice each month. At schools where students lived on campus he would normally show up during the dinner hour. Thus, on a cold clear evening in early November 1942, Wit set up camp in the hallway just outside MIT's student dining hall. Seated in a folding chair behind a card table stacked with Bay State Skyriders' promotional materials, he began his search for pigeons to sign up for nine weeks of flight training. His first pigeon of the evening turned out to be Danny Ehrenreich.

"Hey, kid, how 'bout a free demo flight? I'll even let you take 'er up. Whaddya say?"

Without hesitating, Danny replied, "Sure, why not?"

——

In June 1943, with the war in full swing, Danny completed his third year at MIT. Shortly after that he received a letter from the dean's office notifying him that he was one of only six in his class to be elected to Phi Beta Kappa. Danny thought that was nice, but the letter hardly even registered with him. No longer was he thinking of engineering; instead—and to the great disappointment of his parents, particularly his father—it was flying, thanks not only to Wit Welch's salesmanship but also to his Bay State flight instructor's expertise which resulted in Danny receiving his private pilot's license after only seventeen hours aloft. And if flying really was what he wanted to do, then he'd better forget about his senior year at MIT and enlist—because it didn't take a genius to see that the war effort was tilting in favor of the Allies and that the war would soon be over.

———

The fact that Danny was half a bubble off plumb became apparent when, as one of the top students in his USAAF basic flight training class at Woodring Field outside of Enid, Oklahoma, he early on opted for bombers rather than fighters. "You nuts or something?" one of his cadet classmates asked him. "Why in the world would you wanna do that?" "Because," Danny replied, "I just like fighting the war as part of a group—and I wanna bomb the daylights outta the enemy." "Yeah, but those bombers are big slow birds. You can't maneuver 'em, and they're like flying death traps. Anyway, they're no fun to fly." "Fun?" Danny responded. "Who's talking about fun? I'm talking about fighting a war, killing Germans and Japanese."

There was no dissuading him. Danny had made up his mind: he would become a bomber pilot.

James Washburn's Promises

Chapter 8

When Second Lieutenant Daniel Hawthorne Ehrenreich first climbed through the hatchway located on the starboard side of the fuselage of the brand new Boeing B-17G Flying Fortress (aircraft serial number 41-24787) and entered her interior, it was love at first sight. The three other officer-members of his flight crew immediately followed him inside. These four, along with a senior enlisted flight engineer, would ferry her over the pond (with an initial stopover in Iceland and then on to Prestwick, Scotland) to her final destination, Parkham Airfield at Framlingham Air Station 153 in East Anglia, where she would join the 570th Squadron of the 390th Bomb Group, Eighth U.S. Army Air Force, and commence combat operations. This trip from the States to Framlingham would be Danny's first assignment as pilot-in-command.

"Hot damn!" Noah Wilson said as he ran his hand over the smooth surface of the tiny navigator's table located aft of the nose cone, his digs once the aircraft was airborne. Then he turned to Danny. "Hey boss, I been thinkin': How 'bout naming her after Mitchell? Maybe something like 'Killer Billy'?" Billy Mitchell, a U.S. Army Air Force one-star general, had been court-martialed for advocating the use of air power as the primary means of fighting wars. That was years before. And now he was revered, particularly by bomber crews.

Danny smiled. "Sorry, Noah, she's already named: *Sluggo's Awakening*."

Chapter 9

When Danny and the crew of *Sluggo's Awakening* completed their tenth mission, personnel at Framlingham labeled them "veterans." And then, about three weeks later when they came back from their fifteenth mission, they were branded "old men." "Old men," Danny knew, meant that after only ten more missions they'd be heading back to the States. But Danny also knew that it was bad luck to play the numbers game. Much better—and safer—to focus on the mission they were flying this day, their sixteenth. And their target: Berlin.

Berlin! They had been there before—on their eleventh mission—and had damn near bought it when a 20 mm cannon shell fired from an attacking FW-190 had slammed into their starboard side and gone careening out their port side but not before passing directly between the two staggered waist gunners and less than an inch below the heavy wire control cabling which stretched horizontally along the inner surface of *Sluggo's* fuselage. Danny had thought about this often and had come to the conclusion that the Man Upstairs must have been looking out for them at that particular moment; otherwise, how would they have survived?

And today? Berlin all over again, only this time with an escort of those little red-tail friends who seemed to stick to them like glue!

———

As he had done so often in the past, Danny took a deep breath and then thought of Bailey Shirk berating him in class in front of all the others: *"Ehrenreich! Pick your head up, man! For God's sake start listening and learning or you'll never amount to anything!"*

121

"Never amount to anything?" Danny smiled. How wrong ol' Bailey had been. Here he was minutes into his sixteenth bombing mission as pilot-in-command of a phenomenal flying machine loaded with six thousand pounds of destructive force, and responsible not only for his own life but for the lives of nine others. If that wasn't amounting to something, what was?

Danny reached down and advanced Sluggo's throttles to full power. The aircraft shuddered slightly before commencing its maximum rate of climb of three hundred feet per minute.

Watching Sluggo's altimeter intently, a short while later Danny began speaking over the intercom through the microphone strapped to his throat: "Pilot to crew. We've reached ten thousand feet so put your oxygen masks on." Danny hesitated, and then continued. "And that goes for you too, Shorty."

"Shorty," the tiny ball turret gunner from the Deep South, was the crew comedian, and in addressing him Danny hoped to relieve some of the tension and fear they were all beginning to feel.

"Can't rightly focus on poon tang with that damn mask on, sir."

"Never knew you could focus on anything else, sergeant. Now get that mask on."

"Pshaw! You're just tryin' to depopulate the world, sir."

"No he's not. He just wants us all to share in those Framlingham maidens," Sergeant Stanley Hope, the left waist gunner, piped in.

"I ain't sharing nothing with nobody, least of all you, Stanley," Shorty replied.

"How 'bout me?" First Lieutenant Francis "Frank" Bennett, the co-pilot, asked.

"You, yeah, sir. We need you in case Lieutenant Danny falls asleep. But the others, particularly Stanley: never!"

"Jesus, you're stingy, Shorty," navigator Noah Wilson interjected. "I'll need some of that stuff just to keep us on course."

"Sorry, sir, not enough to go round. Framlingham virgins is a rare ..."

"Okay," Danny interjected. "Enough chatter. Let's keep the intercom clear from here on out. You know the routine: time to check your guns, say a few prayers, and think about getting to the target and back in one piece. Once we've landed you all can join me in fighting over the local heifers. Until then, let's focus on the mission."

Moments later Danny heard short bursts of machine gun fire as the men of *Sluggo's Awakening* began test firing their fifty caliber machine guns.

Chapter 10

Able Flight was at twenty-eight thousand feet some ten nautical miles west of Berlin heading in a northerly direction.

"Jesus, look at that!" Able Three called out. "Flak everywhere. Our 17s are at ten o'clock, right in the damn middle of it. One in the back of the formation just took a direct hit. He's falling behind."

"I see him," James replied. "Let's go." Tuning to the bombers' frequency, James radioed, "Hold your fire, 17s. Four little friends incoming your nine o'clock."

Still spread out in tactical formation, the four Mustangs banked to the west, descending toward the wounded B-17 now almost half a mile behind the formation. As they drew nearer, they saw that it was beginning to lose altitude.

"Left inboard engine's leaking oil like a sieve," James said. "Tail's half shot away. You all go on up with the others. I'll take care of this one."

———

Now alone, without the backup of Able Two, his wingman, James flew up along the port side the stricken B-17. As he drew opposite its cockpit, he saw the pilot wave to him. Seconds later the propeller of its left inboard engine stopped spinning.

James Washburn's Promises

Chapter 11

"All right," Danny said, speaking to *Sluggo's* crew over the intercom. "We've been hit by flak. I've had to feather our left inboard engine. I think a piece of our tail may be gone."

"I saw it fall way, sir." It was Stanley Hope, the left waist gunner.

"Anybody hurt, Stanley?" Danny asked.

"Nobody in back, sir."

"Noah?"

"None up front, boss," the navigator replied.

"Okay, I think we're still good. So here's what I want you to do: First, Shorty, get the hell out of your ball turret—and stay out. Next, everybody start jettisoning. Everything but the Norden goes—guns, ammo, the lot. Do it now!"

The Norden bombsight was super-secret and under no circumstances could Danny allow it to fall into enemy hands.

"Hold off on the Norden until we're over the Channel," Danny added. "But everything else goes now. And for Christ's sake, hurry up. We gotta lose weight or we'll fall outta the sky."

———

Co-Pilot Frank Bennett was sick with fear. He didn't want to die. But that was what was going to happen to him and the others. He was sure of it.

"Now what do we do, Danny? Tail's about gone. How're we gonna steer?"

"We'll use the outboard engines."

"But we'll be defenseless! No guns! And we're limping along at less than two hundred knots. We're gonna be a sitting duck for the Jerry fighters."

"No we're not. Didn't you hear the incoming radio call?"

"Huh?"

"Take a look." Danny pointed out his window at the Mustang.

"I'll be damned!"

"We'll both be damned if you don't get back there and help with the jettisoning. Stop worrying about the Jerry fighters. Our little Red Tail Angel is gonna watch over us."

"All the way back to Framlingham?"

"All the way back, Frank."

James Washburn's Promises

Chapter 12

Flying as precisely as he could, James brought *Promises* to an altitude approximately one hundred fifty feet above the 17 where he began weaving from side to side, trying as best he could not to get ahead of the wounded bird. If the German fighters came in from above or below—as they usually did—he probably wouldn't be seen, at least not at the onset. And if they attacked from either side, maybe they'd see his silhouette; and maybe they wouldn't.

What about a frontal attack? That had been the Jerries' latest M.O. in an attempt to kill the pilot and co-pilot. He'd have to be on the lookout for that and for a six o'clock approach.

Although there were other strategies, he'd decided to wait it out until the enemy made the first move—and then take defensive action.

For James, the actual flying for the past hour hadn't been difficult—or even stressful. The bomber was now flying straight and level, although at a slow speed. So far so good. He'd just continue his weaving while, at the same time, scanning the skies above and below and in all directions.

He glanced at the instrument panel. The fuel situation wasn't great. In another hour he wouldn't be able to make it back to Ramitelli—which meant he'd either have to bail out over the Channel or try for a landing on British soil.

And then he heard it: a whooshing sound as a cluster of 2.2-inch rockets zoomed by just beneath him. An Me 262, the *Luftwaffe's* new jet fighter! Christ, just one of those rockets could have brought down *Promises* or the 17! Where in hell had they come from?

127

James looked to his right and saw what he thought were faint puffs of exhaust. Then he looked left, to the south. Despite the sun's reflection off the surface of his canopy, he saw it: a black speck several hundred feet below him which appeared to be growing larger. Instinctively, he advanced Promises throttle to full power while kicking in left rudder and pushing the stick hard left and down—at the same time making sure he avoided the bomber below. He was on a collision course with the speck which by now was beginning to resemble an aircraft. His strategy: he and the 262 would be closing on each other at a rate of roughly one thousand knots. In just a few seconds James would put up a wall of lead through which the attacker would have to fly. Coming in as fast as he was— and if he hadn't seen *Promises*—James figured there'd be no way he could make any kind of a meaningful course correction. Maybe, just maybe, he might get the German before he fired off any more of his rockets—that is, if he had any left.

The two aircraft were close enough! Now! James commenced continuous firing of *Promises'* six wing-mounted fifty-caliber machine guns. He hoped he was right because his guns only held eighteen hundred eighty rounds!

James Washburn's Promises

Chapter 13

The crewmembers of *Sluggo's Awakening* were in a state of shock. Moments before a powerful explosion had occurred some three hundred yards off to their left. Its bright fireball—which illuminated the sky with flashbulb intensity—sent out shockwaves of such magnitude that, when they finally reached Sluggo, caused its fuselage to shudder and rattle, giving those inside the impression that it was about to break apart.

Shorty and two others rushed to the left waist gunner's bay where they could view the explosion's aftermath—heavy black smoke, dust and ash seemingly in suspension, and falling debris. "Lord God!" Shorty muttered. "I think our Red Tail just bought it."

And then, beyond the explosion, they saw the Mustang turning back toward them. As it approached, it wagged its wings.

———

"Listen up," Danny said over the intercom. "Our Red Tail just radioed that he's short on fuel and out of ammo. He'll be sticking with us all the way back to Framlingham.

"So Noah," he continued, addressing Sluggo's navigator, "let's find him the shortest way home."

Chapter 14

That he was out of ammunition really didn't much matter to James. By his best estimate, they were over Holland or Belgium, not far from the coast. They were in friendly airspace—airspace in which the Allies had achieved air supremacy months ago. It was highly unlikely that they'd encounter any German fighters.

James took a deep breath. The worst was over.

Twenty minutes later he saw the coast below. They were home free. All he had to do now was stay close to the bomber whose navigator had undoubtedly been this route many times in the …

And then he saw it: a tiny black speck which appeared to be growing larger by the second. Looking straight ahead into the afternoon sun, he could just barely make out the silhouette of a Focke-Wulf 190 as it bore in for a frontal attack! Damn!

The entire B-17 crew—those ten men—were about to be senselessly annihilated. Ten lives lost—and for what?

But wasn't this war? Why should he save those men? Weren't they complete strangers? Why should he be sacrificed? Hadn't he done enough? What duty did he owe them?

"What duty? Why James Lincoln Washburn, I am surprised at you! Don't you know? Don't you remember that promise you made so many years ago?"

"Miss Carlton?"

"Yes, James, Miss Carlton. And now the time to repay your debt has arrived. You do remember that, don't you?"

"Yes, ma'am. I'm sorry. I guess I forgot."

"Well, sometimes we all forget. Good thing I'm around to remind you. Now, young man, will you please

fulfill your promise. The one you made to me, to your father and to Dr. Richman."

"Yes, Miss Carlton. Right away."

"I knew you would, James."

James reached over and advanced *Promises'* throttle to full power, at the same time concentrating on the incoming 190.

James Washburn's Promises

Chapter 15

Ever since their safe arrival back at Framlingham, Shorty, the diminutive ball turret gunner, had taken to wearing a large cross on an unusually long chain. Military regulations be damned, he wore it outside his shirt where it dangled from his neck almost touching his belt. He just didn't much care what anyone else thought. Sometimes he would hold it, occasionally rubbing it. This gave him a feeling of protective comfort, something he desperately needed after their harrowing sixteenth mission.

It was early morning and Shorty and the others were seated in the hospital corridor waiting to thank the man who saved their lives. At Lieutenant Danny's request, Shorty and the left waist gunner, Stanley Hope, had gone into Framlingham the day before and purchased an overly large arrangement of cut flowers to give to the pilot. All Shorty knew about him was that he was a major and that he had miraculously survived.

They had been waiting for over an hour when the door to the hospital room opened. Two officers were about to exit, but then changed their minds and went back into the room. One officer was short; the other was tall ... and *black*. "Jesus," Shorty thought, "a stinkin' nigger! Nigger army air force officers! What was the world coming to?"

Ten minutes later the white officer came out. A two-star general. He pulled Danny aside. They spoke for several minutes before the general left.

Danny walked over to where *Sluggo's* crewmembers were seated and addressed them. "Okay, we go in two at a time. This guy's in pretty bad shape. Multiple fractures of both legs when the planes collided; plus he cracked and chipped several vertebrae. He's also got some deep gashes in his upper torso, they think from his chute's straps or maybe from getting all tangled up on his way down into the Channel. So limit your visit to ten minutes maximum. Also, be respectful because there's a lady in there. This will be the only time we can say a few words to him because I'm told they're gonna be flying him home to Chicago tomorrow. I guess his war is over."

Danny paused for a moment.

"Shorty, you and Stanley go on in first. His name's Major James Washburn. And like I said, there's a lady in there so be respectful."

Shorty and Stanley Hope got up and, with each of them holding on to a handle of the floral arrangement's heavy vase, headed for the door to the hospital room.

Chapter 16

Shorty was uneasy. He hated niggers and he knew there was one in that room—an officer no less. And they stunk. Yet Lieutenant Danny had told him there was also a lady in the room, and to "be respectful." But how could that lady and the pilot stomach being around a smelly nigger? Shorty's unease was rapidly increasing.

Shorty and Stanley were now at the doorway to the hospital room when someone inside gently pushed open the door. It was the lady. She must be a nurse, but she wasn't dressed like one. Shorty stared at her in amazement, noting her unusually unattractive appearance:

Tall, gawky lookin', attired in that wrinkled gunny-sack-of-a-dress, and wearin' the weirdest hat I've ever seen with all them points on it. And those buck teeth 'a hers—seems like they're just about ready to fly outta her mouth!

Yet there was something about her that seemed familiar to him. He wasn't quite sure what it was.

"Please come in," the lady said. "How lovely. You brought flowers. Let's put them over here by Colonel Donald."

Colonel? A stinkin' nigger colonel! The strangeness of the room and its occupants had begun to take hold of Shorty. He was barely functioning.

"Move it, Shorty!" Stanley whispered. "Put the vase down where the lady said."

"All right," Shorty replied weakly.

"Gentlemen," the colonel said, "I'd like you to meet our nation's First Lady, Mrs. Eleanor Roosevelt."

The president's wife! That lady! Now Shorty began to gasp. And then he looked over at the bed on which the pilot was lying.

"No!" he cried out. "Not another dirty stinkin' ..." Suddenly he sank to his knees clutching the cross, overcome by confusion—and guilt. He began to shake uncontrollably as he wailed aloud, "Why? He done saved my life. He done saved all our lives. I don't smell nothing. I really don't." Then he paused for just a moment as if drawn back in time: "Why did I do what I done? Why?"

Tears were now streaming down his cheeks as he held on to the cross with all his might. And then he felt a gentle arm resting on his shoulders. It was the lady.

"We all understand, young man," Mrs. Roosevelt said. "You're having an awakening right now, aren't you? Something like an epiphany?"

Shorty looked up at this kindly lady with the soothing voice—no longer quite as unattractive as before.

"Come," she said. "Let me show you something."

Gently she took Shorty by the hand and walked him over to Colonel Donald. "The colonel here is a West Point graduate. His father is a general. The colonel commands the 332nd Fighter Group, the 'Red Tails.' He's one of the finest pilots in the United States Army Air Force."

Grasping Colonel Donald's hand, she said to him, "Colonel, please allow me."

Turning back to Shorty, she continued: "Now, young man, look at this hand. What do you see?"

Shorty shook his head. He wasn't sure how to answer.

"Well, let me help you," Eleanor Roosevelt said. "This hand belongs to an American. There's only one slight difference: skin color. His is darker than yours. But isn't it silly to hate him because of that?" She smiled.

"Now come over here." She gently guided Shorty back toward the bed. "I want you to meet Major James Washburn, the man who saved your life and the lives of the others in your bomber. Like Colonel Donald, Major

135

Washburn's skin is darker than yours. But is that a reason to hate him? I can't imagine that it is.

"When you become a father will you teach your children to hate Major Washburn? I hope not. After all, he gave you back something of real value, your life. And your children? You'd never have any without Major Washburn, now would you?"

Shorty stood motionless.

"One more thing, young man: Suppose instead of having darker skin Major Washburn were a redhead. Would you hate him because of that?"

Shorty shook his head.

"Would you hate him if he had blue eyes?"

"No," Shorty said.

"Then why would you possibly hate him and other Negroes because their skin is a different color?"

"I guess I wouldn't, ma'am. I cain't."

"I'm so glad to hear that. We desperately need Americans like you who find out how senseless racism really is. I think your little discovery here this morning might mean a great deal to Major Washburn—probably even more than all those medals he's going to receive." Eleanor Roosevelt glanced over at James and saw that he was smiling.

"Think about what you've learned this morning, young man." She noticed that Colonel Donald was pointing to his watch.

"Oh, my goodness, I believe it's time for you and this other nice young man to leave—or the others won't get a chance to meet Major Washburn."

"Thank you, ma'am," Shorty said to Mrs. Roosevelt who had suddenly grown beautiful in his eyes. Shorty turned to James: "Thank you too, sir, for saving my life."

And then Shorty did the unthinkable. He reached out and shook Major Washburn's hand.

———

"My, that was a bit of a happening, wasn't it?" Eleanor Roosevelt said.

"I was told he's the only southerner in the group, ma'am. I doubt that you'll have to spend as much time with the others."

"I'm sure you're right, Colonel. But we'll see. I'm going to meet them all.

"And before I forget: You, James ... you'll be back in the States in a few days. When you're up to it, the president and I would like you and your parents to come to dinner at the White House. Nothing fancy. Just an evening with friends. Can I count on you to call my secretary and set this up?"

"Certainly, ma'am," James replied.

9:00 a.m., Saturday, August 2, 1969
Terminal Building, Moton Field
Tuskegee Institute

Judge Washburn and his grandson, Jamie, sat on folding chairs in the seldom-used terminal building at Moton Field. It was in this very building more than twenty-five years before that Tuskegee's first class of thirteen flight cadets—Jamie's father and Benton Donald among them—had received ground instruction.

Over the past two days Skip Taylor had been escorting the judge and Jamie around Tuskegee Institute, Moton Field, and the site where TAAF used to be while, at the same time, recounting to them the exciting and often exasperating history of the 99th Fighter Squadron and the 332nd Fighter Group—and how Jamie's father had saved the ten-man crew of Sluggo's Awakening *from almost certain death. He had even shown them photographs of* My Promises *at Ramitelli and* Sluggo *on the runway at Framlingham with half its vertical tail assembly shot away. Throughout, Jamie had been listening to Skip intently and had been busily taking notes, particularly about his father's acts of heroism. His stuffy overly strict father a war hero? Hard to believe. Yet there they were: those telltale photographs.*

"Something else, Jamie," Skip had said. "Take a look at this." It was a list of his father's military decorations.

———

"Gosh, Grandpa, I didn't know."

"Well now you do, boy. And that's why I brought you down here. Good to know a little family history."

"Did you and Grandma and Dad ever have that dinner at the White House?"

The judge shook his head. "Nope. Shortly after

138

your daddy got back home, the president and Mrs. Roosevelt left for Warm Springs, Georgia—I guess maybe because the president wasn't feelin' too good. And a few weeks later he died. So we never did have that friendly get-together at the White House. But for about seventeen years after that whenever Mrs. Roosevelt came to Chicago she'd always call us, and we'd have her up to our house for dinner. Quite a woman, that lady. Way ahead of her time. Made a big difference to a whole lot of people."

"Do you think there would have been any Tuskegee fliers without her, Grandpa?"

"Doubt it. She was just like your grandmother: whenever she put her foot down, you knew a whole lot of things were gonna happen. She got the program started. But people like Ben Donald, your father, and the other Tuskegees put it on the map. They were the ones who proved to the world that Negroes could fly airplanes."

"Skip Taylor helped too?"

"Sure did. But hold on. I think I hear our airplane."

"Our airplane?"

"Yep. There it is. Just landed. It'll be taxiin' over here in a minute or two. It's gonna take us on up to Birmingham where we'll catch our flight to Toronto."

"Toronto! Where's that, Grandpa?"

"Canada. The place where we Washburns got our start."

"I don't understand. Are we Canadians?"

"Not exactly, boy."

"But I thought we were going home."

"Who said anythin' about that? We're on our way up to Canada so's you can learn a little about an important ancestor of ours."

"We have family in Canada?"

"Whoa!" The judge chuckled. "Why don't you hold all those questions for now. You'll find out soon

enough." The judge looked down at his grandson who appeared confused. Protectively, he placed his arm around the boy's shoulders.

"C'mon, let's go meet our plane. By the way, the pilot told me he'd be givin' you a flyin' lesson on the way up to Birmingham. Said he thought you might like that."

———

The judge and Jamie were standing on the tarmac just outside the terminal building when they saw a two-engine Beechcraft C-45 with air force markings taxi to within thirty feet of them and then come to a full stop. A few minutes later a tall black air force officer got out and walked over. The man shook hands with Judge Washburn and looked over at Jamie.

"Jamie," the judge said, "I'd like you to meet an old friend: General Benton Donald. He's gonna be takin' us on up to Birmingham."

Jamie's eyes widened: The Benton Donald! His father's former commanding officer!

"How do you do, sir," Jamie said, extending his hand, which the general grasped.

"Nice to meet you, young man," General Donald replied in a deep, friendly voice. "Let's get in the plane. You sit up front next to me. Your grandfather can sit in the cabin. Once we're airborne, I'll let you fly her on up to Birmingham."

Excerpt from Jamie's Notebook, Page 92

I can see how Skip Taylor hooked Dad and General Donald on flying. What a great feeling to pull back on the yoke and feel the plane go up. I wonder if Dad would take me flying? Maybe even give me some lessons? Would my breathing problems stand in the way? I wonder?

Someone I'd really like to learn more about: Mrs. Roosevelt. Grandpa told me she was pretty famous and did some exciting things besides flying upside down with Skip Taylor. Reminder: Ask Grandpa to recommend a good book about her.

Isaiah Washburn's Tale

6:25 p.m., Saturday, August 2, 1969
Toronto International Airport
Toronto, Canada

Jamie and his grandfather were standing near the baggage area awaiting the arrival of their luggage.

"Your first time out of the country, boy?"

Jamie nodded. "It gives me a funny feeling, Grandpa. Everything's so different. Signs and announcements in English and French. Don't Canadians speak our language?"

"They do. But occasionally you'll hear a strange twang. Like a lot of 'eh's'—that kinda thing. And some people 'round here speak French."

"What about money?"

"There's Canadian dollars. Worth a little less than ours. After our bags arrive, I'm gonna go get me some."

"Grandpa, you said something about an important ancestor. Who's he? And when do I learn about him?"

"Isaiah Washburn, Jamie. You'll hear all about him when we go on over to Beverley House in the morning. One of their docents is gonna be takin' us back in time, tellin' us about three famous men sittin' together in the Beverley House vestibule more than a century ago. One of them, Isaiah Washburn, will be tellin' the other two the story of his life startin' out when he was a boy and endin' years later when he was a man.

"Tomorrow's gonna be a long day. An important one. I'll be puttin' in a wake-up call for six a.m. when we get to the hotel ...

"Hold on. I see a luggage cart on its way over here with our bags on top. C'mon, let's go grab 'em."

145

Part 1 of Isaiah Washburn's Tale
List of Characters
["B" denotes black; "W" denotes white; * denotes a real person]

Sir John Beverley Robinson (prominent Canadian anti-slave jurist, owner of Toronto's Beverley House) W*

John Rankin (abolitionist) W*

Frederick Douglass (born Frederick Bailey, changes name to Frederick Douglass, former slave and famed abolitionist) B*

Isaiah "Izey" Bailey (slave, small boy, later adult and changes name to Isaiah Washburn, manumitted, half-brother of Frederick Douglass) B

Betty Bailey (slave and grandmother of Isaiah Washburn and Frederick Douglass) B*

Thomas Auld (master and owner of Isaiah Washburn and manager of Wye Plantation) W*

Lucretia Auld (wife of Thomas Auld) W*

Benjamin Washburn (New Orleans attorney, brother of Lucretia Auld) W

Susie Washington (slave, Wye Plantation) B*

Robert "Rob" Ensor (captain, brig *Creole*) W*

Madison Washington (slave being transported aboard brig *Creole*, husband of Susie Washington, leader of slaves' mutiny aboard brig *Creole*) B*

Ruffin, Morris, Jenkins and Burden (four slaves taking part in *Creole* mutiny) B*

John F. Bacon (US consul in the Bahamas) W*

Sir Francis Cockburn (British governor general of the Bahamas) W*

Sir George Cockburn (anti-slave British admiral, brother of Sir Francis) W*

Zephaniah Gifford (first mate, brig *Creole*) W*

Lucius Stevens (second mate, brig *Creole*) W*

Henry Speck (seaman, brig *Creole*) W*

Part 1

Midday Arrival In Toronto

Beverley House, Toronto, Canada
12:10 p.m., August 1, 1862

Although not particularly memorable to most, Friday, August 1, 1862, would be an uplifting day for those attending the gathering. It would be a day accompanied by almost no public fanfare, its ambience highlighted only by sunlight shining through scattered clouds, a vaguely detectable scent of an early fall in the air, and a pleasant cool breeze which, in one case, drifted gently through two large open windows into the vestibule of Beverley House, one of Toronto's preeminent residences. The day would mark the twenty-eighth anniversary of the official end to slavery in Canada and almost everywhere else in the British Empire, the result of the House of Lord's passage of the Slavery Abolition Act of 1833, which, on its effective date, August 1, 1834, freed nearly eight hundred thousand slaves.

Each year August 1st was celebrated by the wealthy owner of Beverley House, Sir John Beverley Robinson, First Baronet of Toronto, former Chief Justice of the Queen's Bench of Canada, and currently Presiding Judge of its Court of Error and Appeal. Throughout his adult life Sir John had vigorously fought the evils of slavery. In fact, his eloquent legal opinion on the subject as Upper Canada's Attorney General in 1819 was not only legendary but had ensured freedom to thousands of fugitive slaves crossing over into Canada before the 1833 act became law. And now, at age seventy, plagued by ill health and knowing that soon he would be passing over into the next world, Sir John longed to meet some of the luminaries of the abolitionist movement, particularly that former slave about whom

147

Gerrit Smith had so enthusiastically written to him. What was the man's name? He was having difficulty remembering.

At his expense, Sir John had invited them all to his home this day. Beginning at 4:00 p.m. there would be a reception followed by a banquet; there would be speeches; and, finally, there would be awards of gratitude presented by a representative of the Queen.

Sir John realized that the trip to "York"—he still referred to Toronto by its former name—would be a difficult one for his invited guests, and he suspected that many would be unable to attend. America's civil war would most certainly interfere with travel; and one guest, Harriet Tubman, had already enlisted in the Union army as a nurse. Yet he hoped that most would be there.

———

It was shortly after the noon hour. Three strangers sat in the vestibule of Beverley House not completely sure why they were there.

Of the three, two were former slaves. One, the eldest, had been freed fifteen years before and now resided in New Bedford, Massachusetts; the other was granted his freedom only a few months ago and was currently living on the Peterboro, New York, estate of wealthy abolitionist Gerrit Smith. For each, the trip to Toronto had been arduous. But now they were in Canada where by law slavery was outlawed.

By contrast, the third man was white. He was tall, gaunt, and attired in traditional Presbyterian preacher's garb. He was also much older and certainly far more exhausted than the two black men. Although his journey on horseback from his homestead in Ripley, Ohio, had required only six days, it had taken a severe toll on his body. Thank the Good Lord that two of his sons had accompanied him as far as Detroit. How he wished that they had boarded that barge and crossed over with him into Canada where one of Sir John's horse-drawn carriages had transported him to Beverley House. But they had not. Apprehensive, he wondered how he would return home by himself. Perhaps his sons were awaiting him in Detroit. They had not mentioned this. An oversight, he was sure.

As he sat there, he saw the two Negroes seated to his far left. One he recognized. The other, an unknown. The two were speaking loudly, engrossed in animated conversation, and had not noticed him. Or had they? As he got up and walked over to where they sat, he heard them laugh and then saw them embrace.

"Would you be Frederick Douglass?" he asked, addressing the older of the two.

"I am. And this gentleman is Isaiah Washburn, an attorney. Although we don't remember one another, can you believe that we have just learned that we are brothers!" He turned to Isaiah and smiled.

"And you, sir, must be the famous Reverend John Rankin?"

So he had been noticed! He was surprised—and pleased. "Famous? Hardly. You are the famous one, Mr. Douglass, and it is indeed a great honor to meet you. And you also, Mr. Washburn. But how is it that you are brothers but not of sameness in name?"

"The same mother," Frederick Douglass replied, "but of our fathers we know little. All we have are suspicions. We do know that Isaiah and I were owned by the same man, Thomas Auld, but not at the same time; and that at different times Auld and his maternal grandfather, Captain Aaron Anthony, were managers of Wye Plantation, the plantation nearest our cabin where our mother and grandmother worked in the fields. But it is unlikely that Auld is my natural father because I don't believe he was at Wye until after I was born. But Anthony was at Wye long before I was born. So I suppose Anthony could be my

149

natural father. And Auld—who is still managing Wye Plantation—could well be Isaiah's father. But, as I said, all of this is pure conjecture ... because there were so many other men, overseers for the most part, who could have been our natural fathers. Remember, our mother was treated as a breeder and gave birth to many children; and she was also a source of pleasure—which undoubtedly explains why she died at such a young age."

"Of course," John Rankin replied sympathetically. "But you are brothers nonetheless."

"Technically, half-brothers," Isaiah said, speaking for the first time. "As Frederick has said, it is highly unlikely that we have the same father. As you can see, Frederick and I don't resemble one another. I am darker than he is, and he is far more learned and a better speaker in public than I am. And also a great writer."

"He is that. I have read both his autobiographies. Fascinating. But he never mentions siblings—brothers or sisters."

"No, he does not. I'm sure there were many we don't even know. You see, some were sold and sent away; and others died. And then Frederick left the cabin for Baltimore and I was sent to the Deep South."

"You were a slave in the Deep South! My God, how is it that you are here? I am told escape from there is next to impossible."

"A long story, sir. And with Frederick's permission, I will tell it since we have enough time before the reception begins."

"I am as anxious to hear it as you are, Reverend," Frederick said. "From what I can gather, we all are here because each of us has, in some small way, contributed to the abolitionist cause. Perhaps when we hear from Isaiah we will understand why he has been invited—and, of even greater interest to me, why someone as eminent as Gerrit

Smith has offered him the hospitality of his home. So please, Brother Isaiah, tell us."

Isaiah Washburn paused for a moment before beginning to speak of those times so long ago—more than twenty years before—when, as a small boy, he was forcefully taken from the cabin of his beloved grandmother and cast out into a world of ugliness.

———

"Although we never knew one another—probably because Frederick had already left—he and I spent our early years in the same tiny cabin located in the impoverished Tuckahoe District of Talbot County, Maryland, not far from Chesapeake Bay. Like most slave children, I don't know when I was born and I've never had a birthday to celebrate; nor did I ever know much about my master, Thomas Auld, who managed nearby Wye Plantation for its owner, old Colonel Edward Lloyd. You see, just before I was to start work in Wye's fields I was sent away. That said, later events led me to believe I must have been born sometime in 1833 or 1834.

"My first memories are of the tiny one-room windowless cabin with a loft in which I lived along with my two older sisters and my precious grandmother who raised me—and, I also understand, Frederick. Unfortunately, I never knew my mother who died shortly after I was born.

"Our cabin was constructed of wood scraps with mud filling in the cracks. It had an earthen floor and one doorway but no door. From the top of the door jamb Grandma hung a ragged swatch of heavy cloth that helped keep out the rain and snow. Inside, opposite the doorway, there was a large fireplace made of mud with a few bricks embedded in it. This was where Grandma cooked our food. At nights I would curl up and sleep next to it while my sisters and Grandma slept in the loft. Out back, some forty feet behind our cabin, Grandma dug a large hole that we all used to relieve ourselves. When the hole filled, she covered it over and dug another.

"My only item of clothing was something resembling a sack. The bottom was open and there were slits for my arms and head. It was washed once a week at the same time my Grandma bathed me.

"The years before I left were happy ones. Although I seldom saw my grandmother and two older sisters during the day because they all worked in the fields from dawn to dusk, I found other slave children my age to play with— that is, when I wasn't given tasks to perform like taking care of smaller slave children. And even though at play we had no toys, we invented them—out of sticks, stones, and clumps of dirt. The only bad things I remember during those years were the times when the master or some overseer would come by to visit Grandma. When this happened, she would shoo us out of the cabin. That's when we heard noises coming from inside, sometimes Grandma's wails and screams, other times just banging and grunting. And whenever they left, Grandma was almost always naked and weeping—and often covered with blood.

"But, as I said, for the most part those years were happy ones—that is, until I reached the age of about eight when my life unexpectedly changed."

From Chesapeake Bay
to a Mutiny at Sea

Isaiah Washburn's Tale

Chapter 1
[October 22, 1841]

"Izey, where is you? You comes right now! Hear?"

Betty Bailey, Isaiah's grandmother, stood in the cabin's doorway as dawn broke that fall day in 1841. Her two older granddaughters had left for the fields hours before.   But following the master's orders, instead of joining the girls that day she remained in the cabin to care for her tiny precocious grandson.   There was something about Isaiah that had caught the master's attention, and he seemed concerned with the boy's well being.

"Where is you anyways? Drat!" In frustration, she brought the forefingers of her hands to her lips and began to whistle—a loud piercing whistle sending out that special signal she taught Izey to recognize: "Twheet, twheet, twheet, twheet, twheeeeeeeeeeeeee!   Twheet, twheet, twheet, twheet, twheeeeeeeeeeeeee!   Twheet, twheet, twheet, twheet, twheeeeeeeeeeeeee!"

Several minutes later there was a rustling noise and the boy appeared smiling and covered with dirt.

"Lordy! You is the dirtiest little one I ever seen. You stays exactly where you is while I gets a bucket of water. Massa may be by an' I don't want him seein' you like this."

The little boy stood in place while his grandmother went around to the creek's edge behind the cabin. Bending over, she filled a pail with water before returning.

"This is gonna be cold, but you stays standin'. Hear?"

Izey didn't move as his grandmother took off his dirty cloth garment and then began pouring water over him.

"You go on inside while I washes your sack. Hear?"

Izey obeyed.

———

"Now while that sack's dryin', you an' I'ze gonna have a little talk.

"We gots two things to talk about: first, what I expects massa's plannin' for you; an', second, what you can do about it.

"Massa's taken a shine to you and that ain't so good. He don't do that except if he sees you linin' his pockets with gold. Know what that means, Izey?"

The small boy nodded, but at the same time his eyes seemed to narrow in anger. "That he's fixin' to sell me. Right, Gram?"

"My oh my, you is the smartest! Exactly! An' what that means for you?"

"That I suppose to get a new massa an' go far away?"

"That's it, boy. An' maybe we never sees each other again."

"No!" Isaiah cried out. "I ain't goin'!"

"What you mean you ain't goin'? You crazy or somethin'? 'Course you's goin'. You knows massa can do whatever he wants with you."

"But, Gram!"

"No 'buts,' Izey. That's the way it was with your other brothers an' sisters. They was sold an' jes' went away. Disappeared. An' that's what will probably happen with you."

Tears of anger began streaming down the tiny boy's cheeks.

"No!" he cried out again. "I ain't goin'!"

"Now you be a man, Izey. No cryin'. That's the way it is. *Unless you changes things.*"

"Changes things? How, Gram? I don't understand." Isaiah stopped crying.

"When the day comes an' the massa decides it's sellin' time, you know you ain't gonna be sold to work in no fields. If you was, you'd be stayin' right here. No, you's gonna be workin' in some house or store or hotel—or maybe even some office. Like what happened to that older brother of yours I done told you about, that Frederick Bailey.

"An' after you's sold an' gets to your new home you keeps your eyes an' ears open. Look an' listen! An' most important, learn to read an' write. Even if they says no, you jes' do it! That's one of the two keys: learnin' to read an' write. Hear?"

Isaiah nodded.

"Good! Learnin' to read an' write is important. It opens up all kinds of doors! But if that key's only in the white man's hands, it jes' locks us up tight so we never gets out."

Isaiah's grandmother paused for a moment. "An' the second key, Izey, is the way we's treated. We's treated as property, not as people. That key say we belongs to white folk an' they can do to us whatever they decides. They can beat us, work us to death, sell us, hang us from some tree—whatever they wants. That ain't right, an' that key, Izey, you's gonna use to change things."

"I still don't understand, Gram."

"I don't either. But I knows in my heart that being treated as property 'stead of people is gonna get slaves their freedom. I jes' knows it. An' with that brain of yours you's gonna make that happen."

"I is?"

"You most certainly is, Izey. Promise me you's gonna do that!"

"I promises, Gram."

"I knows you's gonna keep that promise, Izey. I jes' knows it.

"Now while your sack's dryin', you go stands by the fire an' stays warm."

His anger subsided, Isaiah walked slowly over to the fireplace. As he did, he thought about what his grandmother had said. On the few occasions he had played with the master's children he had never thought of himself as anything but their property—something like a pet or a toy. But he wasn't an animal or a possession. His grandmother was right. He was a person.

Now more than ever he vowed to keep the two promises he had made to his grandmother: he would learn to read and write; and he would free as many slaves as he possibly could—although he had no idea how he would go about doing that or why slaves being treated as property would help him do that.

Isaiah Washburn's Tale

Chapter 2

Several evenings later Betty Bailey was standing outside the cabin. She rushed back inside. "Hush! They's comin'!" The sound of hoof beats could be heard.

"You girls, get! Go on back, out of sight. Do what I done told you to do.

"An' Izey, you stays put. I think they's comin' for you."

"I'ze scared, Gram."

"No use bein' scared, baby. You won't change things jes' sittin' in this cabin. Jes' remember what I done told you."

"About readin' an' writin', an' that we's property?"

"That's it. An' one more thing, Izey: that I always loves you."

———

There were three white men on horseback. They dismounted in front of the cabin. One was Thomas Auld, Izey's master; the other two were overseers.

"I just want the boy," Auld said. "You two do what you will. The ol' lady's all right, but a bit used up. She's caring for a couple of fresh fillies, though."

"I seen them in the fields," the smaller of the two overseers said, grinning, then licking his lips. He withdrew a leather pouch from his shirt pocket, removed a thick square of tobacco from it and, biting off a plug, began to chew. "That older one ain't bad." He laughed and let fly a well-aimed glob of brownish spittle in the direction of the cabin's doorway.

"Yeah? Just what I was thinkin'," the other overseer interjected. "Whaddya say we arm wrestle over that one, 'cause I'm feeling like I want her too?"

"Now, gentlemen, as I said, do what you will. But first help me take the boy into custody."

The two overseers nodded. Whips in hand, they followed Thomas Auld into the cabin.

———

The three stood just inside the doorway, the master in front of his two overseers. They could see Betty Bailey standing by the fireplace facing them, hands on hips. Next to her stood Isaiah. The master couldn't help staring at her, remembering the first time he'd had her. That was years ago. And today she was still a fine looking woman, probably as headstrong now as she had been then—something he liked.

"I'm here for the boy, Betty."

"Why is you doin' this, Massa Thomas Auld? You knows he's too young. Jes' give him few more years with me. That's all. Few more years."

"Can't. He's sold. He'll be on his way to Orleans in two days with a group of young ones. They'll all be working inside. Damn sight better than the fields. Might even get a mistress like your fancy-ass Frederick got. So let's have him."

Betty Bailey turned to her grandson. "You go on over to massa."

Isaiah walked slowly over to Thomas Auld who grabbed his shirt garment and pulled him out through the doorway.

———

Betty Bailey saw that the two overseers were still standing there, now with uncoiled whips. "We want them girls of yours," the smaller one said.

Unafraid, Betty made her way outside. She returned a few minutes later with her granddaughters.

"Lord God, they stink!" the smaller of the two overseers cried out, bringing the crook of his arm up to cover his nose. The other overseer hastily headed for the doorway. "Jesus, I'm leavin'," he said.

"What they been doin'? Rollin' in manure?"

"Cleaning out the family hole, that's what," Betty replied.

"Well, listen here, lady: I'll be back sooner than you think 'cause I'm hankering for a round of tussle with them girls, particularly that one." Menacingly, the small man pointed at the eldest granddaughter before coiling up his whip and stomping out of the cabin.

———

Relieved, but just for the moment because she knew that she had done nothing more than postpone the inevitable, Betty Bailey looked over at her granddaughters: "Both you come over here an' I'll get you cleaned up."

Isaiah Washburn's Tale

Chapter 3

For Isaiah, the trip from the cabin to the Wye Plantation's main house where the Auld family resided was his first on horseback. When they departed, Auld roughly dropped the boy onto the saddle behind its pommel where he sat directly in front of the master. With the master's left arm around the boy's tiny waist, the two galloped along the winding trail for close to half an hour before arriving at the main house where they immediately dismounted. Susie Washington, a large middle-aged black woman, approached.

"Take the boy back to your quarters. I want him bathed and dressed in some decent clothes. And cut his hair. God knows what's crawling around in there. I'll be by late tomorrow afternoon to look him over. And he's to mind you. Understand?"

"Yassuh, Massa Thomas," she replied, grabbing Isaiah by the ear and tugging him in the direction of a large one-story wooden planked building off to the side of the main house.

———

Isaiah had to run as fast as he could to keep up with Susie. He was terrified that if he tripped she might tear his ear off. And once or twice when he slowed down the pain in his ear became unbearable.

"Please, let go. I'ze comin'."

Suddenly Susie stopped, releasing him. And then, just as suddenly, she smacked his buttocks as hard as she could.

160

"What the massa say about you mindin'? I guess you don't hears too good, does you? Well, you jes' shut that mouth of yours an' stops your whinin'. Elsewise I'll gives you somethin' to whine about. Hear?"

Isaiah was doubled over in pain; yet he forced himself to nod.

"That's better. An' what they calls you?"

"Izey."

"Izey? That ain't no name. What's your real name, boy?"

"Isaiah."

" 'Isaiah,' huh? That's a bible name. Maybe that's why you's gonna be workin' inside."

But as Susie looked carefully at this tiny boy she noticed something disturbing: a determined look of defiance which to her spelled trouble. Had her master seen this? Was this why Isaiah was being sold? And, if so, this might explain why he was being sold to someone her master loathed. Susie recalled overhearing her master scream at his wife that her brother, Benjamin Washburn, was nothing more than an "overly-educated jackass attorney and a goddamn nigger lover." Now Susie understood what was taking place: her master was ridding himself of a potentially troublesome slave at a decent price, while, at the same time, palming him off on his wife's unsuspecting brother.

———

When Isaiah entered the wooden-planked building, he found himself in a large room containing a number of boxes and a stool below which were cuttings of hair. At the side of the room he saw a doorway. Its door was closed, and he thought he heard children's voices coming from its other side.

Susie pointed to the stool. "Get that sack off an' sits down."

Isaiah obeyed.

"Now holds still."

She reached for a pair scissors and began cutting his hair. Within ten minutes it was neatly trimmed. Then, examining his head, she said, "What I suspected. Full of lice. Stays put!"

She disappeared through the doorway, only to return a short time later with a large brown bottle filled with liquid.

"This here's gonna sting, so don't move. An' close your eyes tight!" She began pouring the liquid onto his head.

Isaiah squeezed his eyes shut. At first, the pungent liquid felt cool. Then it began to burn. Within a matter of minutes he felt as if his scalp were on fire. He started to gasp and tears began running down his cheeks. But he didn't say a word.

"I'ze sorry, little one. It won't last long."

———

An hour later most of the burning had subsided. Susie approached.

"Lemme see." She began parting Isaiah's hair as she carefully examined his scalp. Then she blew on it. Tiny black specks fell to the floor. Taking hold of a heavy comb, she combed out as many of the dead insects and insect eggs as she could.

"They's mostly gone. Get down an' come over here." She pointed to the tub.

"Get in an' puts your head underwater; then come on up." Isaiah obeyed.

"Now stand there while I washes you."

Susie took a large wad of wool, soaked it in water and rubbed it into a pail of soft soap. Then she began washing the boy, scrubbing him repeatedly. Finally, she took a handful of soap and rubbed it into his hair.

"All right, duck under the water and get all that soap off. After that, I'ze gonna see if we can find you some clothes in one of them boxes."

———

Late the following afternoon Isaiah and five other slave children stood in a line in front of the wooden planked slave quarters building bathed and dressed, their hair neatly trimmed and combed. The four boys had on gray pants and white shirts, and the two girls—one not more than four years old—wore red and white checked gingham dresses. All six had on polished leather shoes. Susie stood proudly in front of them.

"Well, now, ain't that a sight! Massa sure be pleased." She turned and looked in the direction of the main house. She saw Thomas Auld and a stranger approaching. The stranger was well dressed and carried a riding crop. To Susie, he appeared to resemble her mistress, Mrs. Lucretia Auld, Thomas' wife. Perhaps this was the mistress' brother, the man Master Thomas despised.

A few minutes later the two men arrived. Thomas Auld looked over the children, nodded to Susie approvingly, and then introduced her to his wife's brother, Benjamin Washburn. Shortly afterwards, the two men began to speak.

———

"Thomas," Benjamin Washburn said, a twinkle in his eye, "seeing as I overpaid so dearly for these young ones, how about tossing in that ol' lady?" He pointed to Susie who was standing some twenty feet away.

"Can't. She's been with us too long. Sort of a fixture around here. Helps with my slave tradin', particularly children. Anyway, your sister wouldn't allow it."

Thomas Auld thought for a moment about how he could extract even more money from his wife's know-it-all brother. "Tell you what, Ben. Seein' as we're family and all, I'll hire her out to you, but only for eight weeks. She'll help you take the young 'uns on down to Orleans. You'll be needin' that."

"For how much?"

"Oh, say, five a week? But you gotta see that she gets back here."

Not realizing how unfair these terms really were, Benjamin Washburn nodded. He reached into his pocket and withdrew a small leather pouch. Untying its drawstring, he took out four ten-dollar gold pieces and handed them to Thomas Auld.

Isaiah Washburn's Tale

Chapter 4

Joined by Benjamin Washburn, just before dawn the following morning Susie bundled the children into a horse-drawn wagon for their journey to the nearby Chesapeake shore. For twenty-five minutes the horse and wagon clumped along a bumpy dirt road before reaching a ship's cutter which was floating in shallow water next to the beach. Although the trip had been short, it had been hard on the children, particularly on the youngest girl who was not doing well—a matter of great concern to Susie. Susie knew why. The little one was deathly afraid, and she obviously missed her mother.

As their wagon halted at the water's edge a few feet from the cutter, a tall ugly man ran up to Benjamin Washburn and saluted. In his left hand he held a whip.

"You be Washburn?" he asked.

"I am."

"Well, then, I'm here to greet you. I'm *Creole's* first mate, Zeph Gifford. And I see you got them little blacks you booked passage for. We'll chain 'em up and get 'em in the cutter. Once aboard *Creole*, they'll be ridin' solitary in one of the holdin' areas 'til we get to Hampton Roads where we'll be takin' on the others." He stopped momentarily and then pointed to Susie.

"And what about this here lady? She comin'?"

"She is. She'll be taking care of the little ones. And I don't want any of 'em chained up. Children are too frail; and the lady's gotta have free movement to care for 'em."

"Captain ain't gonna like it. All blacks supposed to be chained up; elsewise there could be trouble."

"I don't give a damn whether you or the captain likes it. These children cost me a bloody fortune, and I'm not riskin' it by chainin' 'em up. Understand?" He glared at Gifford.

Unused to being ordered about—even by a lawyer as well-known as Benjamin Washburn—Gifford's eyes narrowed and his grip tightened around the whip's handle. He was about to uncoil it, but then he relented.

"All right, have your black lady get 'em up forward. You can ride aft with me."

As Benjamin Washburn stepped into the boat, two of the sailors began to snicker. This was a first: a passenger issuing orders to Gifford! To the second mate, Lucius Stevens, perhaps; but not to Gifford. One of the two sailors, Henry Speck, a highly popular member of the crew and a particular favorite of the captain's, began laughing aloud.

"And who you be laughin' at, Speck?" Gifford said in a loud menacing voice while, at the same time, reversing the whip's handle in his grip. An instant later, he stood directly behind the man. Suddenly there was a loud thwack as the heavy butt end of the whip came crashing down on his skull. Stunned, Speck turned around in surprise before losing consciousness and slipping to the boat's flooring. As his eyes closed and he fell into unconsciousness, blood began to seep from a pronounced welt in his skull.

"Serves you right; sure damn does!" Gifford said as he kicked Speck's body aside. "And you," he said pointing to Susie, "get yourself over here. Take his seat and row with the others."

"I cain't, sir," Susie replied in a quivering voice. "I never done that before. I gots to care for the young ones. That's why I'ze here."

"I said move, lady!" Gifford began to uncoil his whip.

"But ..." Susie turned in the direction of Benjamin Washburn who was making his way toward Gifford with clenched fists.

"You and I are going to get things straight once and for all, Gifford: You belay that whip and stay away from my property. Otherwise, you'll be overboard."

As he spoke, Gifford saw that Washburn was a much larger man than he first appeared to be—at least six foot two, heavy-set and well-muscled. He had also used the term "belay." Had he been to sea? Wasn't he a lawyer? Most probably he was bluffing.

"And who's gonna put me overboard, lawyer man? Lawyers cain't do that, can they?"

Far faster than Gifford expected, Washburn's hand was at his throat and he felt himself being pushed over the gunnels. Instinctively, he reached for the large knife sheathed to his belt.

"He's goin' for his knife!" Susie screamed out. She reached for an oar and, as hard as she could, shoved its end into Gifford's stomach. Bending over in pain, Gifford fell over the gunnels into the shallow water. Seeing this, the crew members began to laugh.

"I'll kill that bitch!" Gifford screamed.

"You'll do nothing of the sort, man," Benjamin Washburn replied. "Susie here was following my orders. Now climb back in and let's get on out to the brig. You take the unconscious man's oar. We need to get moving. And if you're one to hold a grudge, we can arrange a

167

duel—your choice of weapons. But I warn you, you'll be the worse for it. And whatever happens, stay away from Susie and my children. I paid dearly for them and they belong to me!"

Both humiliated and cowed, Gifford took Speck's seat, picked up his oar and then ordered one of the men to shove off. The cutter was now underway. In just under ten minutes they would pull up alongside *Creole*.

Unlike Benjamin Washburn, First Mate Zephaniah Gifford was in fact one to hold a grudge—forever! As he rowed with the others, he began formulating a plan in his mind: *Before Creole reached New Orleans he'd slit that lawyer's throat and then have his nigger lady time and again 'til he tired of her. Then he'd throw her overboard. Picturing her rotting corpse adrift in the gulf, he thought to himself, "Now that'd be some mighty fine carrion for the sharks!"*

Isaiah Washburn's Tale

Chapter 5

Alongside *Creole*, Benjamin Washburn breathed in deeply. Sea air! He felt dizzy and elated—and strangely nostalgic—as he gazed skyward, his eyes focused on the uppermost tip of *Creole's* mainmast some one hundred eighteen feet above her deck. Then he glanced forward at her shorter foremast. Typical of brigs of the early nineteenth century, *Creole* was two-masted and box-rigged.

Box rigged! How as a young man he had lived up among those spars on brigs closely resembling *Creole*. He remembered yearning for a life at sea and how his family had dashed his hopes by forcing him to return to New Orleans to manage their most important holding, *Hotel Washburn*.

Still looking up at the sky, his thoughts drifted back to that first day he walked into the front desk manager's office of that old dilapidated hotel. How was he going to turn her around? Yet, in just three years' time he transformed her into a veritable gold mine—and the finest establishment of its kind in New Orleans.

Ironically, though, once the hotel became profitable and respectable, he became bored and lonely. Was twelve hours a day behind a front desk to be his lot in life? And then, as if answering his prayers, an elderly guest sued the hotel claiming that one of its employees stole from him. On advice of his father, he retained kindly Simon Northcutt to defend against this spurious claim (or so he considered it).

His first meeting with Simon had been seminal, serving as an important introduction to both the law and his niece.

"Now, Ben," Simon began, "I'll win this case, but only with your help. You'll be working with my niece, Melinda, and this is what I'll need."

Simon had gone on to describe the elements of theft, and what he needed by way of proof to overturn the plaintiff's claim. As he held forth, the wheels of Benjamin Washburn's brain began spinning furiously. For the first time in years he was no longer bored. It was at this moment that he noticed Melinda, a fine looking young woman who was standing next to her uncle. *In fact, a very fine looking young woman!*

And then it came to him: he would contact his younger brother, Walton, and have him manage the hotel in his absence (an absence which, though he never suspected it at the time, would turn out to be permanent).

———

Over the next five weeks he and Melinda worked closely together helping Simon prepare for trial. When the lawsuit was eventually settled, he felt cheated, for, as with a life at sea, he yearned for something which was taken from him. Still, there would be other trials and no family pressure keeping him from them—or from becoming a lawyer, something he now realized was his calling.

Yet, he had another passion: *a very fine looking young woman*. He had never met anyone quite like Melinda. Her beauty, charm, refinement and graceful ways enchanted him. More than anything else, he wanted her in his life—*forever*. When the opportune moment arrived (as it did several months later), he would ask for her hand in marriage.

Isaiah Washburn's Tale

Chapter 6

"I say, Benjamin!" a loud voice called out from above.

Benjamin Washburn looked up and saw a large man leaning over *Creole's* rail waving a sea captain's hat. The man had a full head of uncombed thick black hair, a ruddy complexion and an oversized bulbous nose forming part of a large wide smiling face. That voice! Could it be?

"Ahoy, Bennie! Do you not remember? Yes, 'tis me!"

"Ensor?"

"Aye, none other. Risen from the depths."

"But I heard ..."

"Heard what, old salt—that I went overboard and perished? Ha! Not true. For here I am! So come aboard and enjoy a pint or two with your former mate and comrade, Rob Ensor."

Then addressing his first mate, Zephaniah Gifford, in the cutter below, he continued, "I say, Zeph, help Washburn and his blacks come aboard."

———

The two friends sat at a small round wooden table in the captain's cabin. Rob Ensor leaned forward, his right hand loosely grasping the handle of a pewter mug half-filled with rum. Benjamin Washburn sat opposite him leaning back in his chair, his empty mug resting on the table before him.

"Aha, and here we are, Ben Washburn, with much changed these many years. You, a prominent Orleans lawyer, married to a handsome woman, highly respected, and wealthy, I'd wager. And Rob Ensor? A common sea captain with no family or gold, but happy and content with laughs and comradeship aplenty. Am I right, old friend?"

"Right you are, Rob, save for the wealth. Two or three hundred in gold stashed away, but no more. All my wherewithal is in those young blacks I brought on board. That's why they cannot be chained. I want them well and healthy."

"To sell in Orleans?"

"No. All but one to work inside our hotel."

"Yes, I've heard of it: *Hotel Washburn*."

Benjamin Washburn nodded.

"And the one?"

"My wife, Melinda, wants him for the house."

"But chains shouldn't bother 'em, Ben."

"On the contrary. They're young, tender … and frail. Suppos'n they fall sick? Or need fresh air? The little girl's pretty delicate."

"You've got that black lady."

"I do. And she can't care for them while she and the children are chained." Benjamin Washburn paused.

"I got a whole lotta money tied up in 'em, Rob. A whole lotta money! Almost everything I got."

Captain Robert Ensor shook his head. "I can't go along with you, Ben. I just can't. Insurance won't cover slaves 'les they're chained. Wish I could, but I just can't. They gotta be chained."

Benjamin Washburn rested his left elbow on the table, cupping his chin in his left hand. He closed his eyes and thought for a moment.

"Well, how about this? Suppos'n you give me a key. For emergency purposes only. Case one of 'em needs unchaining. That's all."

Now it was Rob Ensor's turn to think. "All right. But I'm trusting you, Ben. Don't be lettin' me down."

The two men shook hands.

———

"Now you listen carefully, Susie. This is a master key. For emergencies only. In case some of the children have to be unchained. Guard it carefully. Don't let it out of your possession. Understand?"

"I does, Massa Benjamin. An' I promises I be watchin' over that key."

Isaiah Washburn's Tale

Chapter 7

Shortly after Benjamin Washburn and the slaves boarded *Creole,* the wind died. Since there was little to be gained in attempting to get underway until it picked up, Captain Ensor ordered the ship to remain at anchor. Alone in his large luxurious stateroom, Benjamin Washburn fell into a deep sleep. Six hours later he heard knocking at the door. He walked over and unlatched it.

"So, old friend, and how'd you sleep? Well, I'll wager?"

"Like a newborn, Rob."

"Aye, 'tis the sea in your veins. The wind will come up shortly and we'll be on our way to Hampton Roads for a batch of slaves. This time men and women. Adults. And bad business it is for the sexes to be mixed. Ship's got twin holding areas aft. I'll be putting the women in one of them and the men in the other. Your slaves will ride with the women." He waited for Benjamin Washburn's reaction, but there was none. He continued.

"Might be a tad crowded with the women in there, Ben, but the little ones will adjust."

Still no reaction.

"So it's settled then?"

"Settled my arse! You know that my contract calls for private slave quarters while we're in transit. I paid for that, and that I'll be gettin'. Nothing less! Now either refund my fare and take us back to shore, or abide by my contract!"

"I would if I could, old salt. But I can't permit the males and females to commingle in the same holding area. The commotion they'd raise. All that ruttin'. Can't do it."

"Then return my fare and get us the cutter. Now!"

"Can't do that either. 'Least, I don't have your fare to return. The cutter—yes, I could do that if that's what you really want."

Benjamin Washburn stopped to think. "Tell you what, Rob: my slaves will sleep in here, and I'll board with you in your cabin. That way you can keep the men and women slaves apart without harming my young ones. What do you say?"

"Slaves in our best stateroom? That's a first, by God! We've got some time. I'll let you know."

"Won't work, Rob. I must know now. Otherwise, we go back. So what'll it be?"

Captain Ensor frowned. "All right, dammit. But you waive all claims against the ship's owners. Agreed?"

"Agreed."

"And you pay for any damage to the stateroom."

"Agreed," Benjamin Washburn replied a second time, still irritated that someone he trusted would knowingly attempt to breach his agreement. And sharing a cabin with Ensor for the remainder of the journey? Hardly the pleasant sea voyage he'd been anticipating.

Isaiah Washburn's Tale

Chapter 8

"Lordy, Lordy! Look at this! I ain't never seen nothin' like this! Lordy!" Susie mumbled to herself.

The children by her side, Susie stood in the middle of the posh stateroom thunderstruck.

"Why is we here, Massa Benjamin? Where does we sleep? An' the chains. Gotta be scratchin' things. What does we do? Please, Massa. Please!"

"Let me explain, Susie. In a few hours we'll be taking on a shipment of over a hundred slaves. They'll be chained like you. Captain wanted the women in the same holding area with you and the children. Squeezed together, and with all the cavortin' and commotion that'd be goin' on, I knew it'd be mighty hard on the children. Probably some of them would die. And I'd paid for private quarters for you all, something I told the captain.

"Captain and I had a little disagreement, and we settled it by allowing you all to stay in here. I'll be sleepin' in the captain's cabin."

"But Massa, what about them chains? They be scratchin' things."

"You can take off the childrens' chains while they're in here. But put them back on when you bring them up on deck. Understand?"

Susie nodded.

"All right, then, I'll be goin' on back to the captain's cabin for the night. Lock the stateroom door. Don't let anyone in."

———

Shortly after Benjamin Washburn exited the stateroom, Susie addressed the children: "All right, now, line up over here an' I'll take off them chains."

Isaiah was last in line. After Susie unlocked the chains binding his wrists, she bent down to remove a second set from his tiny ankles. As she was doing this, she looked up and saw tears streaming down his cheeks.

"What's the matter with you?"

"It ain't right."

"You crazy? What ain't right?"

"We's people, not property. Ain't right to treat us like we's things. We ain't that an' you knows it!"

"You hush up or I'll grab hold of that ear again. Understand?" Susie waited, but Isaiah looked down and didn't say a word.

"Now you go gets some sleep. Hear?" Susie pointed to a corner of the room.

Walking slowly over to where Susie pointed, Isaiah curled up on the floor and almost immediately fell asleep.

"Where that boy get them ideas?" Susie wondered as she began to undress. She knew, though, that Isaiah was right—that she and the children weren't property. They were folks—just like white folks. Only difference was their skin color. "An' skin color?" she thought. "Why, pshaw, that don't make all that kind of difference lessen you be a massa an' says it does."

Chapter 9

At 3:30 a.m. Susie heard a loud thumping noise. The *Creole* seemed to hit something. Almost immediately after that it came to an abrupt stop. Men began to shout followed by distinct crackling noises which Susie instantly recognized as bodies being whipped. Women started screaming and men began to wail. Then she heard the tramping of footsteps on the deck just above the stateroom. She also heard First Mate Gifford's voice: "Not a damn word. Especially from you, Doctor. Women over here, and men over there. Now! Move!"

More whipping, and still more screams and shouts. Above the din, she heard a powerful, deep voice: "No use makin' trouble. Do as we's told. Quiet an' in good order. In step."

And then she heard Gifford again: "That's a good boy, Doctor! The kinda nigger I like. Where'd you learn that?"

"From you, Gifford, on another ship years ago, when you whipped me bloody for no damn reason. Long before I escaped to Canada."

"But you're back, ain't you, Doctor? On this here ship and with me again. Ha! And tell me, what do I call you while I put a strong lash to your black body a second time?"

"Madison. Madison Washington."

When Susie heard the man's name, her eyes widened, her jaw dropped and she began to gasp. Hardly able to catch her breath, she slowly, almost deliberately, fell to her knees. "It's Madison. He done returned!" she whispered looking up at the stateroom's ceiling, holding her hands together in prayer. "Thank the Good Lord! My man done come to fetch me!"

And as she prayed, she reached into the pocket of her skirt just to make sure: *the key was still there*.

Isaiah Washburn's Tale

Chapter 10

Three days later Susie put the children in chains and brought them up on deck. Benjamin Washburn walked over to her.

"Everything all right, Susie?"

"Chains is too heavy for the little ones. Kinda pulls them down. Cain't walk with them, Massa."

"I can see that. Take them off."

"But you done said ..."

"I know what I said. Go ahead and take them off. I'll explain to the captain."

"They needs food. Almost nothin' since the first day. I hear the slaves gots a new cook, but I ain't seen hardly any food from him."

"I'll have some sent to the stateroom. Now you and the children go aft. Sit out in the fresh air for a while—and don't be botherin' anybody."

"Thank you, Massa."

———

Susie and the children sat near the *Creole's* stern. It was sunny and warm, cooled only by a pleasant breeze propelling *Creole* on her southward journey. Susie tilted her head back and looked up at the sky. She felt relaxed and strangely secure as she began to daydream: *"Madison, where is you, baby, 'cuz I needs you somethin' terrible?"* Followed by more daydreaming: *"That Benjamin Washburn. He be pretty nice to ol' Susie. Givin' her that big room for the children an' takin' off them chains. Maybe he thinks we's more than property."*

And then she heard a strange noise, something resembling a moan which seemed to be coming from a nearby pile of blankets. Looking closely, she thought she saw several of the blankets rise and fall ever so slightly. She got up to investigate.

Next to the blankets she saw dark reddish smears. Then the moans again and more movement.

"You in there? You somebody?" She poked the pile of blankets. With this, more moans could be heard.

"Whoever you is, I'ze comin'!" Susie began to remove the blankets one by one. When she had laid aside half the blankets, she noticed a hand. Black skin!

"Lordy, who this be?"

Frantically she pulled away the remaining blankets. There, lying on the deck was a partially clothed man, his wrists and ankles shackled, his shirt torn away from his torso. Deep bloody welts crisscrossed his back.

"My God! Madison!" Susie cried out. "It's me, Susie. What happened? Who did this to you?"

"I was cookin' in the galley when Gifford comes in. He's the one," he replied in a whisper."

"I be right back. I promises."

———

"Massa Benjamin, I needs help."
"One of the children?"
"No, Massa. Please come."

———

"Who did this, Susie?"
"He say 'Gifford.' That's all."
"I see. And do you know this man?" He pointed to a prostrate Madison Washington.

Susie looked down.

"Well?"

Susie continued to look down. "I ain't seen him for years."

"Who is he, for God's sake?"

"My ..."

"Answer me!"

"My husband."

"Husband? How in God's name ..."

"He be a good man, Massa. Never makes trouble. An' we ain't no bother. No children. We gots nothin' except ..."

"Except what?"

"Love. That's all we gots, Massa. I swears it."

"Love? What do you know of love, Susie? What could you possibly know of love?"

"I knows the same as you, Massa," Susie replied looking directly at Benjamin Washburn. "It's that special feelin' that makes somebody a part of you—that makes him the most important person in the world. Your very best friend. I ain't seen him for years, but he still that."

She looked up at Benjamin Washburn, but he appeared stunned, even speechless.

"Please, Massa, help! I gots to get him moved. Put some lard on his back. Give him food an' water. Please!"

Benjamin Washburn knew he had to speak to Ensor about this. He had to find out what had warranted such a beating. At the same time, he also knew that Susie was right: this man had to be ministered to at once or he would die.

"Unchain him, Susie. Then we'll carry him down to the stateroom. Hurry! I'll come back for the children."

Isaiah Washburn's Tale

Chapter 11

By early evening Madison Washington regained consciousness. He began to moan.

"Noise is good. Means you's livin'. Now you jes' be restin'. In a few days you be almost yourself again. Lemme put some lard on your back."

"Susie?"

"Your wife, baby. She's right here. Lovin' you like always. Now you rest easy. Hear?"

Susie thought she heard Madison softly sobbing. She reached for the bowl of lard that Benjamin Washburn had brought her earlier in the day. Scooping out a handful, she slathered it on her husband's back. When she touched him, his moans grew louder.

The children sat on the floor several feet away watching quietly.

"What happened to him?" one of the girls asked.

"Is you married to him?" the second girl chimed in.

Annoyed, Susie turned to the two youngsters. "Now you jes' hush. Hear?"

Isaiah Washburn's Tale

Chapter 12

Susie, who had spent almost every waking hour over the last six days caring for her husband, was exhausted. And the children? Ashamedly, she had almost completely ignored them. If their owner, that strange Benjamin Washburn, hadn't brought food, they all most assuredly would have starved.

Susie began to think: *"That Benjamin Washburn: he a different kind of massa. Never met one like him. He be hardly massa at all. Jes' a kindly man, that's all. He treats us so different, like we's humans."*

What was even more puzzling was his relationship with tiny Isaiah. To Susie, it appeared as if the two had struck up a friendship; and Master Benjamin was starting to teach Isaiah something, for they would sit together and the master would read to him from a book. Once she saw the master and Isaiah in deep conversation. And then a few minutes later, after the master left the stateroom for the evening, Isaiah climbed up on her knee and she felt his tiny hand reach into the pocket where she kept that key the master had given her.

"What you be doin', boy? You gets that hand of yours outta my pocket! Hear?"

He quickly withdrew his hand and jumped down off her knee. Somehow, though, she knew he'd be back trying once again to take that key from her. But why? Had the master told him about it? Or maybe even told him to steal it from her? Nonsense! If the master wanted his key back, all he had to do was ask her for it and she would return it to him. Well, then, what was little Izey up to?

Isaiah Washburn's Tale

Chapter 13

In the early evening two days later while Susie slept, Madison Washington awoke. He sat up in bed. His back had more or less healed, and its bloody welts were now replaced by long ugly scabs. But, thankfully, most of the soreness had left him. He stretched, rubbed his eyes and then for the first time saw the tiny boy standing several feet away intently staring at him.

"What you wants, boy?"

The boy tried to speak, but couldn't.

"I said what you wants? Who is you?"

"Izey," the boy stammered. "An' we's gonna free 'em."

"Free 'em? What you means, 'free 'em'? Who we's gonna free?"

Izey looked down at the floor. "The men slaves. I got Susie's key. An' I seen 'em. We can do it, Mr. Washington."

"You crazy? They finds out you gots that key an' they throws you to the sharks! Now you gives it to me! 'Least if they finds that key I be sharks' feed, not you!"

Izey handed Madison Washington the key.

"Why they calls you 'doctor,' Mr. Washington? You a real doctor or somethin'?"

Madison Washington laughed. "No, I'ze no doctor. But everybody calls me that, maybe 'cause I can read. That's all."

"An' write?"

"Only a little. Someday I be writin' better."

"Where you learns all that, Doctor Washington?"

186

"In Canada, boy. Four years at a school. Four long years."

"That's what massa gonna do for me: teach me to read an' write. He done told me."

"Don't be believin' no massa, boy. They lies. All of them."

"No! He don't lie. An'..."

"What, boy?"

"Nothin', except you gots to go get the men slaves an' take over the ship. Now! Hurry!"

"Where'd all that craziness come from, boy? Who done told you to be tellin' me that?"

"Nobody. Jes' me! I done told you that. Please, Doctor Washington, go free the men slaves. Now! Hurry!"

Izey turned and ran to the far corner of the stateroom. Turning his back, he squatted and folded his arms around his knees, placing himself in a near-fetal position—as if to leave Madison Washington alone with his thoughts.

"Craziness?" Madison Washington thought. "Maybe that Izey's not so crazy after all. Maybe I'll do what he done told me to do. In fact, I think I jes' will! I'll go to the galley an' get me some knives an' ..."

Yet deep within his thoughts Madison Washington knew that most slaves confined aboard ships would be close to death after five days, for they would be so tightly chained together in the sweltering, suffocating tiny crawl spaces allotted to them that movement of any kind would be next to impossible; that they would be forced to wallow in feces and urine; and that they would be given only the minimum amounts of food and water—just barely enough to survive. And of those who were strong enough to take part in a mutiny, how many would be willing to join him?

187

He knew he would find only a few—perhaps no more than half a dozen. Still, he would try even though he felt his chances of success were poor.

But what Madison Washington did not know was that luck was on his side. Unlike the typical slaver, *Creole* had not been built as a slave ship but rather for coastal trading. Her slave holding areas had been added as an afterthought and had ceilings high enough so that slaves confined in them could sit, kneel or even stand and, ultimately, survive the voyage. Like another ship of its time, *Amistad*, it seemed that *Creole's* shipwright had designed her to facilitate a slaves' mutiny rather than prevent one.

Isaiah Washburn's Tale

Chapter 14

"If I'm gonna do it, boy, it's gotta be tonight. Only a half moon. Gotta do it before the moon gets any bigger." The tiny boy listened as Madison Washington addressed him.

"I'm off to the galley; then to where the men slaves is. I'll soon be startin' a takeover of this here ship. Won't be easy, but I'll try."

"I'm comin' too, Doctor Washington. You needs help. It's dark up there on deck. An' I knows the way better than you."

"All right, then, come along. But don't be bumpin' your head when we crawls into them low slave decks."

"What you mean, 'low slave decks'? Ain't like that. Jes' two big rooms next to each other—one for the men, the other for the women. That's all."

"You mean they ain't squashed together like dead fish?"

"Not like that, Doctor Washington. Jes' big rooms where they can be standin' or sittin' or lyin' down."

"Big rooms, huh? Never heard of anythin' like that for slaves. Why, boy, this here ship was built for a mutiny! Let's go up on deck!"

Isaiah Washburn's Tale

Chapter 15

Izey peered around a coil of rope on the deck.

"What you sees, boy?"

"A man over there. Standin' guard."

"Quiet then. Let's you an' me slip into the slaves' galley. Get them knives on that table. Grab a handful. But be careful not to be cuttin' yourself."

The large man and small boy entered the galley. A short time later they were once again out on the open deck. Through the dim moonlight Madison Washington saw the guard at the same time he saw them. It was Gifford. He held a pistol in his left hand and with his right hand was withdrawing a cutlass tucked in his belt. "Who goes?" he shouted.

"Only me, Madison Washington, Mr. Gifford. I done come up on deck to air them long scabs on my back so they dries up. I don't wants no trouble, only healin'. An' I knows I was deservin' of that beatin' you done gave me. I promises ... no trouble."

"Well step on over here. I wanna see that back of yours. And who's that with you?"

"Only a small boy carrying some food. I ain't eaten in four days."

"Come on over then." Gifford lowered his pistol, but he now held the cutlass in his right hand. "And lemme see your hands. Looks like you're holding on to something."

"Only food, Mr. Gifford. Here, I'll show you."

Bending over slightly to conceal what he was carrying, Washington walked over to where Zephaniah

190

Gifford was standing. "Here," he said as he plunged a knife deep into Gifford's stomach. "I done told you I don't wants no trouble. Only carryin' food, that's all."

"Ahhrugh!" Gifford cried out in agony, dropping the pistol and cutlass and grasping his stomach. Within a matter of seconds blood began to seep through his shirt.

"No trouble at all, Mr. Gifford," Madison Washington repeated as he continued shoving the knife in with all his might and then, in a tearing motion, pulling it up toward the man's sternum.

"An' now, Mr. Gifford, time for you to be swimmin' with the sharks." With that, he let go of the knife's handle, and, as Gifford gasped and sagged, he lifted him over his shoulder and carried him to *Creole's* railing where he threw him into the sea.

"An' that, Izey, is the end of one evil man! We best be getting' over to where the men slaves is."

"Over here, Doctor Washington."

Isaiah Washburn's Tale

Chapter 16

There were sixty-seven of them who had just been unchained, and they were crowded in closely around Madison Washington listening as he spoke.

"I already done killed that Gifford, but I don't wants no more killings. No more! The captain ain't bad, an that second mate's a good man. So leave 'em be unless they's gonna kill you. An' if you do what I jes' told you, we be done with all this in no time." Madison Washington saw that the men were still listening to him.

"So who's with me?"

Seven men stepped forward.

And then one of the other men asked, "Where we goin' after we take over the ship, Madison?"

"Goin' back to Africa where we all come from. We gots people over there."

"No!" Izey said in his loudest tiny voice. "Not there, Doctor Washington. We gotta go where the Queen rules, where all slaves is free—to the Ba-ham-as!"

"How you knows about that place, boy?" another man asked.

"I jes' knows it. That's all." He looked up at Madison Washington nervously, as if asking for help.

"Now you all stop botherin' Izey. He's jes' a little boy. Let's forget about where we's goin' an' take over this here ship. An' here's what we be doin':

"You, Ruffin, come with me. We's goin' to the captain's cabin. Take all his guns an' swords. Make him surrender.

"Morris, you go after the second mate.

"An you two." He pointed. "Go round up the passengers.

"An' you other three, capture the rest of the crew.

"Anybody else with me?"

A dozen more men raised their hands.

"Good. Then Jenkins an' Burden, you be with Morris. An' the rest of you help take over the crew. Now let's go! But keep quiet. We needs to surprise 'em all."

—

The *Creole* mutiny was anything but organized. Of the nineteen mutineers, not one had ever before fired a shot, wielded a cutlass or led a revolt, and not one had offered any semblance of a detailed or coordinated plan of attack. Yet the mutiny succeeded, and historians have concluded that it did so only because to those who took part in it a lifetime of agonizing servitude was intolerable *even though not one of them save Madison Washington had ever known a single day of freedom.* One observer later remarked that it was interesting that *Creole's* mutineers, all uneducated slaves, had confirmed what one of America's most prominent and eloquent patriots had proclaimed many years before: "Give me liberty, or give me death!" Patrick Henry had cried out. And so also by their acts and deeds did *Creole's* mutineers cry out, most notably Madison Washington and a small boy who years later would become one of the great luminaries of abolitionist movement.

=====================

["B" denotes black; "W" denotes white; * denotes a real person]

Melinda Washburn (wife of Benjamin Washburn) W

Simon Northcutt (New Orleans attorney, uncle of Melinda Washburn) W

Elvira (slave of Melinda Washburn, later takes name Elvira Washburn) B

Jenny (slave of Benjamin Washburn, later takes name Jenny Washburn and becomes Isaiah Washburn's adopted sister) B

Henry Clay (US senator, Kentucky) W*

William Graham (US secretary of the navy) W*

Oliver Wigglesworth (chief counsel, US Naval Department) W

Roger B. Taney (chief justice of the United States) W*

Part 2

Mid-Afternoon In Toronto

Beverley House, Toronto, Canada
2:40 p.m., August 1, 1862

"And where in your journey are you now, Brother Isaiah?" Frederick Douglass asked. "I seem to recall that you told us you were sent to the Deep South. Yet we find you stranded in mid-ocean somewhere between the Chesapeake Bay and New Orleans. What happened next, pray tell?"

"I too must confess that I am 'at sea,' " Reverend Rankin interjected, savoring his play on words. "I am certain your tale doesn't end aboard *Creole*. Or does it?"

Isaiah Washburn looked at these two magnificent men. It was obvious he had captured their interest—perhaps even their imagination—and this pleased him.

"Patience, my friends," he said. "I see that we have well over an hour remaining before Sir John's reception begins, and, as you have correctly surmised, I still have much to recount. And so, with your permission, I shall continue."

"Please do so at once, for I must admit that I am intrigued by your journey—as I am sure Frederick is." Reverend Rankin looked over at Frederick Douglass.

"Indeed I am. So do proceed, Brother."

"And so I shall," Isaiah replied. He paused for a moment to gather his thoughts before beginning to speak once again:

——

"I was up on deck early the following morning, and, except for the absence of Captain Ensor who remained in his cabin recovering from a concussive blow to the head

195

and a near-mortal wound to his pride, you would never have suspected that a mutiny occurred just hours before. Second Mate Lucius Stevens was at the helm and Madison Washington and one of his lieutenants, Elijah Morris, stood directly behind him. Oddly, I noticed no tension between the three; in fact, Stevens would occasionally turn and, in a friendly manner, banter with Washington and Morris. Sometimes one of them would even laugh. I thought that perhaps this might have been the result of Washington's order to his men enjoining them from further killing following Gifford's death, but I may be wrong.

"This particular morning was also special for me in a way I shall never forget. It seemed to be telling me and the others that God had come down from on high to bless our little mutiny, for the sun shone brightly, the sky was of a clarity I had not seen before, and a strong cooling wind out of the West seemed to be forcing *Creole* along—as she had never been forced before—toward a predetermined speck somewhere out there on the horizon.

"Even though overly protective, Susie took leave of us children for just a few minutes to speak with Madison. When she returned, I learned that we were running southeasterly before a twelve-knot wind at what seamen describe as 'speed made good,' our most efficient speed; and that, in carrying out Madison's orders, the Second Mate had charted a course for the Bahamas, a group of islands under British rule. On hearing this, I felt deeply honored for I then realized that Madison had chosen *Creole's* destination because of what I told him and the others the night before. Yet I wondered why Second Mate Stevens and Captain Ensor had been so submissive in following Madison's orders. Why, four days later, had they guided *Creole* into the port of Nassau without protest? Soon I was to discover the answer—they had other plans for us.

"One other thing bears mentioning: Benjamin Washburn. You would have thought our owner would have been upset, downcast, or even enraged. After all, he was about to lose an unheard of amount of money when we, his valuable properties, were set free. But, instead, to me he appeared triumphant, as if he had vanquished some inner demon.

"And how did I feel? Happy that Madison, Susie and we children would soon be on our way to freedom, yet sad since I was the cause of our master's financial loss— because by that time I realized I had grown to love him.

"On our arrival in Nassau I could stand it no longer. Overwhelmed by guilt, I confessed. Not caring what the consequences would be, I told Benjamin Washburn everything about my involvement in the mutiny including my theft of the key from Susie and how I was at Madison's side when he took over the ship. I spared no detail. And Benjamin Washburn's surprising reaction? Much to my relief and puzzlement, one of gratitude."

———

"November 9, 1841, the date of our arrival in Nassau, marked the beginning of an approximately thirty-day hiatus in *Creole's* journey. When we made fast to the dock that morning, Second Mate Stevens disappeared only to reappear several hours later in the company of two men I had not seen before: John F. Bacon, United States Consul and, in my view, a scoundrel of grandiose proportions overflowing with insincere niceties and an outpouring of lies; and—most fortunately for us—Sir Francis Cockburn, Governor General of the Bahamas and a member of the illustrious Cockburn family which, by reputation, despised slavery—so much so, in fact, that one of Sir Francis' elder brothers, Admiral Sir George Cockburn, had, during the War of 1812, launched a series of raids against American plantations situated near the Chesapeake Bay freeing hundreds—if not thousands—of slaves. From what I could gather, while en route back to the ship Stevens had lodged two requests with Bacon and Sir Francis: that *Creole's* slaves, 'being the property of United States citizens,' be prevented from escaping, and that the nineteen mutineers be jailed forthwith. What followed I can only describe as an overly-polite yet somewhat humorous tug-of-war in which Sir Francis' pleasant and prolonged persistence drove Stevens and Bacon to the point of maddening distraction before Sir Francis finally refused their requests and offered all of the slaves unconditional freedom. Quite frankly, from the very inception of the negotiations I believe Sir Francis had no intention of allowing *Creole's* slaves to remain in chains. It not only flew in the face of British law which he was obliged to uphold, but it also violated a core belief which he and other members of his family held sacred—that black or white, we were all of the Good Lord's making and equally revered by Him.

"Finally, after close to a month, the interruption in my journey came to an end. All of *Creole's* slaves were told they could leave the ship. They could remain in freedom in the Bahamas or anywhere else under British rule. That was when Susie brought us together in Benjamin Washburn's stateroom where we were staying. We children were all there, as was Benjamin Washburn."

From Mid-Ocean to Nassau;
Thence to the Deep South and Beyond

Isaiah Washburn's Tale

Chapter 17
[December 12, 1841]

That this sumptuous stateroom had been her home for almost five weeks was something Susie would never be able to accept in comfort. Nor, for that matter, would she ever be able to forget the almost unbearable worries associated with it. Had the children scratched the furniture, torn the upholstery, or soiled the carpeting? Were there any signs of Madison's recovery? Blood perhaps? Damage to the bunk he'd been tossing and turning in? Were there any food scraps lying about? Or water stains? And so many other things! Despite its luxuriousness, Susie desperately wanted to leave the stateroom for good. "This here's for white people, not us black folk," she thought.

She looked down at the children. There they were, just a few feet away, quietly seated on the floor in a circle. They certainly were adorable. And, as with all children, she loved them—particularly that Izey. "That boy's gonna be somethin'," she thought. "No wonder massa's taken such a likin' to him."

Still staring at the children, she heard Benjamin Washburn walk over. Now he was standing just beyond the circle of children. Susie clapped her hands. "Hush! Massa wants to say somethin'."

——

"Well, Susie, I doubt that the children will understand this, but we are moored at a place ruled by Queen Victoria. And wherever she rules, there is no slavery. Do the children know that?"

Susie shook her head.

"And do you know that?"

"I'ze not sure, Massa. I never been to such a place."

"Well, Susie, you and the children are at that kind of place now. And because it's where the Queen rules, you are free. No longer slaves. No longer my property. There are no masters here. You're free to go; to leave the ship. Do you understand?"

"I thinks so. But where we go, Massa?"

"I just spoke to Madison. You and the children will go with him. The British governor, Sir Francis, will find a place for you all to stay. I understand that once you get settled, the children will be starting school."

"But what we do for food, things to wear?"

"Don't be worrying about all that, Susie. There are people on the island who will help."

"Never done nothin' like this. I'ze scared."

"You just stay with Madison, Susie. He'll watch out for you and the children." As he said this, Benjamin Washburn looked down at them with sadness.

"I'll be missing you all. But, Susie, I wish you and the children Godspeed." He was about to leave the stateroom when he heard a tiny voice.

"Wait! Please, Massa. I ain't goin'. I'ze stayin' with you." It was Isaiah.

Confused, Benjamin Washburn stopped and turned toward him. "Izey, what in the world are you talking about? If you come with me, you'll still be a slave, my property. Here in the Bahamas you can go to school, learn to read and write, live in freedom. And you'll be living with Susie and Madison. They're fine people."

"You been good to me, Massa. We know things 'bout each other nobody else do. We be friends. You's almost like a daddy to me. Never anybody treats me like you do. I wanna be your property. I wanna learn from you, do what you do—be a lawyer man. Cain't learn that here, Massa. Please!" The little boy looked up at Benjamin Washburn. There were tears in his eyes.

"You been good to me," he repeated. "Don't wanna be where you ain't. Never!"

Suddenly little Isaiah got up and rushed over to Benjamin Washburn grasping his arm. "Please!" he said again.

"Izey, you sits back down! Hear?" Susie cried out. But then she noticed Benjamin Washburn holding up his hand, as if to silence her.

"Izey, why? You can become a lawyer here in the Bahamas. Why go with me?"

"Cuz," Isaiah looked up at Benjamin Washburn with an expression of determination, "I gots to. I gots to be where black folks is treated as property so's I can change that. My gramma says that ain't right, and I done promised her I'd be usin' my head filled with readin' and writin' to do that. An' black folk ain't treated like property 'round here, is they?"

"No, they're not. But if you were to come with me you know I'd have to treat you as a slave. I couldn't permit you to go out alone, and maybe when we got off the ship I'd even have to put you in chains so nobody would try to steal you. Do you understand that?"

"That's all right."

201

"And maybe my wife wouldn't understand all this. She might even beat you. Maybe you'd have to live in my office—or somewhere else outside our home."

"That's all right, too."

"And what if you did slave's work in my house? Or in a hotel? Or somewhere else?"

"I can do that. Only thing I wants is to learn to read an' write; an' later to become what you is, a lawyer man. That's all."

"What do you think, Susie?"

"I don't know, Massa. 'Spose'n you dies? Or your wife and children hates him? What about all that?"

"I have no children, Susie. And I'll give him his freedom when he reaches eighteen. But my wife? I really don't know. After all, she was raised in the Deep South. She's a good woman, but ..."

"Don't know what to say, Massa. I think Izey should come along with us."

"No, I ain't. I'ze goin' with massa!"

Isaiah Washburn's Tale

Chapter 18

"So one of them little blacks decided to stay on board, eh?" Captain Rob Ensor asked Benjamin Washburn. It was midday and the two were standing on deck as *Creole* tacked southwesterly toward the Gulf of Mexico.

"I tried to talk him out of it, but he insisted on coming."

"Damn fool, that! Well, he'll bring a pretty penny at auction in Orleans, I'll wager. Probably more than a thousand. They pay up for young ones, you know."

"He's not for sale, Rob. He's for my wife. Sort of a coming home gift. And she needs him for the house."

"Ah, the joys of matrimony! A present for the little woman, and a house to be cleaned. Not for the likes of Rob Ensor. Besides, I'll have problems of my own once we dock. I'll be dealing with *Creole's* owners and insurers. I'm certain I'll not be her captain a month from now, for I'll be the blame of that mutiny." Captain Ensor thought for a moment.

"And will you be making a claim for them slaves of yours, Bennie?"

"Have you forgotten that I agreed to a waiver?"

"Ah yes, and so you did. Well, then, we're in the same tub, aren't we? Me without a ship and you without all but one of your slaves."

Isaiah Washburn's Tale

Chapter 19

Undernourished and small as he was, it was difficult for Isaiah to walk weighted down by the heavy iron collar which Benjamin Washburn had placed around his neck in a manner which seemed to be choking him. The collar was hinged in the front, and in the back a metal loop was welded to each of its ends. The loops were held fast together by a heavy chain link which was also welded in place—or so it appeared. However, on closer examination, it became apparent that the link only dangled loosely from the two loop ends and could easily be removed, and that the collar itself was not nearly as tight as it appeared to be. Benjamin Washburn had attached a heavy leather leash some ten feet in length to the collar. To hide his deception, he had placed an overly large hat on Isaiah's head, so large in fact that it fell over his ears coming to rest on his shoulders where it effectively covered up most of the collar.

After Benjamin Washburn and Isaiah descended *Creole's* gangplank in the late afternoon of Tuesday, December 21, 1841, they began walking into the city on their way to the Washburn residence; and as they did, people looked on and started laughing—for here was an owner who managed his slave with panache! What could be more fashionable, more appropriate, or more demeaning than to put a collar around a young slave's neck, attach a leash to it, and then, holding the leash in one hand and carrying a whip in the other, parade him in public along the walkways of New Orleans? One onlooker was so impressed he began to applaud. Others joined in.

Hearing this, Benjamin Washburn bowed in feigned appreciation, all the while cracking his whip and urging Isaiah on. More than anything else—for he feared that Isaiah might become the object of a kidnapping—Benjamin Washburn wanted the world to know that this young black belonged to him.

Isaiah Washburn's Tale

Chapter 20

Even though Isaiah only had a brief glimpse of Thomas Auld's house at Wye Plantation before leaving for the Chesapeake shore, to him the Washburn residence seemed surprisingly small by comparison. It was two stories in height and unusually narrow, no more than thirty feet across. Its white wooden exterior and its black front door also puzzled him for he thought that all homes would resemble the red brick Georgian design of the Auld house.

When Isaiah and Benjamin Washburn entered the home, the commotion that followed also surprised him. Three persons—an attractive woman in her thirties, an elderly man with long hair and an even longer beard, and an overweight black lady wearing a calico dress, a kerchief on her head, and a white apron—all began talking at once while staring in wonderment at Benjamin Washburn. Finally, the attractive woman rushed over and embraced him.

"Dear God, you're home! It's been a dreadful two months wondering how you survived that mutiny, my husband. But you seem fine. Are you? Please tell me that you are! We were so worried."

"I'm fit all right, Melinda, but a whole lot poorer. All save one of the slave children I purchased from brother-in-law Thomas are gone, freed by British law once the mutineers brought *Creole* into port. And Thomas' prize slave, Susie, is also gone. I've only been able to salvage this young boy, and he's not really a slave."

Hearing this, the elderly man spoke up: "Well, by God, if he's not, then what in hell is he—some kind of a black varmint? Look at that ridiculous hat, his iron collar, and that leash!"

Somewhat embarrassed, Benjamin Washburn removed Isaiah's hat and collar. "He's a fine young man, Simon. He chose to come with me rather than remain in freedom. And I only put that collar on him to attract attention. I wanted people to know he belonged to me."

"Must be daft to relinquish his freedom for a collar," the old man replied, now looking at Isaiah. "Come here, boy, and let's have a look at you." He pulled Isaiah over.

"Look up here, boy. I wanna see them eyes of yours."

Isaiah did as he was told.

"Well, he don't look daft to me, Ben. Looks to be a pretty smart young fellow."

"He's that and fearless as well."

"Fine and good. But why'd you bring him here?"

"It's a long story, Simon, and ..."

"Now hold on, Massa Benjamin. An' you, too, Mr. Simon Northcutt. This here's a small boy. Clothes need washin' an' so do he. Probably hungry and tired too." The black woman turned to Isaiah. "What's your name, boy?"

"Isaiah, but they calls me 'Izey.' "

"Well, Izey, I'ze Elvira. An' don't you be payin' no mind to these folks. They sounds mean, but they ain't. This here man is Mr. Simon Northcutt, the best lawyer in Orleans. An' I belongs to this beautiful lady, Mrs. Melinda Washburn. She's Mr. Simon's niece an' Massa Benjamin's wife; I know'd her since she was drinkin' mamma's milk. An' I sees you knows Massa Benjamin."

207

"He's my massa."

"Elvira," Benjamin Washburn said, "why don't you take Izey on back. Give him something to eat and get him washed up. Maybe find him a place to sleep."

"Exactly what I intends to do, Massa Benjamin."

Then, turning to Melinda, he continued: "I'm exhausted. I think I'll turn in."

"And I'll be off," Simon Northcutt said. "But Ben, any chance we could sit down sometime tomorrow or the next day? I need to speak to you. And I'd like Melinda there."

"I've got to have a chance to readjust to being back, Simon. Let's meet the day after tomorrow in the early afternoon. Is two o'clock all right?" he asked, turning first to his wife and then to the old man.

"That's fine, dear."

"And you, Simon?"

"Fine by me too. See you both then."

Isaiah Washburn's Tale

Chapter 21

Two days later the three were seated in the living room of the Washburn home, Melinda next to her husband on the couch, and Simon Northcutt in a chair facing them. Clearing his throat, the old man began to speak:

"I know you've hardly settled in from your two months away, Ben, but there's a reason—an urgent one—that I wanted to speak to you.

"Over the past few weeks three groups of slave owners have come to the office trying to pressure me into representing them in a lawsuit against *Creole's* owners and insurers; and, at the same time, those owners and insurers have been after me to represent them. So within the next week or so I've got to choose sides—or stay out of this thing entirely. I was hoping that maybe you could help me make a decision by explaining to me what the devil took place aboard *Creole*—because so far you're the only person I know who was there at the time of the mutiny."

With his right hand, the old man reached into a side pocket of his vest and withdrew his spectacles. For a few seconds he twirled them between his thumb and forefinger before finally putting them on.

How many times in the past had Benjamin Washburn seen him do that? He'd lost count. A nervous habit perhaps, but always a sign that something important was afoot.

"I don't want to beat around the bush, Ben, so let me speak my mind. Before you got here, Melinda and I talked about that mutiny. We were both puzzled. How

209

could a mutiny occur if every damn one of those slaves was chained up in one way or another? Fact is, it probably couldn't. So I had Melinda do some checking. She talked to a couple of seamen down at the waterfront that'd previously sailed on *Creole*. They had nothing but good things to say about her captain, a Robert Ensor. Said he was a stickler for doing things by the book, and that the minute a slave arrived on board he was padlocked in chains, not always in the same way every other slave was chained up, but locked up in chains nevertheless; and that every slave stayed that way until the end of the voyage. Oh, maybe a few slaves might have their chains removed for a short time every so often, but only when they were under guard and watched carefully—and never in sufficient numbers to set off a mutiny.

"So what happened aboard *Creole*? Only thing I could come up with was that somebody got hold of a key and freed those slaves. I suppose it's possible that one or two slaves might have slipped out of their chains. But all nineteen of the mutineers at the same time? Not likely."

The old man was silent for a moment. Then he looked up. "Anything to add, Melinda?"

"Not really." Turning to her husband, she continued: "Those two seamen I spoke to were as puzzled as we are. With Captain Ensor in command, they felt that mutiny was a virtual impossibility. I believe they were as convinced as we are now that someone came into possession of a key."

"So," continued Simon Northcutt, "that's where we're at, Ben. I'm not sure who to be representing. And, frankly, this whole thing doesn't pass my smell test. If my instincts are correct, whatever happened aboard *Creole* had something to do with you and that little boy and why you brought him along with you.   But, then again, my instincts are only about ninety percent correct."

For the first time since sitting down in the Washburn living room with his niece and her husband, the old man smiled.

Isaiah Washburn's Tale

Chapter 22

"Those instincts of yours, Simon! I only wish mine were half as good!" It was now Benjamin Washburn's turn, and he too smiled.

"To a degree, Simon, you're correct: Isaiah and I did have something to do with the mutiny, and I will tell you about that shortly. But, strangely, the person who precipitated it was *Creole's* first mate, Zephaniah Gifford, a sadist if ever there was one, a man who deserved to die—and the only man killed during the mutiny. Without Gifford there would have been no mutiny; and without the mutiny I would have been deprived of one of God's greatest gifts, something which changed my life forever."

"And what was that, dear?" Melinda asked, somewhat surprised.

"I'm going to have to start at the beginning, Melinda, because the gift I received from that mutiny wasn't just one thing; it was a combination of several—a few small things which in my mind became one."

———

Melinda and Simon Northcutt had been listening for well over an hour as Benjamin Washburn related in detail his entire journey, from the time he, Susie, and the children first boarded *Creole's* cutter on the Chesapeake shore to his disembarkation in New Orleans with Isaiah in that ridiculous disguise. Finally, he finished. For perhaps ten seconds there was an uncomfortable silence, broken only when Simon once again began to speak.

"You know, Ben, you've not told us everything. Several nagging questions remain. Most important of all, you previously mentioned receiving one of God's greatest gifts which you said changed your life forever. Are we not entitled to know what that was?"

"Of course you are—particularly since it's now an integral part of me, a very appendage of my soul. But before I tell you about that, what are those nagging questions of yours?"

The old man leaned back in his chair. "First, Ben, what in God's name motivated tiny Isaiah to steal the master key from Susie so that those male slaves could be unchained and the mutiny started up? Damn dangerous thing for him to do, I'd say. And after you've answered that one, how in blazes did he know to go to the Bahamas—that those islands were ruled by the Queen and if *Creole* docked there her slaves would be free? And last of all, with what you had to lose, why didn't you come to the defense of the slave owners while you were in Nassau?"

"Before I answer, Simon, I'm wondering if there are some things I need to clear up for you, Melinda?"

Melinda Washburn looked directly at her husband. "Ben, I found the description of your voyage fascinating, but hardly revealing. From the time we've spent together since your return, I've sensed that something happened to you while you were away. You're still the same husband I married, but you've changed in ways I'm having trouble identifying.

"Another woman, perhaps? No, our trust in one another runs too deep for that—and deceit is not your style.

"Gambling losses? Hardly. Again, you've never been interested in cards or the roll of the dice.

"The significant loss we suffered when the children you bought were freed? I doubt that this bothers you all that much. Yes, the loss amounts to a tidy sum—but that's all that it is, the loss of a tidy sum. And knowing you, you long ago rationalized this away by convincing yourself that through your law practice we would be able to survive financially. So, as I said, I doubt that the loss of those children bothers you all that much.

"This leaves me with a single question, dear: What is it that's swirling about in your head—that made it so difficult for you to fall asleep these past two nights, that's interfered with our ability to communicate as easily as we did before you left? Or, to put it differently, how and why have you changed? I know the answer to this question may be difficult for you to come by, but come by it you must, because, as your wife, I'm entitled to know. And, as your closest friend of many years, Simon also deserves an answer. Are you in trouble, my love? Have you broken the law? Are you ill? Or, as I suspect, have some of your core values changed? Please, Ben, tell us."

Benjamin Washburn was silent. In truth, he knew his wife was right. He had changed, and she and Simon deserved an answer. But how to explain it? He was having difficulty as Melinda continued.

"I understand that it's not easy—perhaps impossible—to answer my question, dear. So let me make a suggestion: Why don't you think back to your voyage. There has to be a single defining moment—or perhaps several of them—which moved you deeply, so deeply, in fact, that you've undergone a significant change of some kind. Would that help?"

"It might, Melinda. I do remember two such instances."

Isaiah Washburn's Tale

Chapter 23

Benjamin Washburn felt himself being transported back in time. He was once again at sea aboard *Creole* where he was about to experience two seminal events which would change his life forever. And now he began to describe them.

"The first was that haunting conversation I had with Susie:

'And do you know this man?'

'I ain't seen him for years.'

'Who is he, for God's sake?'

'My …'

'Answer me!'

'My husband.'

'Husband? How in God's name …'

'He be a good man, Massa. Never makes trouble. An' we ain't no bother. No children. We gots nothin' except …'

'Except what?'

'Love. That's all we gots, Massa. I swears it.'

'Love? What do you know of love, Susie? What could you possibly know of love?'

'I knows the same as you, Massa. It's that special feelin' that makes somebody a part of you—that makes him the most important person in the world. Your very best friend. I ain't seen him for years, but he still that.'

"I remember being deeply affected by what Susie said. I knew that this was a defining moment in my life, a moment I would never forget—for here was a slave, a chattel, a mere possession, *an item of property* who was experiencing the most treasured of human emotions: love. And if she could experience that, then how could she be anything but a human being, a person in the most complete sense?

"Then the second—which I may have failed to mention—when, shortly after Susie and I placed a mangled, beaten, and bleeding Madison Washington in that bunk, tiny Isaiah took hold of my hand and what followed was the startling conversation we had which revealed to me his brilliance, courage, and unbending determination:

'He say he been beaten by that Gifford. But why? Cain't nobody beat somebody like that. It ain't right. So why, Massa? What he done?'

'I don't know, Izey. I'll try to find out.'

'But Massa, no matter what he done, ain't right he be beaten like that, is it?'

'I think it's wrong, but ...'

'You gonna beat that Gifford back?'

'I can't.'

'I don't understand.'

'Gifford is a free man and Madison Washington is a slave. He's considered property and anyone can beat him.'

'If the slaves is freed then they cain't be beaten like that?'

'That's right.'

'Well then, how they free a slave?'

'Oh, many ways. One way is for the owner to sign a paper saying he's free. Another is to go to a place where everyone is free?'

'Where that?'

'Wherever Queen Victoria rules. She's rules the British Empire which is almost everywhere.'

'Near where my gramma lives?'

'Not there.'

'Africa?'

'Not there either. But not far from where our ship is.'

'Where that?'

'Some islands. The Bahamas.'

'Ba-ham-as. So if this ship go there, slaves is all free and cain't be beaten?'

'That's right.'

'I likes the Queen, an' we's goin' to the Ba-ham-as.' "

Isaiah Washburn's Tale

Chapter 24

Simon Northcutt had removed his spectacles and his eyes were half-closed, but he hadn't been sleeping; he'd been listening intently to Benjamin Washburn. He finally looked up and shook his head in amazement.

"I'll be damned if you haven't dropped a child prodigy in our laps, Ben. That little fellow took it upon himself to steal that key, see to it that those slaves were unchained, and set that mutiny in motion; and then, by God, he told them to head for the Bahamas after they'd mutinied. If he were writing music, he'd be another Mozart. But he's chosen a different profession: freeing slaves. And I think he's just getting started. Only question I have is what in tarnation do we do with him?

"Something else, Ben: that first seminal moment you describe—the one in which you were having a conversation with that slave lady. Seems to me when you heard her take on love you were so moved that you decided to scrap slavery—which would explain why you didn't try to help those slave owners back in Nassau."

Then, turning to his niece, he asked, "That the way you see it, Melinda?"

"Indeed it is. For want of a better term, Simon, Ben has become an abolitionist, and I readily join him. He has simply confirmed beliefs we've both held for some time but never really talked about."

"So where does that leave me?" Simon asked, almost half-talking to himself. "I know too much. I can't represent those slave owners; and I sure as hell can't represent *Creole's* owners and insurers. Fact is, I really don't want to."

"Doesn't surprise me, Simon," Benjamin Washburn said. "But what's more important, how do you feel about slavery?"

"Always was, always will be a scourge upon humanity," Simon Northcutt replied. "A shameful practice if ever there was. I've always hated it, but I'm so damn weak-kneed I never came out against it. I guess I was afraid of doing that. It would have destroyed my law practice here in New Orleans. And I won't openly oppose it now—unless I want to wind up in the poor house."

"I don't think we have to become outspoken abolitionists, Simon—just quiet ones," Melinda said. "We can begin by taking that boy under our wings and helping him along by teaching him to speak properly and to read and write."

"And read law," Benjamin Washburn added.

"Yes, that too, dear."

"Where will he be staying?" Simon asked.

"With us, of course," Melinda replied. "Elvira can take care of him. And when he's old enough to start learning the law, he can move into your office, Simon."

"Fine with me."

"Another thing," Benjamin Washburn added. "Manumission. I'll draw up and sign three sets of papers giving him his freedom at eighteen. Let's each of us hold on to a set. He may want to remain a slave as part of his work in freeing other slaves. We'll let him make that decision when he's old enough. Meanwhile, if something happens to me, each of you will be able to show that he'll be granted his freedom when he comes of age."

———

Alone with her husband later on, Melinda asked, "Ben, will all this end your political aspirations—because I know how important they are to you?"

Benjamin Washburn shook his head. "I doubt it, Melinda, provided we keep what you, Simon, and I discussed confidential. Remember, I hadn't planned on running for Congress for at least a decade, maybe longer. And hopefully by then being an abolitionist won't prevent the voters from sending me to Washington."

Isaiah Washburn's Tale

Chapter 25

The time since Isaiah's arrival at the Washburn residence had not passed easily for Melinda, for she had never expected to become the boy's full-time tutor. Yet after spending only a few weeks with him she reaffirmed in her own mind what she, her husband and Simon had previously concluded, that Isaiah's manner of speech had to be changed drastically and he had to be taught to read and write. And so with resolve she set about transforming him into an educated young man. Along with lessons in elocution designed to erase all vestiges of "plantation-talk," she would teach him the basics of reading and writing and a smattering of American history. At first, this seemed a daunting task. Nevertheless, to her surprise, after only several months she discovered that Isaiah was a gifted student with an ear for voice patterns, a remarkable aptitude for verbal skills and a craving for knowledge. And now, after the passage of four years, his transformation was complete, for he had become a young man who, but for the color of his skin, would most certainly have been taken for a graduate of any one of New Orleans' finest private schools.

And so Benjamin and Melinda agreed that the time had arrived for Isaiah to begin the next phase of his education.

———

Simon Northcutt and Benjamin Washburn were seated at a table in the back of one of New Orleans better-known restaurants, *Antoine's*.

"Must be pretty important for us to be lunching here, Ben. What's on your mind?"

"Isaiah, Simon. Since his arrival he's matured nicely, don't you think?"

"Wouldn't know. What I've seen of him—and that ain't much—gives me the impression he's too damn quiet. Not much of a talker."

"I agree. Hardly says a word. Too busy reading everything in sight. Never saw anything like it: always got his nose in a book. And now he's spending hours reading law cases. But he does talk with Melinda on occasion and she tells me there's a vast improvement in his manner of speech."

"So you're thinking it's about time he moved into my office and started reading law? Is that why we're here?"

"That's why I invited you to lunch, Simon. Melinda and I think he's ready. Question is, are you ready to take him in?"

"I'd be glad to have him, Ben. A little company would do me good."

"Well, then, it's settled. I'll arrange to have him move into your office by the end of the week.

"Something else though, Simon: the boy hasn't had any exposure to slavery at its ugliest. I think he needs to experience that."

"Meaning?"

"I think we ought to take him to the auction. Let him see firsthand. What do you think?"

"Mighty dangerous, Ben. He's liable to get stolen, beat up. Those people over there are crazy."

"You, me and Melinda could go along with him. And we'll dress him up like a dumb sickly slave. Keep him in chains. Maybe have him limp—something like that. Do you think that would do it?"

"Maybe. Still, I don't like it. I'd say you're lookin' for trouble. But I'll join you if that's what you want."

Isaiah Washburn's Tale

Chapter 26

They were an odd lot of four: Simon, Ben, and Melinda—and a bent over chained slave in disheveled clothing shuffling alongside them dragging one leg in a decided limp. It was approaching noon on this stifling day in July 1845, and they were on their way to the site of the slave auction, the rotunda of the recently rebuilt *City Exchange Hotel* located at the corner of St. Louis and Chartres streets. More than anything else—for he feared that Isaiah might become the object of an assault or a kidnapping—Benjamin Washburn wanted the auctioneers and others in attendance to know that this young slave belonged to him.

"Now don't forget to act the way I told you to, Izey: slow-witted and sickly. If anyone asks, you're only along to help us find a runaway slave. We'll be searching all parts of the auction for him. That should give you a chance to witness slavery at its worst. So far as we know, that fugitive might have been recaptured and brought here aboard the coastal brig *Emile* which arrived in port this morning. You'll probably see more than one pathetic coffle of slaves coming to auction from her holds or from one of the holding pens. While we're looking around, I may have to whip you a time or two. If I do, it will only be on your back where you're wearing all those layers of clothes—so I hope to God I won't be injuring you."

"I understand, sir," Isaiah replied. "And what do I do if someone wants to look at my teeth, or have me take my shirt off, or even lower my pants?"

"I'll intercede," Melinda said. "You're our property and not for sale."

"I still don't like it one bit," Simon Northcutt interjected. "We can go back if you want, Izey."

"No, I really don't. We'll do fine, and it is important for me. Being as cloistered as I've been has insulated me from the real world and the way Negroes are treated. I do remember some of that from my childhood, but a slave auction is something I must see. If I ever have a chance to speak out against slavery, I've got to be able to describe its horrors."

"And horrors you'll see, my boy. That I promise!" Simon Northcutt shook his head in disgust.

Isaiah Washburn's Tale

Chapter 27

As they entered the magnificently domed rotunda, Benjamin Washburn reached for Isaiah's garment and pulled him over. Whispering in his ear, he said, "Izey, many of the slaves you'll see arrived illegally from Africa. If they did, they've come from a holding pen across the street where they spent the night. Normally they don't speak English or French. And they'll be confused and scared to death. The others who've been here a while or were born here may be faced with unbearable separations: husbands and wives, parents and children, siblings. Maybe that's the cruelest part of all."

Isaiah nodded, but didn't say a word.

"First, though, let's go to one of the rooms off the back of the rotunda where the slaves are being readied for sale." Benjamin Washburn again pulled Isaiah by his garment, this time through a doorway just behind one of the auction blocks. Melinda and Simon followed.

They were now inside one of a series of private rooms, this one larger than the others and occupied by several dozen people including at least twenty slaves. Over to the side there was a fire pit in which several branding irons rested in white-hot coals. To his astonishment, Isaiah saw a middle-aged woman naked from the waist up dragged to the pit's edge where she was made to kneel. A large ugly man wearing a leather apron then reached into the pit, took hold of one of the branding irons and proceeded to press its red-hot end against the woman's back. Isaiah heard a sizzle first, followed a crackling noise as her skin beneath the iron curled and blackened, accompanied by the woman's pitiful screams. The man withdrew the iron and placed it back in the fire pit. "Next," he called out with the nonchalance of someone who had just hammered a nail or sawed through a piece of wood, and Isaiah saw another half-naked slave dragged to the pit's edge.

"They're branded either before or after they're sold, Izey. A way of permanently marking them as slaves." Turning, Benjamin Washburn continued, "Let's all go over here."

They walked over to where a group of naked slaves—men, women, and children—were anointing themselves with lard. A tall man wearing a top hat and holding a whip stood nearby. Next to him lay piles of clothing. The man walked over to Benjamin Washburn and raised his hand to his hat's brim. Then pointing to Isaiah, he asked, "He for sale, your honor?"

"Definitely not. I paid a small fortune for him awhile back—before he got sick. Belongs to me and my wife." He nodded toward Melinda. "We brought him here to help find a runaway."

The man grunted, nodded, and walked back to where he'd been standing.

Benjamin Washburn leaned toward Isaiah. "If you look carefully, each of these slaves has been branded. Probably several days ago. Now they're being prepared for sale. The current wisdom is that the lard makes them look healthier.

"All the beards have been shaved off and they've been bathed. Now they're applying the lard. After it sets a few minutes, they'll put on clothing: cheap suits for the men and calico frocks and head kerchiefs for the women. The young ones will be dressed pretty much the way Susie dressed you and the other children just before leaving Wye Plantation. Everyone will be wearing shoes.

"Look over there: the implements of slavery."

Isaiah saw a man standing guard next to clubs, whips, chains, handcuffs, and ankle shackles piled up on the ground. Close to where the guard stood he also saw several long serrated knives coated with congealed blood resting on top of a small wooden box.

"Occasionally when a purchaser wants to make sure his slave won't escape, he'll ask that the ankle tendon be severed. That's what those knives are for. It's done on the spot with as little indifference as a butcher lopping off a piece of meat from the bone. Disgusting and permanently crippling. The slave won't be able to escape, but his value will be reduced because he'll have difficulty walking. That's why it's not commonly done these days. A barbaric practice."

Isaiah nodded.

"All right, let's go on back into the rotunda. It's 11:30 and the auction starts at noon."

Isaiah Washburn's Tale

Chapter 28

When they entered the Rotunda proper once again—now closer to auction time—they were greeted by a cacophony of loud noises and hundreds of people milling about. It was then that they became aware of the extreme humidity, disgusting odors, and almost unbearable heat of the place, along with its inherent dangers. So perilous were their surroundings that, without saying a word, Benjamin and Simon immediately took up positions on either side of Isaiah watching that no one tried to snatch him away or otherwise assault him.

Walking a few feet further into the Rotunda, they were now in the midst of where the auctions would take place for, some thirty feet in front of the Rotunda's circular inner wall, they saw that a series of wooden auction blocks had been set up, each spaced approximately one hundred feet apart. The auction block which they approached, Block Number 22, was, like all the rest, two and one-half feet high and large enough for one person to stand on. Number 22's auctioneer, identified by his top hat and black suit with its unusually long coat, stood directly in front of the block while a guard holding a curled whip sat on a stool next to him. Behind the auctioneer, and off to either side of the block, there was a line of slaves with shackled wrists awaiting sale. According to custom, the men were in the line to the auctioneer's right and the women and children in the line to his left; and the slaves in each line were arranged by height so that the tallest was furthest away from the auction block. Because of this, family members were invariably separated. Also, according to custom, slaves were sold one at a time in a curious manner: the auctioneer would alternate from one line to the other, always selling the tallest unsold slave. However, if a seller so desired, he could specify that two or more of his slaves be sold in a single sale. This was done most often not out of compassion but rather because the seller felt that such a "joined sale" would generate greater revenue.

During the minutes remaining until noon potential buyers would now have their last chance to examine the slaves being offered for sale. While standing near Block Number 22, Benjamin, Simon, Melinda, and Isaiah watched as would-be buyers inspected the slaves—sticking their hands in mouths feeling for loose teeth, squeezing arm and leg muscles, poking abdomens, and even exposing private parts looking for promising breeders. One ill-kempt, unshaven, overweight man who looked to be in his forties kept leering at a beautiful young female slave in her late teens or early twenties. Then he approached the auctioneer and the two spoke for a few moments. The man handed the auctioneer some gold coins before dragging the girl into one of the nearby smaller private rooms. Several minutes later the girl's screams could be heard, and sometime after that the man and girl emerged from the room. The girl was weeping. Her clothes were in tatters and blood flowed from her mouth. Suddenly she bent over and vomited. Seeing this, the girl's owner who was standing in the crowd began yelling at the auctioneer in protest. Hearing the owner's cries and then looking at the girl, the auctioneer blanched in anger, most probably because of his foolishness in allowing the man to carry the girl off for a moment of pleasure in exchange for a few gold coins. Mortified at the thought of his reputation being sullied, the auctioneer motioned to the guard, and the two rushed at the man and began beating him. The commotion finally ended when the man, in an attempt to compensate for the property damage he'd caused, reached into his pocket, pulled out his money pouch and emptied its contents into the auctioneer's hand. Humiliated, the man departed. Seeing all this, the slaves began chattering excitedly, only to stop when the guard turned toward them brandishing his uncoiled whip.

Precisely at the stroke of noon, the auctioneer began his chanting, signaling the start of the auction. It was a strange staccato-like outpouring of words describing in detail the attributes of the slave to be sold—who, by then, was standing on the auction block—and the minimum bid. Then the bidding began, also a strange procedure because some of the bidders said nothing but, instead, used subtle hand signals in placing their bids.

At last, the first sale ended, and the slave who had been sold, a handsome muscled man in his late thirties, was taken down from the block by his new owner and made to stand at a designated place nearby. A conversation then followed between the two, which Isaiah and the others overheard:

"What they call you, boy?"

In response, the slave bowed his head in deference to his new master. "I'ze 'Clyde.' As that auction man done said, I'ze an expert in the kitchen an' can make most anythin' you likes."

"That's why I bought you, boy. So best we get goin' back to the house and I can show you around. The missus is looking for help in cooking up meals."

"No, please wait, Massa. I'ze gots a wonderful wife up there: Ella." He pointed to an attractive female slave waiting in line to be sold. "We's always together an' she's a wonder in the kitchen. No childen. Jes' us two. Cleans house nice like, an' serves the foods. Helps me with pots an' pans an' dishes after meals. Massa, she the best and we together for almost eighteen years. Only be here now 'cuz our old massa done passed on over."

He looked up pleadingly at his new master. "Please, Massa, buy her so she can be with me. Please do that, Massa. Please. If you do that, I be the most loyal slave there is for the rest of my life."

"Would if I could, boy. But I ain't got them kind of resources. Let's you and me wait for her to come up for sale and see how it goes. Maybe I got enough to buy her. Doubt it though."

"Thank you, Massa."

———

As they waited for Ella's sale, a large man approached.

"Got here late. Looks like you bought the old buck I was after." He pointed to Clyde. "What did you pay for him?"

"Seven hundred fifty dollars."

"Tell you what: I'll give you nine hundred to take him off your hands; and I'll bid on that wife of his up to a thousand. Whaddya say?"

"I don't much give a damn about the wife. Make it a thousand dollars and we've got a deal. And you can forget about the wife."

"You're on, brother," the large man said, as the two shook hands sealing their agreement. The large man reached into the breast pocket of his suit coat and took out his coin purse. He opened it, extracted one thousand

232

dollars in twenty dollar gold pieces, and handed them to the other man.

Clyde, who had been listening to this exchange, was confused. Speaking to his master, he said, "I don't understand, Massa. Is you still my massa, or is this man my massa?" He pointed to the large man.

"I've just sold you to him, Clyde; he's your new master. He may try to buy Ella."

"Oh, that's wonderful, Massa. I thanks you so much. I really does."

"Well, don't be thanking me just yet, Clyde."

The large man, who had absented himself to speak to the auctioneer, returned, this time with a riding crop in hand. "Okay, there, Clyde, let's get moving." He pointed to the lineup of male slaves. "Get on over there." He brought the riding crop down hard across Clyde's cheek. "Now, bucko!" he said, this time shoving the slave with his foot in the small of Clyde's back.

"I don't understand, Massa," Clyde said as he raised his hand to the side of the face where a welt was beginning to form. "What I do? Where I go? What about Ella? Ain't you gonna be buyin' her?"

"Shut up, bucko, and get movin'!" This time he brought the riding crop down across the back of Clyde's neck with even greater force while applying a boot foot again to the small of his back.

Confused, Clyde rejoined the line of male slaves awaiting sale.

———

"C'mon," Benjamin Washburn said. "We're leaving." The four started walking in the direction of the main entryway.

"What's going on, dear?" Melinda asked as they were about to exit the Rotunda.

"Man's a slave speculator. He's going to try to resell that slave for more than he paid for him. Probably will."

"Damn shame," Simon said. "They're good people."

"Of course they are. They're all good people," Benjamin replied. "But don't you be putting your hand in your pocket or you'll be buying up every one of them."

"I've never spoken out against slavery. Maybe by freeing them I can at least make my voice heard in some small way."

"Sure you can, Simon—and then how about taking up residence in the poor house? You know damn well you can't afford to pay out well over two thousand dollars for that couple. So stop while you're ahead."

"Dear," Melinda said, "I think we should buy that poor young girl who was ravaged by that awful man."

"You too, Melinda?" Benjamin Washburn looked at his wife in disbelief. "Absolutely not! If you want to save the world, that's fine. But you can't go around buying up slaves whenever the fancy strikes you. That girl will survive, and so will Clyde and his wife—even if they're separated."

Now it was Isaiah's turn: "It would be wonderful to have a contemporary in the house. A new sister, maybe."

"Dammit, Isaiah, what in hell are you talking about?"

"Now, dear, the boy's right. He does need someone his own age. And ..."

Benjamin Washburn stood still for a moment, shook his head again and, before walking away, said, "Just stay put, the three of you!"

Ten minutes later he returned. The young girl with the bloodied mouth followed closely behind him still in her tattered dress.

"Well, I did the best I could. By the time I got there, Clyde and his wife were gone—sold to different buyers. The auctioneer told me Clyde carried on something awful, and they had to halt the auction until his new owner could drag him away. Pretty sad, but not uncommon—and not nearly as tragic as parents and children being torn apart.

"The girl was by herself in one of the rooms. Her owner decided not to sell her today, maybe because of the way she looked. I think he considered her damaged goods because I was able to buy her for four hundred dollars.

"By the way, her name is 'Jenny' and she hasn't lost any teeth or cut either lip. She's been bleeding from a nasty gash inside her mouth. With Elvira's help and a new dress, I expect she'll be fine in a few days."

——

As predicted, in just over two weeks' time Jenny's injuries had fully healed. And, to the delight of everyone, she had also become a member of the Washburn family.

Isaiah Washburn's Tale

Chapter 29

"Mighty fine dinner, sir," the man said. "And your slaves: well behaved and respectful. Know their place, they do." The man leaned back in his chair and took a long draw on his cigar. A few seconds later he exhaled a faultless smoke ring reminding Benjamin Washburn that he was in the presence of a consummate politician who now was about to hold forth.

"All told, I'd say you've done well, sir. And the president and I consider your reputation unblemished. That's precisely why I'm here."

"Thank you, Senator," Benjamin Washburn replied. He looked over at his wife who sat at the other end of the table. "Dear," he said, "would you excuse us?"

Melinda Washburn knew the routine well. Without saying a word, she got up from her chair, nodded respectfully to their guest, the Honorable Henry Clay, Senator from the great state of Kentucky, and quietly left the room.

"Lovely lady," the senator added.

"Now, Washburn, am I correct in assuming you're an experienced seaman?"

"I suppose so. In my youth I spent over three years up among the spars of box-rigged brigs. In those days I longed for a life at sea. Unfortunately, family business brought me back here where I eventually opened my law practice. But I've never lost my love of the sea. The trip down here some years ago aboard *Creole*—even with all her problems—reminded me of that."

"Glad you brought that up. I understand that mutiny caused you to incur substantial losses."

"It did, Senator: five slaves. But that was nine years ago and I've tried to move on since then."

"And indeed you have. But are you aware that you're eligible to receive compensation from Great Britain for your losses—roughly eight hundred dollars per slave?"

"Never heard of that, Senator."

"Well, look into it. By my calculations, your losses should bring you somewhere in the neighborhood of four thousand dollars. Not an insignificant amount, I might add."

"I'll do that, Senator. Thank you."

"But that's not why I'm here. Seems that we—President Fillmore and I—need your services up in Washington. We're looking for an Under Secretary of the Navy. Someone to run the department.

"William Graham, the current secretary, is a good man, but misplaced. Can't relate to naval officers and, just between us, gets sicker than a dog whenever he sets foot on a ship. Likes the title, but hates the job. So don't worry about working for the man. Chances are, you'll never see or hear from him."

"I know him, Senator. He's been down here a few times. Even been to my office where we collaborated on a matter. I think he respects me; I certainly like and respect him. So I have no concerns about working for him. But I have other concerns."

"What exactly, sir?"

"Well, for one thing there's my law practice. I'm on my own and my clients rely on me. Then there are my three slaves. And I'd have to get rid of this home and find another. Finally, there's New Orleans: it's an important part of our lives. We like it here. My wife's lived in the South all her life. And her uncle who lives here, Simon Northcutt, is very dear to her. I know she'd miss him. Lord only knows how she'd adapt to Washington."

He looked up and saw that his guest was smiling. "Whoa!" Senator Clay said, raising his right hand. "I hear this all the time. And, frankly, there's merit to what you say. But here's what I have the authority to offer you: First, the government will buy your law practice and your house and possessions—including slaves—all for a fair price. Second, we'll arrange for your family's transportation aboard a naval vessel to Washington. And, third, when you arrive we'll buy a house and household goods for you, get you slaves to replace the ones you left behind, and get you settled—all at our expense. Happens all the time. So this should ease your concerns—at least most of them. But your wife's uncle … not much I can do about him." He waited for a moment before continuing.

"Lastly, you'll have a substantial salary and a pension. And I know you and Mrs. Washburn will enjoy living in Washington. It's a damn exciting place."

"Two questions, Senator: I know Mrs. Washburn would never give up our slaves. Can we bring them with us? And what happens after President Fillmore leaves office?"

Again, the senator smiled. This time Benjamin Washburn noticed a slight shaking of the man's hands. Maybe he wasn't as well as he first seemed to be. After all, he was getting up in years. "The slaves—not a problem, Washburn. Bring them along if they're that important to you. And so far as a change of administration goes, you'll be guaranteed a position for life at an under-secretary's level until you retire. Maybe not as Under

Secretary of the Navy after Fillmore goes, but something of equivalent rank and responsibility."

"I'll have to think about all this, Senator."

"I understand," Senator Clay replied, again puffing on his cigar. "Let me know by the end of the week."

Isaiah Washburn's Tale

Chapter 30

It was hot and humid in Washington that Thursday afternoon, July 1, 1852, as Benjamin and Melinda Washburn reverently entered the imposing room containing the coffin of the man who had persuaded them to move to Washington, Senator Henry Clay. Clay, who died two days before, was the first person in the nation's history granted the honor of having his body placed in state in the Capitol rotunda.

As they joined the procession of admirers slowly circling the open coffin, Benjamin Washburn thought back to his dinner with the senator almost two years before—when Clay had promised him the position of Under Secretary of the Navy. True to the great man's word, he now held that position. And, despite his title as a mere under secretary, he knew that President Fillmore, although stubbornly supportive of slavery and the recently reenacted Fugitive Slave Act, had come to rely on his counsel on most other subjects, even those not involving the navy. Yes, in the truest sense, he was now a Washingtonian. This, happily, had led to a social life far more exciting than that offered by New Orleans. Perhaps this was why Melinda had grown so fond of her new circumstances.

And what of the other members of his household? Each of his three slaves—Elvira, Jenny, and Isaiah—had taken to using his surname, something he found strangely complimentary perhaps because they had done so of their own choosing. Even stranger, he knew that he loved them. That they were Negroes made not the slightest difference to him. Sometimes he even wondered if they loved him and Melinda in return. They would never tell him this, because slaves just don't do that—although there was that one time aboard *Creole* when Isaiah, as a small boy, had refused to leave him. That certainly must have been a declaration of love. He hoped so.

They were now abreast of the coffin and his thoughts turned to beautiful Jenny. She seemed forever grateful to him and Melinda for rescuing her. How bizarre it was that that ugly attack on her person had resulted in the good fortune of bringing her into his family. And what a wonderful addition she had become: as a sister to Isaiah, as a daughter to him and Melinda, and as a delightful companion to all. How many times had he sat there mesmerized by her music—her magnificent singing voice and the alluring way she played the piano. Where had she come by this? Somewhere, back in her ancestral chain, there must have been at least one gifted musician. Perhaps many. He was certain of that.

And the boy? Lord, what a mind! Ever racing, ever creating! But for the color of his skin, Isaiah would be one of the nation's outstanding attorneys. As it was, he had arranged for Isaiah secretly to assist the Naval Department's chief counsel, Oliver Wigglesworth, in his day-to-day work. Wigglesworth had reported back to him that Isaiah was not only brilliant but that he possessed the uncanny ability to quickly analyze the most complex set of facts and then opine on how it should be resolved— something which Wigglesworth often had difficulty doing. As time passed, Wigglesworth came to rely more and more on Isaiah's legal talents. Currently he had him ghostwriting the most complicated legal opinions which came out of his office.

Now they were about to exit the rotunda. They would be returning to their Washington home shortly, a home which, in less than two years, had become a place of happiness and love.

There was, however, one thing which Benjamin Washburn had yet to deal with: manumission. Should he immediately free the three? Or could that wait until sometime in the future? He must discuss this with them. And the sooner the better.

Isaiah Washburn's Tale

Chapter 31

Several evenings later, Elvira, Jenny, and Isaiah stood just inside the doorway of the study wondering why they had been summoned. Benjamin and Melinda Washburn sat on a couch in the room's interior. Three empty chairs had been placed opposite them.

"Please," Benjamin Washburn said, pointing to chairs.

Bewildered, the three slaves looked at one another in obvious discomfort. Finally, Isaiah spoke up: "I'm not sure I understand you, sir. Do you want us to sit in those chairs?"

"That's exactly what I'd like you to do, Isaiah. We're about to have a discussion."

Isaiah noticed that both Benjamin and Melinda Washburn were smiling warmly. Respectfully, he, Jenny, and Elvira sat down.

"Well, now, that's progress," Benjamin Washburn said. "I only hope we'll be able to dispense with needless formalities like the one we just went through at our next family meeting." He looked over at his wife who, by this time, was beginning to laugh quietly.

"I expect I'd better repeat that, hadn't I? At least for the sake of emphasis. I did say 'family,' and, indeed, that's what we are. You, Elvira, you've been in Melinda's life for how long?"

"Since she be born, Massa. She be like my own baby."

"We know that, Elvira. And you're as much a part of our family as anyone could possibly be."

"I always hoped that, Massa. But sometimes I'ze scared to ask."

"And you, Isaiah, how long have we been together?"

"I'd say eleven years, sir."

"That's about right. And you chose to be with me, didn't you?"

Isaiah nodded.

"And you, Jenny. Unlike Isaiah who chose us, we chose you. And you've brought us nothing but happiness."

Benjamin and the others could see tears welling up in the girl's eyes.

"So here we all are in this small room: *five Washburns*. We are family: not by blood, but by choice, by shared experiences, by the passage of time, by caring deeply for one another, by … ." But Benjamin Washburn stopped, for he saw Jenny, who was seated between Isaiah and Elvira, reach out with one hand and take hold of Isaiah's hand and, with the other, grasp Elvira's hand.

"We feel the same way, Master Benjamin," Jenny said.

"Thank you, Jenny." Benjamin Washburn glanced over at his wife who appeared expressionless but was beginning to rock slowly from side-to-side. Benjamin Washburn had seen her do this only once before, and that was during another emotionally charged occasion: her mother's funeral.

"So being family," he continued, "there is something I am compelled to say. We are equals." He looked at the three who continued to hold hands, not saying a word.

"And being equals, Melinda and I cannot own any of you. So here," he reached into the breast pocket of his suit coat and withdrew several sheets of paper.

"These are your 'Grants of Manumission.' " This time he handed a sheet of paper to each of the three.

"This means you are free—free to leave if you wish, or free to stay with us and be paid for your work. That is your decision, not ours."

A moment of uncomfortable silence ensued before Isaiah responded: "Thank you, sir, for the high honor of accepting me into your family. I promise I will carry on the name 'Washburn' with respect and dignity for as long as I live.

"And, so far as leaving, I previously was given that opportunity and I refused. Nothing has changed since then. I want to stay.

"Finally, sir, it is my understanding that family members don't work for one another or pay one another; they *help* one another. And that is what I propose to do: I will continue helping you and Mistress Melinda in any way that I can. And I don't expect to be paid."

"And you, Jenny?" Benjamin Washburn asked in a slightly shaky voice, obviously moved by Isaiah's reply.

"I also want to remain, Master Benjamin. I want our family to be together for as long as the Good Lord permits. And, besides, if your skin is black, the world out there becomes a dangerous place."

Benjamin Washburn looked over at his wife who continued to rock ever so slightly.

"Elvira?" Benjamin Washburn asked.

"Where I go, Massa? What difference if I be yours or I be free? I still be with you. That's what God done decided for Elvira. An' that's where I be. So I stays."

"Well, then, it looks like our little family remains intact, at least for the moment. So I think that ends our first family meeting—unless, Melinda, you have something to add?"

"I think, Ben, you may have forgotten to mention that you wanted to discuss something with Isaiah."

"Oh, yes. So I did." He turned to Isaiah.

"Isaiah, may I have a few words with you after the others leave?"

"Of course, sir."

Isaiah Washburn's Tale

Chapter 32

"His name is Roger Taney, Isaiah."

"The Chief Justice?"

"Yes. And I've never met anyone more mean-spirited. I suppose what bothers me most is his 'holier than thou' attitude. He tries to give the impression that he is a deeply religious, sensitive, caring human being, when in fact he is not. But he is believed by many, including other members of the Supreme Court.

"When we lunched together several weeks ago, he referred to the Negro as a member of 'that unfortunate race.' 'Unfortunate!' I had to laugh. He considers the Negro no more unfortunate than a pig or a cow or a sheep! He went on to tell me that he views Negroes as being inferior to whites—just as he told me the framers of the Constitution viewed them. In fact, he used the term 'sub-human.' I think if given the chance he will brand Negroes as unworthy of equal treatment in our society and even go so far as to say that they can never become American citizens and that their only lot in life is to be subjugated by whites.

"Now you and I know that Justice Taney is not alone in his views. But as Chief Justice, he's in a position to do more harm than anyone else. If the opportunity arises, I know he will attempt to destroy the abolitionist movement. He might even go further and declare that all state and federal laws banning slavery are unconstitutional. Why? Because to him a slave is an item of property and, under the Constitution, any law banning slavery would result in the taking of someone's property—and of course you can't do that without going to court.

"He's evil, Isaiah, and it's not inconceivable that he alone could cause this country to be torn apart. And don't ever forget that when the Supreme Court speaks, it speaks as the law of the entire land.

"Now, fortunately, Justice Taney is only one of nine justices on the Supreme Court and, even though he is Chief Justice, he only has one vote. But he's extraordinarily persuasive and, if given the opportunity, I believe he'll do everything within his power to sway at least four other justices to vote along with him in destroying the abolitionist movement and forever relegating the Negro to a life of servitude. That's why I consider him so dangerous."

Benjamin Washburn looked over at Isaiah who was silent. He was obviously thinking.

"Sir, do you think he'll ever get that opportunity?"

"I do. In fact, there's a case winding its way through the court system as we speak. I wouldn't be at all surprised if it eventually reached the Supreme Court. It involves a slave by the name of 'Scott.' Wigglesworth mentioned it to me."

"I'll have to ask him about it."

"Please do, Isaiah."

Isaiah was silent again, and Benjamin Washburn knew that now the wheels in his brain were spinning furiously.

"Sir, it seems to me that whenever a setback comes along, an opportunity also presents itself."

"How so, Isaiah?"

"Well, if I am considered a chattel and unworthy of American citizenship, then I believe I have certain other rights."

"Rights? You make no sense, Isaiah. How can a chattel have rights?"

"Oh, indeed we do, Master Benjamin. So let us wait until the Supreme Court speaks on slavery—if it ever does. If I am never to become a citizen, and if I am only an item of property, then I shall turn the tables on Mr. Justice Taney. Perhaps not in as large a way as we might wish. But large enough. And to do that, I most probably will have to remain a slave. So here." Isaiah reached into his pants pocket, withdrew the Grant of Manumission document and handed it back to Benjamin Washburn.

Isaiah Washburn's Tale

Chapter 33

Promptly at 10:00 a.m. on Friday, March 6, 1857, in the magnificently appointed United States Supreme Court chamber situated on the lower level of the north wing of the United States Capitol, Chief Justice Roger Taney began reading his opinion in the case of *Dred Scott v. Sandford* before a packed audience—which included, among other notables, Under Secretary of the Navy Benjamin Washburn now in his eighth year in office. As Chief Justice, Taney's opinion would become the opinion of the court, although, in reality, it was not because each of the other eight justices had written an opinion of his own—six concurring and two dissenting. After Taney concluded, the other opinions would be read.

As Taney read on in a pleasant monotonous voice, murmurs of approval and disapproval could be heard emanating from the audience. For his part, Benjamin Washburn remained silent, although when he finally realized what Taney was saying he was overcome by sadness, despair, and disgust. Just as Taney had told him at that luncheon years before, the man now repeated himself: the framers of Constitution, he said, never contemplated that Negroes and their descendants would be embraced within the family of citizens and, for that reason, they were forever barred from citizenship.

Did this man really understand what he was saying—that Isaiah, Jenny, Elvira, and their descendants could never enjoy the privileges of citizenship? Did he realize that he was relegating them and those who followed to a lifetime of servitude—and that, because of his words, they would forever be branded as outcasts? And had he considered the impact his words might have on the country—perhaps even sending it to war?

As rage began to well up within him, Benjamin Washburn felt his blood pressure rise. He knew he had to leave this chamber. He would read the remainder of Taney's opinion and the other opinions some other time. Or, if he couldn't bring himself to do that, he would have Isaiah read them.

He nudged the man seated next to him. The man pulled back in his chair allowing Benjamin Washburn to pass and make his way down the aisle toward the exit.

Isaiah Washburn's Tale

Chapter 34

"Well, they've done it, sir—those nine old men. They've sealed our fate. Now Jenny, Elvira, and I can never become citizens. I suppose if we want to live in freedom—enjoying all those constitutional rights you and I have discussed so often—we'll have to flee to Canada or somewhere else in the British Empire. And I've also heard that they've made it illegal for Congress to ban slavery in the new territories!" Isaiah shook his head in disgust.

"I do understand that the Constitution creates checks and balances, Master Benjamin; but to give those nine men such vast power—it's insanity!"

"I'm not sure you're right, Isaiah. You've got to give the country a chance to react. Did you know that one of the two dissenters, Justice Benjamin Curtis, was so angered by the decision he resigned from the court?"

"I heard that, sir. But, still, how is anyone going to change the Supreme Court's ruling so that Negroes can become citizens?"

"I wish I had the answer, Isaiah. I don't. But now that we have the court's decision, can you tell me about that mysterious action you said you'd take if you were denied citizenship?"

"I've committed it to writing. Here, sir." Isaiah handed Benjamin Washburn two handwritten sheets of paper which the latter immediately read.

"Lord, Isaiah, where'd you come up with this? It's phenomenal!"

" 'Phenomenal,' maybe, sir. But as you can see, now is not the time."

"Why not?"

"For two reasons: First, my plan requires that the country be at war—a conflict precipitated by extreme civil unrest between pro- and anti-slavery factions; and, second, we'll need friends in high places—and the new president, James Buchanan, is hardly a friend of the abolitionist cause. When the time comes and we have those friends and the country is at war, we can proceed. And that time, Master Benjamin, is not far off."

"My God, Isaiah, what are you saying?"

"I'm saying that Mr. Justice Taney's decision in *Dred Scott* will become a catalyst setting in motion a national calamity—a civil war of monstrous proportions. I predict that thousands of Americans will die."

"God help us if you're right," Benjamin Washburn replied.

"I hope I'm wrong, sir; but it's all too clear to me that I'm not."

=====================

253

Part 3 of Isaiah Washburn's Tale
List of Characters
["B" denotes black; "W" denotes white; * denotes a real person]

Abraham Lincoln (sixteenth US president) W*
Harriet Tubman (abolitionist) B*
Benjamin Franklin Butler (attorney and US Army major
general) W*

Part 3

Reception Time Postponed

Beverley House, Toronto, Canada
3:55 p.m., August 1, 1862

The tall servant brought his hand to his mouth, coughed, and then cleared his throat, his way of gaining the attention of the three men huddled together in the vestibule's corner. One of the three, a black man, had been speaking while the other two, an elderly white man and a second Negro, had been listening intently. But now the three looked up.

"Excuse me, gentlemen," the servant said, "but Sir John asked me to inform you that the reception has been delayed for at least an hour in order to accommodate the arrival of some unexpected guests. Since the reception will now begin sometime around five o'clock, Sir John was wondering if you would care to take tea at this time? I might add that I highly recommend our cook's scones."

Smiling, Reverend Rankin looked over at Isaiah Washburn. "I say, Isaiah: you've been speaking nonstop for quite a while. I would think that some refreshments might be in order, particularly if you have a sweet tooth as long as mine."

"I'm sure mine is even longer, Reverend. Tea and scones sound most tempting."

"I too concur," Frederick Douglass interjected.

Hearing their responses, the servant bowed slightly. "I will return in a few minutes, gentlemen."

After tea had been served, Isaiah began speaking again:

———

255

"And so it was that implementation of my somewhat grandiose plan was in the making. But before it could be activated, my stepfather insisted that it be subjected to what can only be described as the most meticulous scrutiny, one carried out by a general officer who was also an extremely skilled attorney.

"In looking back, it really all began for me in early March of last year when Lincoln was inaugurated. By then, seven states had seceded from the Union and the Confederate States of America had provisionally been formed. Trying times for Lincoln, as you can well imagine.

"My stepfather was present at the inauguration and heard Lincoln speak. I was told the man was brilliant and dedicated and that, for him, holding the nation together was all that mattered. And in trying to accomplish this—and despite his abhorrence of slavery—he did the unthinkable: he promised not to abolish it in states where it already existed. But to no avail. On April 12th of last year came the attack on Fort Sumter and war. And the very next day, Saturday, April 13th, my stepfather introduced me to the man he had chosen to scrutinize my plan and eventually implement it, Major General Benjamin Franklin Butler."

An Audacious Plan Is Implemented

Isaiah Washburn's Tale

Chapter 35
[April 13, 1861]

"We have a guest arriving in less than an hour, Isaiah," Benjamin Washburn said. "And don't be put off by his military attire. He's also a highly competent and perceptive attorney. I've asked him to review your plan before we present it to the president. He knows Lincoln well and his comments could prove extraordinarily helpful."

Just at that moment Jenny came into the study. "We have a visitor. Someone in uniform."

"That must be General Butler, Jen. Please ask him to join us. And have Elvira bring in some tea. Our meeting with the general may last a while."

———

"Good afternoon, Mr. Secretary. Always nice to see you. And this must be the young man you've told me about."

"Yes, General, this is my stepson, Isaiah Washburn.

"Isaiah, I'd like you to meet Major General Benjamin Franklin Butler from the great state of Massachusetts. I took the liberty of giving him a copy of your plan."

Isaiah and General Butler shook hands. "An honor, General."

"Frankly, young man, the honor is all mine. I've read your plan. It's absolutely brilliant. But unfortunately we have a timing problem."

"Timing problem, sir? I don't understand."

"Let's sit down, and I'll go over it with you and your stepfather. Please understand, though, that I cannot remain here for any length of time. I have important appointments elsewhere now that the country's at war."

———

"For your plan to work, Isaiah, it must be approved by the president. And his approval is not always easy to come by, particularly after Sumter's bombardment yesterday. So let me begin by telling you a bit about his priorities.

"Above all else, he feels that it's his sacred duty to preserve our fragile Union. That's far more important to him than doing away with slavery. Your stepfather and I were at his inauguration where he promised not to abolish slavery in the southern states. He did this in an attempt to hold the country together. Yet despite that promise, and after only six weeks in office, he now finds our country at war—a war, by the way, which threatens to undo everything the Founding Fathers worked so hard to create. And beyond that, I'm sure you're aware that after the secession of seven states over the past few months, four more are now on the verge of leaving the Union.

"And how has Mr. Lincoln reacted to all this? I was with him earlier in the day and to me he appeared stunned—in a state of extreme shock. I further suspect that he feels overwhelmed by the countless tasks facing him—not only as president but as commander-in-chief of the country's military. Can you imagine what being commander-in-chief entails, particularly for a man like Mr. Lincoln who has never worn the uniform? He simply must be given time to adjust to his new role as a war president so that he can begin to deal with our nation's problems—problems which he never anticipated when he sought the presidency. This will take time and, at the moment, he is completely incapable of focusing on anything but those problems. So I suggest that we wait at least four months before approaching him."

"But why wait, General? There are so many slaves desperately seeking freedom?"

"As I said, young man, the president's primary concern is not slavery. He has a war to fight and the remainder of the nation to hold together. It will be impossible for him to focus on the merits of your plan for some time—I feel at least four months. And remember, you will have only one chance to present it to him."

As he got up to leave, General Butler grasped Isaiah's shoulder. "I beg you to wait. Your plan is extraordinarily important, something we all want implemented. And four months is not an eternity."

———

After General Butler left, Benjamin Washburn turned to Isaiah. "Well, what do you think?"

"I'll wait, sir. I don't like it, but I'll wait. General Butler obviously knows the president well, and I'd be a fool not to take his advice."

"A wise decision, Isaiah. I completely agree. We must wait, particularly since our country's problems will prevent your plan from receiving a fair hearing from the president at this time."

Isaiah Washburn's Tale

Chapter 36

"My two men! Let me look at you," Melinda Washburn beamed. "On your way to meet with our beloved president! Given his added duties now that we've been at war for more than four months, I'm amazed that he's willing to spend even a few minutes with you. Well, I must say you both are dressed for the occasion." She looked over at her stepdaughter. "What do you think, Jenny?"

"They both look so regal, Mother Melinda—in those long coats and top hats. I'm so proud to have a father like Master Benjamin and a brother like Isaiah. And his plan: I'm certain the president will be taken by it."

"Let's hope so, dear. And what about you, my husband?"

"I know he'll sign on to it. Not only will it help the war effort, but few can resist Isaiah once he has the floor." Turning to Isaiah who seemed engrossed in thought, he continued: "How do you feel, Izey?"

"I'm as ready as I'll ever be, sir."

"Well, then, let's be off! I predict that in less than four hours thousands of slaves will have a new path to freedom! And you will be the first to walk it."

"I hope so, sir."

Isaiah Washburn's Tale

Chapter 37

They were halted at the main entrance to the President's House[1] by a senior army master sergeant who immediately recognized Benjamin Washburn from his prior visits during the Fillmore administration. Now that the country was at war, the sergeant's demeanor appeared particularly stern.

"Nice to see you again, Mr. Secretary." Then, looking at Isaiah, he nodded, seemingly uncomfortable in the presence of a Negro entering the President's House in formal attire.

"The president and the others are expecting you, sir," he continued, still avoiding eye contact with Isaiah. "Please follow me."

They proceeded down a long hallway, and then climbed to the top of a narrow flight of stairs.

"I'll leave you here, sir. You know the way to the president's office."

"Thank you, sergeant," Benjamin Washburn said.

"I also thank you," Isaiah interjected.

The guard looked over at Isaiah and, for the first time, seemed willing to recognize his presence. "I'm not certain why you're here with the secretary, young man. But whatever the reason, I wish you well." Leaning closer to Isaiah, he continued confidentially, "I hope it has something to do with ridding us of slavery. If it does, I wish you Godspeed."

Taken by surprise, Isaiah nodded.

---

[1] Later known as the "White House"

Later, when the sergeant had left, Benjamin Washburn said, "Not all things are as they appear, Izey. For years Sergeant Thomas has helped slaves escape to the North. Not something I'd expect from a career soldier. I doubt that President Lincoln knows about it; certainly his predecessors didn't.

"But let's go on into the president's office. You've got some important selling to do."

Isaiah Washburn's Tale

Chapter 38

"Please come in," a haggard President Lincoln said, trying as best he could to feign cordiality and friendliness after struggling through the first four months of a war which had so severely drained him. "I've been looking forward to meeting you both. And you, young man," he continued, pointing a long crooked finger at Isaiah, "those legal opinions of yours bowled me over. Where in tarnation did you learn to write like that?"

"I'm sorry, sir," Benjamin Washburn said somewhat puzzled, "but what opinions are you referring to?"

"Why the ones that come out of Wigglesworth's office. Oh, I know, he signs them. But young Isaiah Washburn here writes them. I read one just the other day. Brilliant!"

"How would you ...?"

"How would I get copies and how would I know that this young man wrote them? Do you think for a moment I live in a vacuum, Mr. Secretary? I have to know what goes on in Washington. Most of that I leave in the good hands of Allan Pinkerton. And you may be surprised to learn that your Mr. Wigglesworth works for him." The president's tired eyes began to twinkle slightly and he smiled weakly.

"But those opinions aside, that plan you've come up with to free all those slaves is phenomenal, Isaiah Washburn. And what we're here to do today is implement it."

Now Isaiah spoke for the first time. "But Mr. President, I was all prepared to try to sell you on it."

"I know that, boy. And you'd be wasting your breath. I've been sold on your plan ever since war broke out more than four months ago. Not only will it free thousands of slaves, but think of the devastating effect it will have on the South's economy. Why the loss of all that labor will bury them!"

"And I suppose you got hold of a copy of Isaiah's plan from Pinkerton and Wigglesworth, Mr. President?" Benjamin Washburn asked.

"Exactly, Mr. Secretary. And the moment I read it, I was hooked on it. But hold on. Let's call in the other two. I know they're chomping at the bit to begin work on your plan, young Isaiah."

The president walked over to the door to his office. His male secretary was seated at a nearby desk. "Call them in, Sam," the president ordered.

Isaiah Washburn's Tale

Chapter 39

Minutes later General Butler entered the room accompanied by an unattractive short pudgy black woman in a tattered dress.

"I have it on good authority that you two have already met General Butler. Am I correct?" The president looked first at Benjamin Washburn and then at Isaiah. Both nodded. "Thought so," he continued. "And I suppose you know he now commands Fort Monroe, just outside of Hampton, Virginia—the initial dropping off point we've selected for the first group of slaves granted sanctuary under your plan, Isaiah?"

"We didn't know that, Mr. President," Isaiah replied.

"Well, now you do." The president smiled.

"And this lady is Harriet Tubman. A dear friend; and responsible for freeing more slaves than we all can count." The president approached the short Negro woman and gently placed his arm around her shoulders.

"Now you jes' stops that, President Abe. You flirtin' with me jes' ain't right, 'specially in front of these here folks.

"An' you, boy," she continued, this time jabbing Isaiah in the chest, "What they calls you?"

"Isaiah, ma'am. And I'm deeply honored to meet you. I've heard so much about you."

Harriet Tubman appeared annoyed: "C'mon, boy. What they calls you as a boy, cuz that's when you gots your real name?"

"Izey, ma'am."

"That's better. Now Izey, how comes you speaks and writes fancy like?"

"I've learned it from my stepfather, Secretary Benjamin Washburn."

"That so?" Harriet Tubman asked, turning to Benjamin Washburn.

"Yes, ma'am, it is. I've tried to teach him as best I could."

"Well, then, Mr. Secretary Benjamin Washburn, you done a good job 'cause we's gonna give lots of slaves their freedom 'cause of what Izey done wrote. So listen careful, all of you's. In about two weeks I'ze gonna be at Fort Monroe, General, with three slaves, and you's gonna free 'em usin' Izey's plan."

"I'll be ready, Harriet," General Butler replied.

"I was hoping I could be one of them, ma'am," Isaiah said.

"You? You's still a slave?"

"Yes, ma'am."

"But not a workin' one, is you?" Harriet Tubman paused. "Lemme see them hands, boy."

Isaiah held out his hands palms up.

"Why pshaw! Them hands don't belong to no outside slave. Put them back in your pockets, boy! I cain't be bringin' you in to the general with hands like that."

She thought for a moment. "An' why ain't you free?"

"As his father, I've offered him his freedom on a number of occasions, ma'am. But he's always turned me down. Seems like he feels it would interfere with his plan."

"What! Is he crazy or somethin'?" Harriet Tubman replied in a raised voice. "Now listen, boy," she continued, looking directly at Isaiah, "you gets freed right now. Hear! No waitin'; no excuses. Now!"

"Yes, ma'am," Isaiah replied, feeling somewhat embarrassed knowing that he, unlike so many other Negroes who desperately yearned to be free, had refused his stepfather's many offers of manumission.

"All right, boy, that's over with. Now tell me one more thing: where is you from?"

"You mean which plantation?"

"That's exactly what I means. Tell me."

"The Wye Plantation in Talbot County."

"I knows it."

Now it seemed that Harriet Tubman had finished. She went over to President Lincoln and hugged him. "President Abe, you be well. Hear? We's gonna win 'cuz we loves you." With that, she turned and quickly left the room.

"What a powerful lady," Benjamin Washburn commented.

"She is that, Mr. Secretary. And now I believe we've concluded our business. I wish you all well. And to you, young Isaiah, the thanks of a grateful nation."

"I'm honored, Mr. President," Isaiah replied.

Isaiah Washburn's Tale

Chapter 40

Two weeks later General Butler and the entire Washburn family—Benjamin and Melinda Washburn, their two stepchildren, Isaiah and Jenny, and a very nervous and uncomfortable Elvira—were seated in the general's office at Fort Monroe, Virginia, awaiting the arrival of an irate slave owner who just happened to be Benjamin Washburn's brother-in-law, Thomas Auld. Earlier in the day, Harriet Tubman had delivered to General Butler three field slaves from the Wye Plantation and they had been granted sanctuary by the general.

There was a knock on the door. "Come," General Butler said, and a corporal entered.

"A Reb major is here, sir. Says he wants his property back. Three slaves."

"And did he use the term 'property,' corporal?"

"Yes sir, he did."

"His name?"

" 'Major Auld,' sir."

"Excellent. Please ask him to come in. And please remain here for security purposes."

———

"Good day, Major. I will assume for your sake that you're here under a flag of truce. Something about some property of yours? Is that it?"

"What in hell!" Thomas Auld recognized his brother-in-law and Melinda. "What are you two doing here?"

"I'm here as a representative of the government of the United States, Thomas; and these people are my family members."

"But Ben, you're a southerner; from New Orleans. Melinda ..."

"We *were* from New Orleans, Thomas. But we've lived in Washington for years. I'm Under Secretary of the Navy."

"Well I'll be damned! And aren't you going to ask me about your sister?"

"Of course, Thomas. How is she?"

"She's fine, Ben. But I'm here to recoup my property—three slaves. I'll just take them and be off."

"I expect you'll have to deal with General Butler on that." Benjamin Washburn looked over at the general.

"Indeed. I'm the one you will have to deal with. And unfortunately I am going to refuse your request, Major. This so-called property you seek to have returned is being used to raise crops. That supports the Confederate war effort, and I therefore confiscate them as *contraband of war*."

"What!" Thomas Auld roared. "These are my properties, my slaves. Under any law you are not entitled to pillage my ..."

"Now hold on, Major. Under international law, contraband of war goes to its captor. We all know that. And, as I just stated, these three properties are used in your war effort and I have declared them to be just that, contraband of war—which of course entitles me to confiscate them."

"But they're not property. They're slaves. They can't be contraband. Contraband consists of *things*: guns, cannon, ammunition, crops, ships, food, clothing, carriages, housing—those sorts of things. These are people!"

"People you say, Major? But just a moment ago you referred to them as your properties. Why you even treat them as property. They can be beaten, murdered, sold, rented out, traded, demised by will, inherited. That certainly doesn't apply to people, does it? And our Supreme Court agrees with you. It has classified them as chattels and forever denied them citizenship. No, Major, they aren't people; they're property and subject to being confiscated as contraband of war!"

"But this is unheard of! It's plain thievery! Where in God's name did you come up with this, General?"

"An excellent question. And its source is this young lawyer, Isaiah Washburn."

"And where is he?"

General Butler pointed to Isaiah. "This young man."

"That nigger in those fancy-ass clothes?"

"That free American who, incidentally, you sold to your brother-in-law many years ago. His name then was 'Izey.' "

"Goddamn you, you little bastard," Thomas Auld screamed. "I remember you. And I'll have you strung up sooner than you think, you no good filthy little shit." With that, he lunged at Isaiah.

"I don't think so, Thomas," Benjamin Washburn said as he quickly stepped in between his brother-in-law and Isaiah, followed almost immediately by the corporal. "Just understand something: slaves may legally be property, but they possess all the unique traits of human beings. Their brainpower is equal to yours. In fact, Isaiah is a whole lot smarter than you'll ever be. And with your three slaves delivered to us today, he has now paved a way to freedom for thousands of slaves to follow. So be off with you, Thomas Auld—and my warmest regards to your wife."

"And you, Benjamin Washburn, have turned into a damnable thief! I despise you!"

Still enraged, Thomas Auld spun around on his heels and stomped out of the general's office. And as he did, a chilling thought crossed his mind: *could he be that young black's father?*

======================

Part 4 of Isaiah Washburn's Tale
List of Characters
["B" denotes black; "W" denotes white; * denotes a real person]

Gerrit Smith (abolitionist) W*

Part 4

Time for the Reception to Begin

Beverley House, Toronto, Canada
5:44 p.m., August 1, 1862

Frederick Douglass looked over at Reverend Rankin. "My God!" he said. "My ears are burning from Brother Isaiah's tale. And what a tale it is! What an adventure! From ship's mutiny, to slavery in the Deep South, to the president's office—and then, finally, a payback of momentous proportions to that evil Roger Taney. Lord!"

"Yes, I too am impressed, young Isaiah," Reverend Rankin said. "And your plan: brilliant! Salvation for so many slaves—and what a magnificent contribution to the Union's war effort."

"Hardly," Isaiah replied, slightly embarrassed.

"Hardly? How can you possibly say that?"

"My plan would have been nothing without General Butler and Harriet Tubman. They implemented it—with President Lincoln's blessing. What I'm saying is that my plan turned out to be a collaborative effort and … ."

"Nonsense, Isaiah," Reverend Rankin replied. "You're far too modest. Yes, others implemented your plan. But you devised it. It was created in your mind! Didn't you come up with an idea which paved the way for thousands of slaves to be granted sanctuary as 'contrabands of war'—first at Fort Monroe and then later on as the word spread at so many other locations? And wasn't it your plan which inspired Congress to enact the Confiscation Act of 1861 which forbade the return of slaves to their southern masters if they were used by the Confederate military? My God, man, take credit where it's due! It was your plan, Isaiah! Yours, and yours alone!"

273

"I suppose so," Isaiah replied in an almost inaudible voice. He was beginning to feel uncomfortable. Why was he suddenly being singled out? He hadn't devoted his life to the abolitionist cause as these two men had. They were its true luminaries and he ... why he was only a young inexperienced lawyer with a head full of dreams.

For the past minute or so Frederick Douglass had been silent. He now spoke up: "Like Reverend Rankin, I too shall view this whole idea of slaves being granted sanctuary as contrabands of war as something only you conjured up, Brother Isaiah. And to you I shall be forever grateful."

"And I say 'Amen' to that," Reverend Rankin added.

———

As happened a short while before, the tall servant who previously served them tea reappeared. Again he coughed and then cleared his throat. "The guests have arrived, gentlemen. Please follow me into the hall where the reception is to be ..."

Just then they all heard a strangely distinctive loud piercing whistle: "Twheet, twheet, twheet, twheet, twheeeeeeeeeeeee! Twheet, twheet, twheet, twheet, twheeeeeeeeeeeee! Twheet, twheet, twheet, twheet, twheeeeeeeeeeeee!"

Isaiah and Frederick stared at one another. "It's coming from the front door, Isaiah!" Frederick Douglass cried out. Both men turned and ran at full speed to the main entrance of Beverley House. There they saw a tall white man and a wizened bent over black woman. The man held the woman under one arm, while she tried to prop herself up with a cane. It was Gerrit Smith and Betty Bailey, Isaiah and Frederick's grandmother.

"See them, Mr. Smith." Betty said, pointing her cane first at Frederick and then at Isaiah. "They's my two granchiles, Frederick and Izey. An' they ain't changed one bit—except they's growed big and tall. An' they's famous!" She began to smile. "Real famous!"

Isaiah could see that his grandmother had aged since he left the tiny cabin in Tuckahoe more than two decades ago. She no longer had any teeth; and her hair had thinned and turned gray. For some inexplicable reason the sight of her seemed to transport him back to a time when, as a small boy, she told him he was to be sold, that they would never see one another again, and that he must always be a man and never ever cry.

Overcome by emotion, Isaiah walked over to his beloved grandmother. Falling to his knees before her, he gently wrapped his arms around her frail legs—and, as he did, he felt tears stream down his cheeks and heard prayers he had never uttered before issue forth from his lips:

"Lord, why was it thus? Why did we have to endure such suffering? Why did we have to struggle so? Why did we ..." And then he broke down in uncontrollable sobs before feeling the comforting arms of his half-brother tenderly lift him up.

"It's good to cry, Brother Isaiah. Crying cleanses the soul. I expect you haven't cried in years—and Lord only knows you need to cry. You've been through so much—and done so much good in your short life. So cry, Brother. And don't be ashamed. It's all right to cry."

=====================

For close to four hours Judge Washburn and his grandson had been on a private walking tour of Toronto's recently renovated Beverley House listening attentively while an attractive young docent recounted to them the adventures of their famous ancestor, Isaiah Washburn.

"Well, how do you feel about all this, Jamie?" The Judge looked down at his grandson who appeared to be unusually moved. "Have you at least learned a little about our family history?"

"I never knew, Grandpa."

"Never knew what, boy?"

"That we were such an important part of American history."

The judge smiled. "That's exactly the message I was hopin' you'd carry back with you. Yes, Jamie, we Washburns are Americans to the core. We were there almost from the start. And that's important to know, especially when we're back in Glencoe."

"Are we finally going back, Grandpa?"

"We'll be on a plane to Chicago early tomorrow mornin'. And by the way, did you happen to notice the name of our tour guide on her docent's badge?"

" 'Natalie something'?"

" 'Natalie Alden.' That ring a bell?"

"Is she related to the Aldens in Glencoe?"

"Sure is. There are a whole lot of Aldens livin' in Canada. Mostly in the Toronto area.

"And that reminds me: I've got a little more history for you. You see, after Sir John's reception was held right here in Beverley House over a century ago Isaiah stayed on for a while in Toronto. He was joined by Jenny, his sister. Beautiful and talented as she was, it didn't take long for

276

men to start courtin' her. One of her suitors came from the Alden family: a young lawyer by the name of John Alden. And ..."

"Did they get married?"

"They did. And some years after the Civil War ended they moved down to the Chicago area where John's sister, Nell, was teachin' school. John started up a law practice in Glencoe—then a tiny community of only about fifty—and moved into a large log cabin located on what is now school property. And, by the way, you've been inside that cabin."

"I have?"

"Well, now, haven't you?"

"The only log cabin I can think of is the one next to North School. Is that where John and Jenny Alden lived?"

"It is. So we Washburns are not only a part of American history, we're long-time residents of Glencoe. Our family has probably lived in Glencoe longer than just about any other family."

"Gosh, Grandpa ..."

"Now hold on. How come you haven't asked me about Isaiah? Don't you want to know what happened to him? After all, he was a pretty important Washburn, don't you think?"

"I'm sorry, Grandpa. I guess I've learned so much today and taken so many notes I'm beginning to forget things."

"That's all right. I'll fill you in. Isaiah followed his sister to Glencoe where he went into partnership with John Alden. They called their law firm 'Alden & Washburn.' Got to be pretty well known and highly respected in the community and ..."

"Did he ever marry?"

"Isaiah married John Alden's sister, Nell. A beautiful woman. She became a writer and to this day you can still find some of her books in the Glencoe Library.

277

She and Isaiah had two sons. One died in his teens; the other was my father."

"So Isaiah was your grandfather?"

"Exactly. And your great-great-grandfather—a former slave who actually met with President Lincoln!"

"Did you know him, Grandpa?"

"I did. He was gettin' up in years then, but his mind was sharp—and he told me all about his days as a slave, New Orleans, the contrabands and his wonderful step-parents."

Jamie now began writing even more notes in his notebook.

"What happened to them, Grandpa?"

"Don't know. I never asked him. Wish I had. I suspect that Benjamin and Melinda Washburn remained in Washington, D.C., after the Civil War. That might be somethin' for you to research."

"Did Isaiah and his family live in Glencoe?"

"Yep. They moved in with John and Jenny and their three children. And that's where my father was raised. I can only imagine how full of life that log cabin must have been with all those people livin' in it. There are photos of the two families upstairs in the second floor library. Also some photos of my father in his late teens when he was workin' as a clerk at the Alden & Washburn law firm. C'mon, let's go on up and take a look. Then we'll head back to the hotel and have dinner. Our plane leaves at seven o'clock tomorrow mornin' so we should turn in early."

"What time do you expect we'll be home?"

"Oh, I'd say midafternoon. But don't you be thinkin' that once we're there you'll be free to take off on me—because you won't be! Our travels won't be over until we've finished some important work."

"Work on that dancing thing, Grandpa?"

"That's right, boy: Work on that dancin' thing."

278

Excerpt from Jamie's Notebook, Page 167

Interesting when you think about it—my great-great-grandfather was a slave who met with President Lincoln and came up with that idea about contrabands of war. How much sooner did the war end because of what he did and how many slaves did he free?

I'm getting the feeling Grandpa's about ready to come clean about that dancing thing. I still can't figure out what all our travels have to do with dancing. Or why Grandpa is getting such a buzz out of keeping me in the dark. But maybe that's what you do when you're retired and have nothing else to do—torment your grandchildren.

Glencoe's Small Beginning

Glencoe's Small Beginning – List of Characters
["B" denotes black; "W" denotes white; * denotes a real person]

Mildred Slotkin Gold (Glencoe resident and simultaneously president of the Glencoe Women's Club, PTA and League of Women Voters) W

Stella (Mildred Gold's volunteer secretary) W

Sam Adamson (owner of Adamson Drug Store, Glencoe's Justice of the Peace) W

Jerome Alden (Glencoe resident) B

Norma Alden (Glencoe resident) B

Perry Alden (son of Norma and Jerome Alden) B

Stuart Cliver (Glencoe resident, racist) W

Franklin Price (Glencoe resident, pastor of the Glencoe Methodist Church) W

Rabbi Ed Sorkin (Glencoe resident, local rabbi) W

Trenton Richards (prominent civil rights attorney, later first black associate justice of the US Supreme Court) B

Aaron Reynolds (Glencoe police chief) W

Wanda (Chief Reynolds' secretary) W

Emma Bolton (Dr. Richman's nurse) W

Amy Post (dancing instructor) W

John Stern (Central School teacher) W

Glencoe's Small Beginning

Chapter 1

For fiftyish Mildred Slotkin Gold, a short, slightly overweight, forceful woman with a master's degree from Yale, Wednesday, September 3, 1947, was a day she would never forget. It wasn't because on that day she ascended from president-elect to president of Glencoe's Women's Club, otherwise known as the "GWC," or because on that day she became the first woman in Glencoe history to hold the presidency of three organizations simultaneously, the GWC, the PTA, and the League of Women Voters. It was because on that day Assistant Supervisor Bruno Steiner of the Glencoe Parks & Recreation Department delivered a letter to her the contents of which literally "shocked the daylights out of her" (as she would later tell friends).

"So, Bruno, what are we gonna do about this?" she asked, waving the letter at him. "I can't just sit here and ignore it. And by the way, where'd you get this?"

"It was mailed to every family with an eighth grader. Christopher Wallace's wife called and asked me to come by and pick up her copy. I'm sick about this, Mrs. Gold. After all, they're Glencoe's children."

But Mildred wasn't listening to Bruno's comments about Glencoe's children. Instead, the widespread distribution of the letter only emphasized the enormity of the problem: "God, that means at least eighty letters went out. How come nobody at the village got a copy? The room that lady's renting belongs to the village, doesn't it?"

Bruno nodded. "It's public property."

"Well we've gotta hold a meeting. Figure out what to do." She thought for a moment.

"Call Sam Adamson. Arrange to hold it above his drugstore at 7:00 p.m. tonight. I think he and the Wallaces oughta be there. Also Junior Washburn and James—and their wives; Norma Alden and her husband; Margaret Carlton; and whoever else you can think of."

"I was thinking of people connected with Central School; plus Rabbi Sorkin and Reverend Price; maybe even the police chief."

"You figure it out, Bruno. But as many people as possible. Round 'em up for tonight. I'll run the meeting, although I expect Chris Wallace will take over—which is fine with me. Meantime, I'm gonna have Stella mimeograph the letter so that we can pass out copies at the meeting. Just remember: as many people as possible."

Softening, Mildred continued, "Thanks for bringing me the letter, Bruno."

As Bruno was leaving the GWC's tiny office above the A&P grocery store, Mildred could be heard issuing an order to her volunteer secretary: "Stella, come on in. I've got something urgent for you."

Glencoe's Small Beginning

Chapter 2

There was nothing Glencoe's perennial bachelor, Sam Adamson, liked better than holding court—even when court wasn't in session. Sam was Glencoe's JP (Justice of the Peace) and presided over his courtroom—located above his drugstore on the second floor of the Adamson Building—every Tuesday evening. But any other time he was also pleased ("delighted" is probably a better word) to preside over any meeting of any kind at any location, be it Rotary, a fundraiser, the school board, or a church social. And once at the helm, he wasn't at all shy about making speeches—generally long-winded ones. Thus, when Bruno Steiner called him earlier in the day to set up the evening's meeting, he automatically assumed he was to be its chair. Based upon this assumption, promptly at 7:00 p.m. he stepped to the front of the assembled group of eleven persons and, as was his custom, started things off with a few well-punctuated coughs, some throat-clearing, and his cookie-cutter, generic, late-in-the-day greeting: "Evening folks. Glad you could be here."

Again, more throat-clearing.

"Hold on, Sam," Mildred Gold said, stepping forward. "I think Chris Wallace oughta conduct the meeting seeing as he's got an eighth grader and is much more affected by that damn letter than you are."

"I'm not so sure …"

"Have you read the letter, Sam?"

"What letter?"

A look of annoyance crossed Mildred's face. She turned to Christopher Wallace. "Chris," she said, "take over, will you?" And then she addressed the Washburn clan: "Junior, come on up to the front. You, too, James. And your wives. I want you all involved in this thing.

"Same for you," she continued, speaking to Norma and Jerome Alden.

As an afterthought, she asked: "Anyone not get a copy of the letter?"

Stuart Cliver raised his hand. "No, I didn't. And I want to know why?"

Mildred was immediately sorry she asked the question. Stuart, an average size man with a potbelly and curly gray hair, was almost universally disliked not only for the officious way he insinuated himself into much of Glencoe's business, but also because of his unabashed bigotry, particularly when it came to Negroes and Jews.

"Stella. Mr. Cliver over there." Mildred pointed to Stuart. Stella walked over to Stuart and handed him a copy of the letter—and then quickly moved away, her body language unmistakably communicating dislike.

A minute later Stuart, holding the letter in hand, began to wave it as he rose to speak: "Now here's one gutsy lady. Tells it like it is. I say we all go home; let her do what she's proposing to do."

"You're a damn bigot, Cliver," Christopher Wallace replied, getting to his feet. "Why don't *you* go home! We've no intention of caving in to Miss Post; and what we're gonna do in response to that filthy letter is no concern of yours."

"Screw you, Wallace. Leave her the hell alone."

"And I say it's time for you to leave, Cliver." James Washburn, all six feet four inches of him, turned and, menacingly, walked over to where Stuart Cliver was sitting. "Either you leave or I'll escort you out of here. Understand?"

Stuart Cliver didn't respond so James Washburn repeated himself, this time in a much louder voice: "Understand?"

"All right, all right, I'm going. But threats and bullying don't become your race, Washburn!"

"And bigotry doesn't become you, little man," James replied.

———

"Sorry about that," James said. "I just wanted him gone. His presence will only disrupt what we're trying to accomplish."

"And what is that?" Mildred Gold asked.

"I think what we're here to do is come up with Glencoe's response to the letter, Mildred," Christopher Wallace answered. "And that will require our collective thinking. So, for starters, I'd like to hear from you, Junior. Seems like you always have a twist of your own to contribute."

James "Junior" Lincoln Washburn Jr., recently nominated to be the nation's first black federal judge, rose to his feet, thought for a moment, and then began to speak. "Seems Chris here has been readin' my mind, because I have an entirely different take on this: I say that adversity—and by that I'm referrin' to the letter—gives rise to opportunity." He paused to let what he'd just said sink in.

"I know. You're askin' 'What opportunity?' And the answer is the opportunity which Miss Post has given Glencoe to speak out, to make a positive statement— somethin' I know we can do. How? Easy. We get Miss Post to back down or we cancel the whole damn program. Either way, it will be a wonderful learnin' experience for the children—and hopefully for others across the country. That is, Chris, if you can get us some publicity. And James," Junior turned to his son, "can you do somethin' along those lines usin' your military contacts?"

"Probably, Dad. But I also think you can contribute."

Junior Washburn thought for a moment. "Yes, as a judicial nominee I suppose I can."

287

"Sir, may I speak?" It was Bruno Steiner.

"Of course, Bruno," Christopher Wallace replied.

"Well, I'd hate to have you run Miss Post out of town. Then our kids would lose out."

"We all agree with you, Bruno," Christopher Wallace answered. "But how would you feel if we went along with her?"

"Oh, that would be terrible, Mr. Wallace. We can't let that happen."

"We won't, Bruno. And I think you've just answered your own question: we either get her to change her mind or we cancel. Don't you agree?"

Bruno looked down. "I suppose so, sir."

Christopher Wallace saw that Franklin Price, pastor of the Glencoe Methodist Church, had raised his hand. "Yes, Frank?"

"Chris, I like Junior Washburn's point—that this isn't adversity; it's an opportunity. So I have a question for him: Junior, any law cases we can hang our hat on? Anything similar happen in some other community?"

"Good question, Frank. And the answer is 'yes in a way.' A year ago five Latino fathers went after the City of Westminster in California because it refused to accept their kids into the Westminster school system and instead forced them to attend special Mexican schools. They claimed that this was unconstitutional discrimination, and the federal district judge handlin' the case agreed. The case, *Mendez v. Westminster*, was affirmed on appeal by the federal appellate court, but on flimsy grounds. Still, it was a start. And in some ways it's similar to our situation. Here we're not talkin' about education, but we are talkin' about the use of public property in a discriminatory way. So there's a parallel of sorts."

"Interesting," Reverend Price replied.

"Margaret, anything you'd like to add?" Christopher Wallace could see that Margaret Carlton, principal of Central School, had been thoughtfully taking all this in.

"Yes, Chris. I say we hold a grandiose meeting, preferably in the auditorium. Invite the families of all eighth graders. Give each family one vote. Then give them two choices: Go along with Miss Post and her damnable letter or, if she won't change her mind, send her packing. And if she's sent away, it will be a valuable learning experience for the children—and, by the way, they'll survive. Children always do. They're resilient. It will also give Glencoe a chance to speak out—to tell the world that we won't tolerate racial discrimination."

James, who adored Miss Carlton for her mentoring in years past, added: "I think Miss Carlton and my father are right. This is a great opportunity for Glencoe to make a statement. If Miss Post won't retract her letter and we vote to oust her, then our community will have struck a blow against racism—something which I'm certain will reverberate throughout the country. Maybe even set a trend."

"I agree, son," Junior Washburn said. "It might just be a small beginnin'."

"*Glencoe's Small Beginning,*" Christopher Wallace said. "Maybe that should be our mantra."

Glencoe's Small Beginning

Chapter 3

"Trenton, it's Junior Washburn. How are you?" Junior Washburn had just placed a call to one of the nation's top civil rights attorneys, Trenton Richards.

"Junior, always good to hear from you. I'm fine. Up to my eyeballs in work. But what else is new? And by the way, I'm forever indebted to you for helping us with our brief in the *Mendez* case. I don't think we would have won without some of your arguments. And I think the City of Westminster is still reeling from the shellacking it took. But I've gotta be honest: I'm not happy with the result. I wish to hell the appellate court had done away with 'separate but equal.' "

"It'll be gone one day, Trenton. I promise you that. It may take a few years, but it'll happen."

"I hope you're right, Junior." Trenton Richards was silent for a moment before continuing. "So why the call? What's up?"

"Seems my little village, Glencoe, has a problem of its own."

"Tell me."

"Kids here start a weekly dancin' school in the seventh grade. Takes place in a large ballroom. The boys wear coats and ties; girls have on white blouses, dark skirts and Mary Janes. All of 'em wear white gloves. Girls sit on one side of the room, boys on the other. Then the lady who runs this thing plays some kind of a low-key march on the piano. Boys and girls pair up holdin' hands and march around the room. After that, she teaches 'em the box step and they start fox trottin', waltzin', and doin' some Latin dances. Cutest damn thing you've ever seen. And the children love it. They know that the next year, in eighth grade, the dancin' class will continue with what they call

290

'Fortnightly'—meanin' more advanced dancin' instruction once every other week. And they all look forward to it."

"Sounds great to me, Junior. What's the problem?"

"The problem, Trenton, is that a couple of days ago the lady who runs the dancin' program, Amy Post, sent out a letter to every family with an eighth grader. It's about Fortnightly. She's not discontinuin' it; she's just suddenly barrin' Negro youngsters from attendin'. Out of the goddamn blue. No explanation; no reason. Negro kids are no longer welcome."

"Did they participate in the seventh grade dancing school?"

"Yes. They've always done that. But maybe now she's also gonna change that too. I just don't know."

Trenton Richards didn't respond immediately. Finally, he asked: "Junior, is this officially part of the Glencoe Schools' curriculum?"

"No, but all the kids attend."

"Second question: Where is this held?"

"The dancin' classes are all held on public property. Specifically, in the ballroom which is on the second floor of the Central School Auditorium; and the auditorium is physically attached to the school."

"And by what right is she using the ballroom?"

"Glencoe rented it to her."

"So it's a rental of public property by a private business being used in a racially discriminatory fashion, right?"

"Exactly. And that bein' the case, do you think there's a lawsuit here?"

Trenton Richards thought for a moment before replying: "Offhand, no. If anything, it's a much weaker case than *Mendez*. Also completely different. Doesn't technically involve education or a lawsuit against a municipality—because I'm sure you don't intend to sue Glencoe. It's really only a case to be brought against this lady. And what remedy would you seek? Damages? They'd be minimal since they'd only involve the black children. Cancellation of her lease? Doubtful you'd prevail since you're not a party to it. As I see it, your case amounts to nothing more than black youngsters being treated in a shameful and hurtful manner by a private individual. But from a legal standpoint, no case there.

"I'll get back to you if I have a change of heart. But for now I'd suggest that you think in terms of having your case tried in the court of public opinion. I'm confident you'd get a much better result than in a court of law. And maybe after the whole thing was aired in public, the parents would pull their kids out of the program."

"Thanks, Trenton. Sorta what I thought too."

"Don't mention it, Junior. Always a pleasure. Talk to you later." Trenton Richards hung up the phone.

Glencoe's Small Beginning

Chapter 4

Seated at his desk, Aaron Reynolds, Glencoe's police chief, began to think about why he liked his job so much: mainly, he concluded, because there was hardly any crime in the village he didn't have to deal with law enforcement, something he didn't much care for; instead, he could focus on community relations which he thoroughly enjoyed. Sure, once in a while someone would over imbibe; or occasionally there might be a domestic problem; and from time to time a youngster might do something he shouldn't be doing. But that was about it. Mostly, though, his job involved speaking in public which he felt was his strong suit. He would periodically lecture to various groups on public safety; he would emcee at a variety of private and village events including his favorite, Glencoe's annual pet parade; and he would also give talks to children and parents at Central School on any subject he chose—his latest being the pros and cons of a career in law enforcement. In fact, his job was so unrelated to crime that he almost never carried his service revolver. No need for it.

And then that call had come in: someone threw a brick through the Aldens' living room window. "Damn," he cursed. Tucking his .38 Special in his belt, he headed for the office doorway. As he exited, he advised Wanda, his secretary, that he'd be handling this one.

"I called the Aldens," Wanda replied. "Told them not to touch anything. Maybe we could get some prints."

"Good thinking, Wanda. Thanks."

"Does this have anything to do with that letter, Chief?"

"Don't know for sure."

But what Aaron Reynolds did know for sure was that in the fourteen years he'd been chief he hadn't had to deal with a single racist incident. That is, not until today.

Glencoe's Small Beginning

Chapter 5

Norma and Jerome Alden sat on the couch in their living room. They were stunned—and frightened. Something like this had never happened before. Two hours earlier Norma had been on the phone with a friend, Jerome had been reading the paper, and their son, Perry, had been doing his homework. And then that brick had come crashing through the window, missing Jerome's head by inches.

"You all right, Dad?" Perry had asked, and Jerome had nodded. Norma had moaned: not a scream; instead, a moan of terror.

Now, two hours later, Norma and Jerome awaited the arrival of the police; and Perry had gone to his room. They hadn't heard a word from him in over an hour.

There was a knock on the door. "Thank God," Jerome said. He went to the front door and opened it. To his surprise, it was Rabbi Sorkin.

"Mildred called me, so I decided to come over. You two all right?"

"I think so," Norma replied. "I'm not sure about Perry."

"Where is he?"

"Went to his room over an hour ago. I think he's really shaken up by all this."

"Understandable. Maybe I can help. May I see him?"

Norma looked at Jerome. "What do you think?"

"It's okay with me. Let's try to get him outta his room. Maybe give him something to eat or drink. C'mon."

The three were about to walk down the hallway to Perry's room when they heard a second knock on the door.

It was Chief Reynolds. As he entered, he nodded to Norma, Jerome and Rabbi Sorkin.

"Anything been touched, moved, Jerome?"

"Not a thing."

"May I use the phone?"

"Sure."

"I think I'd better have one of my officers who's trained in fingerprint work come over. I doubt that he'll find any prints on that brick, but it's worth a try. Anything else wind up in the house?"

"Only the brick—at least so far as we know," Norma replied.

"Did you see anyone? Hear anything?"

"We saw a large dark maroon-colored car make a U-turn as it pulled away. I think one of its wheels hit the curb on the other side of the street. I can't tell you the make or the license number, but it was a four-door car. My guess is that it was a Cadillac or Packard—or maybe a LaSalle. Probably pre-war."

"Okay, after I make the phone call I'll wait in the living room for my officer. You three can go ahead and do whatever you were doing when I barged in."

Chapter 6

Rabbi Sorkin gently tapped on the door to Perry's room. "Perry," he said in a soft voice, "It's Rabbi Sorkin. I need to speak to you. Chief Reynolds is here and another officer is expected shortly."

The door opened and Perry stood just inside the room, head bowed.

"Everything's okay now, Perry. And I'm really sorry."

"If they did it because of Fortnightly, I don't have to go. I don't want my parents hurt! But, still, I don't understand. Why, Rabbi? What did we do?"

" 'Why?' That's the age-old question, Perry. And growing up in Glencoe, you've been insulated from racism. I suppose for you it first reared its ugly head a few days ago when that letter arrived. And the brick is just more of the same.

"My take on it is that differences breed hatred. Some people hate me just for being a Jew. Don't ever forget: the Nazis murdered six million of us. Why? Because we follow a different religion. Have for thousands of years.

"And you're black—so some people consider you different. And your blackness therefore breeds hatred."

"But why? I think. I feel. I'm human. I've got the best grades in my class, and Mr. Stern, our science teacher, wants me to go into medicine so I can help other people. I've never gotten into any trouble. And I'm friends with everyone in my class. Even Mr. Wallace told me he'd help me pay for college and medical school. I don't understand."

"And neither do I, Perry. But unexplained hatred exists—as I said, because of differences."

"Just because of my skin color?"

"Just because of that. But only by people who are irrational enough to make a big thing out of what I consider an insignificant difference."

"But why just skin color? Why not hair color, eye color, height, weight—those kinds of things?"

"I can't tell you. Maybe it's because Negroes originally came here as slaves. I just don't know. And I have the same question: why are Jews hated? There's no skin color difference. And remember, Jesus was a Jew.

"No, I've never gotten a satisfactory answer. I've just learned to live with anti-Semitism—as you must learn to live with racism. I try as best I can to rise above it—and sometimes that's difficult to do. But that, Perry, is what you're going to have to learn to do."

"What about the violence, Rabbi? That brick almost killed my father."

"I understand. I don't have the answer. Chief Reynolds will try to find out who threw it. I doubt that he'll succeed. But I suspect that once the letter thing subsides, incidents like that brick will disappear."

"I'm still frightened."

"I would be too, Perry. But I assure you that all this will pass and things will return to normal."

"I don't see how they can, Rabbi."

Glencoe's Small Beginning

Chapter 7

"Hello," Mildred Gold said, answering the phone in the GWC offices.

"Mildred, it's Aaron Reynolds."

"Yes, Chief, what's going on?"

"Officer Stanhill, the fingerprint expert on the force, found some blood droplets on that brick. Apparently whoever threw it cut himself in the process. So we should all be on the lookout for anyone with a cut hand or finger—or wearing any kind of bandage on his hand."

"I'll spread the word, Chief."

"And while I've got you on the phone, anything new on the meeting?"

"We're making progress. I'd say we'll hold it in two to three weeks. But I'm not exactly sure where. Chris Wallace and I are meeting with Peter McAfee to try to get the school auditorium. Also, James Washburn and his father have lined up some people who'll be attending; so has Chris. Assuming we get the auditorium, in about a week I'll be sending out notices. For sure, I'll want Amy Post to be at the meeting."

"Lemme know, Mildred. I really want to be there."

"You're on the list, Chief."

"One other thing, Mildred: I'm pretty concerned about Perry Alden. He's in a really bad way. Any suggestions?"

"I'll give Margaret Carlton a call. I'll ask her to go over to the boy's home and try to calm him."

Glencoe's Small Beginning

Chapter 8

Margaret Carlton was always busy. As Central School's principal, she was overburdened with administrative duties, including what seemed to her to be mounds of paperwork which she never had to deal with as a teacher. In addition, she insisted on teaching one section of seventh grade, something no other principal had ever done. This only added to her workload. And yet, she was never too occupied to rise to an important occasion. Thus, when she received Mildred Gold's call concerning Perry Alden, she immediately dropped what she was doing and drove to his home. Arriving at the front door of the Alden residence, she was greeted by Norma Alden, someone she knew well and respected.

"Come on in, Margaret. What brings you here?"

"I received a call from Mildred. She asked me to stop by and check on Perry."

"Check on Perry? I don't understand. He's fine. Been in his room since he got home from school. Doing homework, I guess. Truth is, he's been spending a lot of time alone ever since that brick incident."

"Mind if I speak to him?"

"Of course not. I'll leave you two alone. And by the way, we'd love to have you stay for dinner."

"Some other time, Norma."

———

A few minutes later Margaret Carlton returned. "It's Perry, Norma."

"Wha…?"

"He's tried to end his life. I'm calling a doctor."

Before Margaret Carlton could say another word, Norma Alden had rushed down the hallway and into Perry's room. Shortly after that, she could be heard wailing.

———

"Dr. Richman, it's Margaret Carlton. Perry Alden just tried to kill himself. He's barely breathing."

"Where's he at?"

"His home. I'm with him."

"I'm on my way. Meantime, call Highland Park Hospital. Alert them that the boy will be arriving within the hour, and have them send an ambulance to his house. I'll want to ride with him to the hospital."

Dr. Richman hung up the phone.

Glencoe's Small Beginning

Chapter 9

"Stay with me, Perry. Don't leave me, boy!" Dr. Richman was riding in the back of the ambulance along with a near-dead Perry Alden. "Faster," he called out to the driver as they sped toward Highland Park Hospital. Perry's eyes were partially closed and he didn't seem to be breathing in any of the oxygen being fed to him through the oxygen mask covering his nose and mouth.

"C'mon, boy, breathe!"

Dr. Richman had hold of Perry's left wrist and was trying to find a pulse.

"Damn!" he cursed.

Three minutes later they were at the entry to the hospital's emergency room. A young intern immediately opened the ambulance's rear door, and two male attendants pushed a gurney in next to where Perry was lying.

"I think we're too late," Dr. Richman said.

"We'll try," one of the attendants responded. "Help me roll him onto the gurney."

———

Twenty minutes later Al Cohen, the emergency room's medical director, and Dr. Warren Richman exited the emergency room.

"I'll leave you now, Warren. You saw firsthand—particularly those rope burns on the boy's neck. Nothing much anyone could have done for him. I'll sign the certificate. Should I list the cause of death as 'cerebral hypoxia'?"

"No. List it as 'damn letter.' "

" 'Damn letter'?"

"Never mind. Just write it up any way you want."

Glencoe's Small Beginning

Chapter 10

In the early afternoon two days later Aaron Reynolds' office intercom buzzed. He reached over and lifted its toggle switch. "Yes, Wanda?"

"They're here, Chief."

"Send them in."

Shortly after that Dr. Warren Richman and Emma Bolton, his nurse, entered the chief's office.

"Sit down, folks," Aaron said. "Coffee?"

"No thanks," Doctor Richman replied.

"Sure," Emma said. "Black, please."

Aaron Reynolds got up, poked his head out the door and could be overheard saying something to Wanda.

"While we're waiting for your coffee, Emma, mind if I ask you a few questions?"

"Of course not, sir."

"How long have you worked for Dr. Richman?"

Emma thought for a moment. "I'd say seventeen years. But we have records in the office if you need to know my exact starting date."

"No, that's okay. Now let's talk about Mr. Cliver. From your call this morning, I understand he showed up in your office two days ago?"

"At around 1:30 in the afternoon."

"Where were you at the time, Doc?"

"Rotary."

"Okay, Emma, tell me what happened."

"Well, Mr. Cliver comes by every few weeks to pick up samples of Veronal for his wife who has trouble sleeping."

"And that's why he stopped by?"

"Yes.

"And while he was there I noticed that he had a bad scrape on the palm of his right hand. It looked to be pretty dirty to me and I was afraid it would become infected, so I cleaned it with a cotton swab soaked in alcohol and applied some sulfa powder to it. Then I gave him a tetanus shot. But when I tried to bandage his hand, he got sort of weird. He said I was making too big of a deal out of it and that all he wanted was a band-aid. I told him I didn't have one that was large enough. When he heard that, he just got up and left. Didn't even bother to thank me."

"Do you happen to recall whether you picked up any dirt or grit on that cotton swab?"

"Strange you should ask—because I do. I distinctly remember a residue of particles that were reddish in color."

"One last question, Emma: do you think you could find that swab for me?"

"I know it went into our trash bin the same day. Trash pickup is tomorrow morning, so when I get back to the office today I'll look for it."

"Let me know if you find it. And as we speak, I'm having some blood drops we found on that brick analyzed. We're trying to determine the blood type. Incidentally, do you happen to know what Cliver's blood type is?"

"I'm sure we have a record of it in the office," Dr. Richman said.

"Okay, I think you see where I'm heading with this. But I guess I'd better fill you in because I already have some pretty damning evidence pointing to Cliver.

"I was at the Aldens' a couple of hours after they called in the brick incident. I spoke to Jerome and he told me he saw a large four-door dark maroon car—probably a pre-war Cadillac, Packard or LaSalle—make a U-turn and speed away right after that brick went sailing through his window. He said that as the car drove off one of its wheels scraped the curb across the street.

"I had Officer Bill Stanhill go over to Cliver's home yesterday and, lo and behold, he discovered that Cliver owns a 1939 maroon four-door LaSalle with a badly scuffed right rear tire. Then he went over to the Aldens' and found a tire mark on the curb on the opposite side of the street which is almost a perfect match to the scuff mark. He's got photos of both the tire and the curb.

"So I think I've pretty much got enough evidence to tie the car to the incident. What I don't have is anything pointing to Cliver as the driver. But if the fragments on that swab match the brick, and if the blood type on the brick matches Cliver's, then my case against him is fairly solid and I'll arrest him."

Doctor Richman, who had been listening intently, seemed impressed. "Nice police work, Chief. For a moment there I thought I was listening to Sherlock Holmes in action!" Smiling, he turned to Emma. "Emma, you know me, and this is way out of my bailiwick—so I've decided to let you take charge of all the evidence gathering."

"Then I think I'd better hurry on back to the office, Doctor."

Just then Wanda entered holding a steaming cup of black coffee. "Your coffee, Emma."

"No time, I'm afraid. Right now I'm in a bit of a rush."

Glencoe's Small Beginning

Chapter 11

Central School's seldom-used auditorium was large for a small grammar school, with an orchestra pit, a balcony, and seating for seven hundred eighty. Traditionally, its main use came at the end of each school year when the eighth grade put on a semi-professional production of a Gilbert and Sullivan operetta, an event widely attended by residents of Glencoe and nearby Chicago suburbs. However, aside from the annual operetta and a few school-related functions, the auditorium remained dark most of the year with few exceptions, the most memorable one being the June 6, 1944, community-wide assembly at which Glencoe Schools Superintendent Dr. Peter McAfee held forth on the importance of the Allied invasion of Europe which was taking place as he spoke and how its outcome could drastically affect our American way of life. Aside from the D-Day special assembly, it was only on rare occasions that Dr. McAfee permitted the auditorium to be used for any purpose not specifically a part of the Glencoe Schools' curriculum. This, though, didn't in the least dissuade Mildred Gold and Christopher Wallace from seeking its use for their upcoming meeting on the "Post Letter" (as that document was now being referred to by locals), a request which Dr. McAfee immediately granted. It appeared to Mildred and Christopher that Dr. McAfee was particularly incensed over the racist implications of the letter, something which he would confirm years later when Christopher Wallace overheard him say after one too many drinks that "I'd be goddamned if I'd allow that bitch to draw any racist color line affecting our children!"

And so it was that the following notice went out to each Glencoe family with an eighth grade student (and also to others, including certain select residents of Glencoe, various faculty members of Central School, the Chief of Police, the Fire Chief, the Justice of the Peace, the press, and special guests of Junior Washburn, James Washburn, and Christopher Wallace):

NOTICE OF IMPORTANT MEETING

September 12, 1947

Dear Friends:

As you are undoubtedly aware, Miss Amy Post, Dance Instructor, has mailed a letter to those Glencoe families with eighth grade students notifying them that Negro children will no longer be permitted to participate in her upcoming advanced Fortnightly dance class.

The Glencoe Women's Club has scheduled an important meeting to discuss the ramifications of this letter (the so-called "Post Letter") and to vote on whether Fortnightly should continue without the participation of Negro children as proposed by Miss Post or whether it should be canceled altogether. [Note: Miss Post has been contacted and has refused to withdraw or modify her letter.]

The meeting is scheduled to be held at 7:00 p.m. on Thursday, September 25, 1947, at the Central School Auditorium. Doors will open at 6:00 p.m. There will be no assigned seating. Since seating is limited, please try to come early. Note that the first five rows of seats will be cordoned off for special invited guests and members of the press.

After those wishing to speak at the meeting have completed their presentations, a vote will be taken either to approve the continuation of Fortnightly in accordance with the Post Letter (that is, to approve Fortnightly without the participation of Negro children) or to cancel it. The vote will be by secret written ballot, and each family will have one vote for each eighth grade student in the family.

A copy of the Post Letter will be made available at a table just inside the main entrance to the auditorium.

Those wishing to speak at the meeting should notify Mrs. Mildred Gold or her secretary by telephone (Glencoe 2164) in advance of the meeting.

The Glencoe Women's Club has selected Glencoe resident Christopher Wallace to chair the meeting. At his discretion, persons who did not notify Mrs. Gold or her secretary may also be permitted to speak at the meeting

There is no time limit established for the length of the meeting; however, it will not be temporarily or permanently adjourned prior to completion of the voting and announcement of its outcome. Tentatively, voting is to be held at 9:30 p.m.

Mildred Slotkin Gold, President
Glencoe Women's Club

Glencoe's Small Beginning

Chapter 12

At approximately 5:45 p.m. on Thursday, September 25, 1947, three light gray Ford vans pulled up to the curb just in front of the main entrance to Glencoe's Central School Auditorium. Each van had the call letters of a local radio station painted on both of its sides and each had a large "PRESS" placard displayed behind its front windshield. The first person to exit was a large overweight man from WMAQ. As he stepped from the lead van, three of his colleagues followed. One was carrying several microphones and cables; the second was lugging a large wire recorder; and the third held a stack of papers and notepads. Then the two other vans—from WGN and WLS—began disgorging passengers and equipment. In less than five minutes, the entire area was flooded with people and paraphernalia.

"Wait here," the large overweight man said, addressing the occupants of the three vans. "I'm gonna find Chris Wallace. Three mikes gotta be set up on stage ASAP."

While the overweight man was walking toward the auditorium, a dark blue four-door Chevrolet without license plates but with white stenciled letters and numbers on its front bumper parked immediately behind the third van. From within two blue-uniformed officers of the newly-formed U.S. Air Force emerged accompanied by two women.

And then behind the Chevrolet a long dark green 1941 Cadillac limousine with blackened windows and federal government plates stopped abruptly—within less than an inch of the Chevrolet. Two large men with crew cuts—probably in their mid-thirties or early forties—attired in charcoal gray single-breasted suits, white shirts and repp ties, stepped out of the vehicle. The first walked some five feet away and, assuming a stance facing the auditorium's entrance, began staring from side to side; the second, opening the limo's rear door, leaned back inside as if to assist one of its passengers. "Now, Jared," a woman's voice could be heard addressing him, "I'm perfectly capable of getting out on my own—and, as I've told you time and again, I need the exercise!"

Just then a line of nine vehicles, a few new, but most much older, pulled up, and men and women began to pour out onto the adjacent sidewalk combining with those already there to create an even larger and noisier mélange of people and equipment—to be joined moments later by a group of reporters from *Life* magazine, the *Chicago Sun*, the *Herald American*, and the *Tribune* who had been walking toward the auditorium.

As if materializing out of nowhere, Christopher Wallace appeared at the far edge of this sea of confusion. Looking about, he raised his right hand, and, as it did for Moses of old, the sea suddenly parted clearing a path for him.

Still with raised right hand, from the crowd's center Christopher began to speak: "Folks, I can't thank you enough for coming. And if you haven't gotten hold of a copy of the Post Letter, it's available on the table just inside the entrance. It should explain to each of you what this meeting is all about, namely, Glencoe's response to that letter." He looked around. The crowd had quieted and was awaiting further word from him.

"We've set aside seats for those of you with the press and a few others in the first five rows, so go on in. Bruno Steiner of Glencoe's Parks & Recreation Department will help you settle in and get your equipment set up.

"Questions?"

"Steve Daley from *Life*, Mr. Wallace. Can I get a photographer up on stage?"

"Come see me about that just before we start, Steve. I'll try to accommodate you.

"Anyone else?"

"Chris, Dave Ralston from WLS. We'll need power near where we sit for our wire recorder."

"You'll have it, Dave. Just work with Bruno Steiner.

"Any more questions?"

There were none.

"Okay, see you all inside. And again, thanks for coming."

———

While all this was going on, Aaron Reynolds, Glencoe's Chief of Police, was about to make an arrest. He was standing at the front door of the Stuart Cliver residence in full uniform. The door opened and he was greeted by Mrs. Cliver wearing a wrinkled dress, a flouncy hat and gloves.

"Chief Reynolds, what a nice surprise."

"Ma'am, is your husband home?"

"Why yes. We're getting ready to leave for the meeting. I'll go get him." She seemed nervous; but, then, she usually did.

Moments later Stuart Cliver appeared at the front door. "Chief, nice to see you. Come on in."

"This isn't a social call, Mr. Cliver. I'm placing you under arrest."

"Me, under arrest? What for? What in hell did I do? I haven't had a ticket in years."

"For criminal assault."

"You've got to be joking."

"Unfortunately, this is no joke, Mr. Cliver. Please place your hands behind your back so I can cuff you."

312

"Cuff me? Jesus! I wanna call my attorney."

"You'll be able to do that once we get back to the station."

"You know what this is, Chief? A damn ruse. You're just trying to keep me away from that meeting, aren't you?"

"Hardly, Mr. Cliver. The lab reports just came in a couple of hours ago. And arresting you at this time has nothing to do with the meeting."

"Lab reports? What in hell are you talking about?"

"Lab reports tying you to that brick-throwing incident—when that brick went sailing through Jerome Alden's window a few days ago and damn near killed him."

"And what about bail? I'm entitled to that, aren't I?"

"You are. I couldn't get hold of Judge Adamson so you'll have to wait on a bail hearing until tomorrow."

"And what in hell do I do in the meantime?"

"I'm afraid you'll be cooling your heels in our jail cell."

Glencoe's Small Beginning

Chapter 13

By 7:00 p.m. the auditorium was packed with people. Some, unable to find seats, were standing or sitting in the aisles. Backstage, Mildred Gold huddled with Glencoe's Fire Chief, Herb Gillman, who didn't look happy.

"Do we have a problem, Chief?"

"Yes. Too many people. And I'm gonna ignore it. This meeting's too damn important. Just go on up there and start things off."

With that, Mildred pointed in the direction of the young man handling the lighting, and he took hold of several large switch handles. Pulling them down halfway, he caused the lights in the auditorium proper to dim. Mildred then stepped out onto the stage and faced the audience.

Holding up her hand in an attempt to achieve quiet, she began speaking into the three microphones placed there by the radio stations.

"Good evening folks. I'm Mildred Gold, president of the Glencoe Women's Club which is sponsoring this evening's event. I want to welcome you all to this extraordinarily important meeting. We're here to face off against what I consider an assault on our small community and, most important of all, our black children, as evidenced by the so-called 'Post Letter.' Christopher Wallace, a long-time Glencoe resident and founder of the international advertising and public relations firm Wallace & Truscott has consented to chair the meeting. But before he takes over, I want to ask Randy Wald, an eighth grade student here at Central School, to lead us in the *Pledge of Allegiance*."

314

Mildred nodded in the direction of Randy Wald's family seated off to the side. Taking his cue from her, a small black boy made his way up onto the stage where, in a surprisingly strong voice, he led the audience in the *Pledge of Allegiance.*

"Thank you so much, Randy," Mildred said. "You do us proud. And now I'd like to turn the meeting over to Christopher Wallace."

———

Christopher Wallace was neither tall nor short. At five feet ten inches and slightly stocky, he appeared average—that is, until his dark piercing eyes gazed upon you. His eyes were the predominant feature of his rather square-jowled face and signaled to the world that his convictions were strong, his sense of fairness even stronger, and that he could never ever be intimidated.

"Ladies and gentlemen, I am deeply honored to chair this meeting. Most of us know one another and fully understand what's at stake: it's not simply deciding whether to continue Fortnightly on Miss Post's terms or to discontinue it; rather, it is an opportunity for all of us to send a message to others that there is no place in our community—or in any other community—for racism. I believe that many of us understand this. I know that the reason so many of our guests and the press are here is because they understand this.

"And so, before I proceed, I would like to introduce you to some of our distinguished guests.

"Former First Lady Eleanor Roosevelt is here. She graciously accepted our invitation to attend this meeting because, like so many other Americans, she has been fighting racial discrimination all her life. She strongly supports the cancellation of Fortnightly.

"A fact or two of interest you may not know about Mrs. Roosevelt: She was the moving force behind the

315

formation of our nation's first all-Negro flying unit, the Tuskegee Airmen—better known as the 'Red Tails' or the 'Red Tail Angels.' By the way, she did that despite a written report from the military brass that Negroes were incapable of flying. And how wrong she proved those generals to be! Thank you so much for joining us tonight, Mrs. Roosevelt."

At this point many in the audience looked in the direction of the first five rows and spotted a very tall woman wearing a pointed black hat.

"And speaking of the Tuskegee Airmen, there are two here with us tonight in uniform so they're easy to spot: their first commanding officer, Colonel Benton B. Donald Jr.; and Major James Lincoln Washburn III, a Glencoe resident of many years and an air force reservist. Would you gentlemen please rise and be recognized."

Hearing this, Colonel Donald and Major Washburn stood up and waved as the audience applauded.

"Colonel Donald is the first black West Point graduate of the twentieth century and the son of the Army's first black general officer. And what he had to endure during his four years at the Point is almost beyond description. He was forced to live and eat alone, and every member of his class shunned him. Still, he persevered, graduating twenty-seventh out of a class of three hundred twelve. Colonel Donald's Tuskegees performed magnificently during the war, flying over fifteen hundred missions and accumulating a combat record which is legendary. He was most famous for ordering his flyers to protect the bombers they were escorting and to forget about chasing enemy aircraft for personal glory.

"Major James Lincoln Washburn III, our Glencoe resident, is another Tuskegee. We all know him. In fact, at six feet four inches, he's pretty hard to miss walking around the village. But just in case you don't know much about his war record, I'll take a moment to tell you about it.

316

"As a Tuskegee fighter pilot, he was one of many tasked to escort bombers. On his last mission he and a flight of three other P-51 Mustangs he commanded were assigned to shepherd a group of twelve B-17 Flying Fortresses back to base after they'd completed a particularly harrowing mission. One of the B-17s, *Sluggo's Awakening*, was shot up pretty badly. Major Washburn ordered the three other P-51s in his flight to escort the eleven 17s that were unharmed while he nursed *Sluggo* home. And that's what he did.

"We have with us tonight all but one member of *Sluggo's* crew and their families. They're here to honor and thank Major Washburn and Colonel Donald and to urge all of you to cancel Fortnightly—their way of saying that racism must go.

"As a show of support for ending Fortnightly, would the crew members of *Sluggo's Awakening* and their family members please stand."

Eighteen adults and twelve children rose from their seats in unison. One went up onto the stage.

"Evening folks. My name is Danny Ehrenreich. I'm now an Associate Professor of Aeronautical Engineering at MIT, but during the war I was *Sluggo's* pilot-in-command. I've been asked by my fellow crew members to convey to you our feelings about racism. Simply put, there's no damn place for it here in Glencoe or anywhere else in our country. We were saved by black pilots like Major Washburn, Colonel Donald and the other Red Tails, and we can't thank them enough. They proved to us and to the world they're as capable of doing anything—including flying—as anybody else. They're equals. And being equals, they deserve equal treatment. So let's make sure they get it. And a good place to start is right here at this meeting. Let's tear up that disgraceful letter!"

———

317

Amy Post, author of the letter, was beginning to feel more isolated by the moment. She was certain they just didn't understand. How awful it was to mix the races. Through an oversight, she had permitted that to occur in the seventh grade dancing class, something she would soon correct. And if these foolish people wanted to cancel Fortnightly, well, so be it. After all, nobody in this auditorium could possibly understand what she had gone through—or the horrors that could result from mixing whites and Negroes.

Glencoe's Small Beginning

Chapter 14

"Well, folks, you've heard from a few of our guests. Right now, I'd like to change the tone of the meeting for a moment. Most of you know about Glencoe's terrible loss: one of our gifted young persons is no longer with us. John Stern, his science teacher, has asked to say a few words on his behalf."

A short man attired in a wrinkled suit, a white shirt with one of its buttons missing, a soiled tie, and scuffed black shoes, slowly made his way up onto the stage, his every movement speaking of sadness.

"I'm John Stern. I don't need an introduction. Glencoe's a family. You know me and I know most all of you." He took a moment to contain his emotions.

"I'm a father. I have eight children. In fact, I informally adopted a ninth, a wonderful young black boy by the name of Perry Alden. Just the other day Perry killed himself. And I'll tell you why.

"Perry was my best student and, from what I understand, had the best grade point average in the eighth grade. He was also a first string guard on the basketball team and an outstanding sprinter. Moreover, he was liked by everyone—particularly his fellow students.

"Perry was also driven. He studied hard and yearned to be a physician. I'm sure he would have been a great one. He always talked about helping others. That was his passion.

"Although his family was not experiencing financial problems, Mr. Christopher Wallace who knew Perry well promised to pay for his college and medical school education. In short, Perry had direction in his life. He was, so far as we were concerned, among the very best of Glencoe's children.

"I was captivated by the boy's interest in science. I grew so fond of him that at some point in time he became something like another son to me. We really never spoke of this; it's just something I felt. I was extremely proud of his academic performance and I wanted very much to see him reach his goal of becoming a doctor.

"This past summer Perry took a job with Dr. Warren Richman. I was told that he did well and that, like Christopher Wallace, Doc also wanted to contribute to his college and medical education. I'd say that's quite a compliment, wouldn't you?

"And so everything was going swimmingly for Perry. He was an outstanding student, highly popular with his peers, and gaining the respect of others wherever he went until ..."

John Stern pulled out a copy of the Post letter from his back pocket.

"Until this goddamned letter arrived at his home."

He stopped for a moment, and then began gazing directly at Amy Post.

"Can you possibly imagine what this letter did to that boy, Miss Post?"

There was no answer, so John Stern raised his voice: "Can you?"

Instead of answering, Amy Post looked down.

"You're a damn coward—that's what you are. You send out nasty letters but don't have the courage to answer me. Well, here's the answer: that letter destroyed Perry. He came to me in a state of shock. He couldn't understand why the color of his skin made all that difference. That letter and everything in it is a bunch of crap, Miss Post. And you damn well know it!

"And what else did that letter do? Lemme tell you, Miss Post: it inspired probably the only racist in our community—and we know who he is—to toss a brick through the living room window of Perry's home narrowly missing his father's head. And that devastated Perry and depressed him even further. He just couldn't understand what was going on. But whatever it was, he felt as if he was to blame.

"So then what happened? Ed Sorkin, our local rabbi, went over to speak to Perry. Being a Jew, Ed had experienced anti-Semitism, something pretty similar to racism. He tried to help Perry come to terms with what had happened. I guess he didn't succeed, because a day later Perry killed himself.

"So you know what your damn racism has led to, Miss Post? The modern-day lynching of one of our finest young talents. With that letter, you lynched him! Do you understand me?"

By this time, John Stern was shaking uncontrollably and tears were running down his cheeks. Bruno Steiner went over to him and gently helped him off the stage. Nobody noticed that Amy Post seemed to be deeply affected by John Stern's accusation, although she was trying desperately to conceal her emotions.

———

"I think this might be a good time for a short break, folks," Christopher Wallace said. "We'll resume in, say, ten minutes."

———

"What do you think, Mildred?" Christopher Wallace asked backstage during the break. "Are we headed in the wrong direction? John Stern became pretty accusatory."

"Press on, Chris. You're doing just fine. I want these people to understand that when you send out letters like that Post Letter or toss bricks through peoples' windows there are consequences—serious ones."

Glencoe's Small Beginning

Chapter 15

Returning to the stage, Christopher Wallace continued:

"You've already heard about the outstanding war record of Major James Lincoln Washburn III. His father, better known as Junior Washburn, is also with us tonight. You might be interested to know that Junior was recently nominated to become a federal judge for the Northern District of Illinois. If confirmed—and there is little doubt about that—he'll be the first Negro federal judge in the country. Sounds impressive? Not really if you know a little about the extraordinary Washburn family and how much a part of our American heritage they are.

"It all goes back to a slave by the name of Isaiah Washburn, half-brother of Frederick Douglass. He was outstanding in ways nobody could have possibly imagined. And if you ever get up to Toronto, visit Beverley House where a docent will fill your ears with the adventures—and accomplishments—of Isaiah Washburn. Isaiah, incidentally, was Junior Washburn's grandfather.

"Well, what about Isaiah? At around the age of eight he led a successful mutiny aboard the slave ship *Creole* freeing close to one hundred slaves. And later as a young man in his twenties he worked with President Lincoln, Harriet Tubman and General Benjamin Franklin Butler, a Massachusetts politician and military man, in devising a scheme which granted sanctuary to thousands of slaves, something which severely crippled the South's war effort and brought an earlier end to the Civil War.

"And did Isaiah have a connection with our village? Indeed he did. In 1862 he and his half-brother, Frederick, were in Toronto where they each received an award and recognition from a representative of Queen Victoria. Isaiah stayed on in Toronto and was eventually joined by his sister, Jenny. In Toronto Jenny met and fell in love with a young lawyer, John Alden. After the two married, they moved to Glencoe, not far from where John's sister, Nell, was teaching school. Isaiah followed them to Glencoe and eventually he and Nell married. And when Isaiah came to Glencoe he formed a law partnership with John Alden. Alden & Washburn is to this day a thriving Chicago law firm.

"So I'd have to say the Washburns and the Aldens have been Glencoe residents longer than just about any other family I know of. And with Isaiah's involvement in the *Creole* mutiny and his help working with President Lincoln and others, I can't imagine families more entrenched in Americana than the Washburns and Aldens. And they continue to be involved in our American way of life with Junior Washburn soon to become our country's first black federal jurist. So why is it, folks, that young offspring of the Washburns and Aldens should be excluded from any Glencoe activity? Or to put it differently, how dare Amy Post even think of excluding extraordinary people like the Washburn and Alden family members from her dancing classes?"

Christopher Wallace paused for a moment before proceeding.

"We have a few other special guests I'd like to recognize:

"First, Glencoe Schools Superintendent, Dr. Peter McAfee. He has graciously granted us permission to use this auditorium for our meeting tonight.

"Second, Central School's principal, Miss Margaret Carlton. Maggie has been a teacher here for years and just recently became principal. Interestingly, she was Major Washburn's second grade teacher.

"Finally, the last special guest I want to mention is Glencoe's beloved physician, Dr. Warren Richman. He has treated us all and done his very best to keep us well and healthy.

"And now the time has come for those of you desiring to speak to come forward and address us no matter whether what you have to say is for or against the Post Letter. I was supposed to have been given a list, but there was only one name on it, that of Mr. Stuart Cliver; and, from what I'm told, he has been unavoidably detained and is unable to be here. So, unless ..."

It was at this point that one of the doors to the auditorium noisily banged open.

Chapter 16

"C'mon, Momma. We's not too late. I'll pull the wagon. You keep on carryin' the twins. And I sees them way down in front—so let's go!"

It was a strange procession: a man resembling a penguin pulling a cart in which a large record player rested along with several record albums, diapers, baby bottles, and little white boxes; followed by a much taller woman holding a twin baby in each arm. The man was strange in appearance. He was just under five feet in height with his hair cut short on the top of his head, but with long hair from the nape of his neck flowing down his back. He wore black shoes, black pants and a black formal coat, its tails almost dragging on the floor. The coat covered a plain white shirt with its collar turned around designating him a man of the cloth. A large wooden cross held by a gold chain dangled from his neck coming down to a point just above his waist.

The man walked quickly to the auditorium's front, stopping at the first row. He turned and waved, and some seated in the first five rows waved in return.

"Jared, I have to greet him."

"Who, Mrs. R.?"

"That young man. He's a friend."

Mrs. Roosevelt stood up and made her way to the aisle. Not caring in the least what others thought, she approached the penguin and hugged him.

"Corporal, I was missing you. I'm thrilled you could come. Somehow I knew you'd be here."

"Thank you," he said. "Mrs. R., this is my wife Janine. And our twin boys: Benton and James."

"Am I allowed to guess how you chose those names?"

"Not much to that, is there, ma'am?"

325

"I suppose not. And now that I see you're a minister, I expect you'll want to be addressing us?"

"That's why I'm here, Mrs. R. I've got some important things to say."

"I'm sure you have, Corporal."

———

Christopher Wallace couldn't help staring at Mrs. Roosevelt and the short man who resembled a penguin. At first he thought he had encountered some crazy person. But Mrs. Roosevelt quickly dispelled that notion. And apparently the man wanted to address the meeting. Christopher looked over in the direction of Major Washburn as if to ask "Should I let him speak?" to which Major Washburn and Colonel Donald both nodded in assent.

"Sir," Christopher called down to the man, "please come up on stage and let us hear from you. I take it you have something of importance to add to the meeting."

"More important than you can possibly imagine, Mr. Wallace," the man replied.

Christopher Wallace was impressed. The little man even knew his name—and they had never met. He obviously was prepared. He most certainly had seen a copy of Mildred's notice mentioning who would chair the meeting. Although how he had gotten a copy was puzzling.

Glencoe's Small Beginning

Chapter 17

The man made his way up onto the stage dragging the cart behind him. His wife and babies followed.

"Set up the record player, Momma," he said.

Then, standing on tiptoe, he lowered the three microphones before beginning to speak.

"Sorry about bein' late. We drove up here from Mississippi. Took longer than we expected what with our new twin boys and this here equipment. But we made it. And I sure need to speak to you all because I know more about what's goin' on here than just about anybody else.

"For starters, what I'm gonna tell you all ain't gonna be pretty. Racism never is. And its consequences … well, just exactly like what happened 'round here a few days ago.

"So bear with me while I catch my breath." The small penguin-like man paused for a moment before continuing.

"First of all, people calls me 'Shorty.' People my size is usually assigned to be bomber ball turret gunners. That's the turret in the aircraft's belly. That's what I was— *Sluggo's* ball turret gunner. And like they done for the rest of the crew, them Red Tails saved my life. And the First Lady, Mrs. R., well, she awakened me. And that's what I intend to do here tonight: awaken you all. Maybe even awaken Miss Post over there. And by the way, that ain't your name, is it *Lia*?"

When Amy Post heard the name *Lia* she suddenly raised her head and screamed. Then she began to sob.

"That's all right, Lia. We's gonna lay everything out here. And maybe you'll tear up that letter; and maybe you won't. No matter, because folks'll understand a lot more than they do now.

327

"So for you all here: My name's Chauncey Miller. I became a Baptist minister after I got out of the Army Air Corps. I gots a small congregation down in Greenville, Mississippi, my hometown and Amelia Polk's hometown. That's her real name: *Amelia Polk*. She's a great talent. And she's lived through some terrible times, all caused by racism."

As he spoke, Amelia continued to sob, for she now she remembered Chauncey.

"You see, Amelia and I grew up in Greenville. She's about a dozen years older than me. But our parents was friends, and we both was taught to hate Negroes—but we called 'em 'niggers.'

"That's an awful word, ain't it? I won't use it again. I only used it to explain what we was taught."

The small man turned to his wife: "Get ready, Momma."

"What's so terrible 'bout racism is what it leads to. You've seen what happened here. Where I grew up it led to murders, and it turned Amelia's momma into a murderer. Using lies and deception, she got two fine Negro musicians lynched. And I was part of it. I did what my daddy done told me to do: I stoned 'em while they was bein' carried to the lynching field.

"They was Harlan and Zachary Jefferson, father and son. They burned the father at the stake after hanging the son. At nights I sometimes hear the father's screams and that popping noise when his son's neck broke.

"And why was the Jeffersons murdered? I don't know, 'cept they was Negroes, and we hated 'em.

"I remember seeing little Amelia try to stop them killings, but they wouldn't let her. See, she was just a little girl and nobody was gonna stop whites from killing Negroes. It was sport. Seems like in some perverted way there was almost something righteous in it ... maybe like going to church on Sundays. And afterwards they sold off

328

boxes of the father's bones and ashes. My daddy bought some of them boxes. Here's one. I keep it to remind me of the evils of racism."

Chauncey held up a small white box.

"Filled with bones and ashes—that's what's in it. All in the name of racism."

As the short man spoke, an unusual quiet fell over the audience. They had never heard about the ugliness of racism as he was describing it.

"Growing up the way I did, I learned to hate Negroes. Couldn't stand 'em. I thought they stunk; I thought they was animals—always after white women and little white girls. I believed this with all my heart until me and the other members of *Sluggo's* crew met up with Major Washburn. And then everything changed.

"See, *Sluggo* was on its sixteenth mission, to a place we'd been to once before, Berlin. The first time we was there we damn near bought it, and the second time around not a one of us was looking forward to going back. We all knew that when we was over the target area we'd be flying through flak thicker than fleas on a farm dog—and that we had about a fifty-fifty chance of getting blown out of the sky. But if we made it out of there in one piece, then instead of high-tailing it bareback back to England along with the other B-17s in our group, this time we'd have Red Tail escorts. And Lord how we loved them little friends!

"Well, seems our luck just about ran out over the target area because flak shot away half our tail. Somehow, Lieutenant Danny was able to fly us outta there. But no matter how hard he tried, he couldn't keep up with the other 17s and we was beginning to lose altitude. That's when our Red Tails showed up. And I wasn't sure what was gonna happen next, 'cept I was beginning to think I was gonna die.

"Lemme tell you a little about them Red Tails. They was different from the other escorts: they stuck to us

329

like glue. They didn't give a damn about chasing German fighters or strafing ground targets. Seems as if the bombers was all that was important to them. I guess because of this we all started calling them 'Red Tail Angels.' Fact is, we considered them to be angels.

"When our four Red Tails arrived, three went with the eleven 17s that wasn't shot up; the fourth stayed with us. I spotted ours flying 'longside of us. Saw him waggle his wings and wave. Fact is, he was so close I could read the name of his plane: *My Promises*. From then on, he became our guardian angel. I just kept my fingers crossed that we'd get back home safe and sound—and trouble-free. But a minute or so after he arrived, Lieutenant Danny had to shut down one of our engines. And then, to stop us from falling out of the sky, he ordered us to jettison everything in sight including our guns. That lightened us up enough so that we was able to fly level. But, still, we was just limping along.

"And then about halfway back to the Channel one of them new German jets comes in after us. 'Oh, Christ,' I thought. 'Now we've had it.' 'Cuz there's no way in hell a P-51 can outfly one of them machines. 'There ain't a damn thing he can do,' I thought.

"Suddenly I saw *Promises* turn into that jet's line of attack firing all six of its guns at once, creating what you might call a solid wall of lead. That jet was flying so fast he couldn't change direction. And damned if he didn't fly right into that wall and blow up setting off the biggest ball of fire I'd ever seen. 'Oh Lord,' I thought, as I saw *Promises* fly right into that fireball, 'he's gonna blow up too.' But a few minutes later I'll be switched if *Promises* doesn't show up—happy, smiling, wagging its wings—like he was sayin' to us, 'Hey, bomber boys, I sure showed that German, didn't I?'

"So now I figured we was home-free. In another forty-five minutes or so we'd be across the Channel heading for Framlingham, and chow, a hot shower, and a warm bed—and the next day maybe even a trip into town. But I was wrong. And also just about then Lieutenant Danny told us that *Promises* had used up all its ammunition going after that jet; and of course we was defenseless because we'd tossed out all our guns.

"Well there we was: a sitting duck. Sure, we had a Red Tail Angel. But what could he do with empty guns? Probably nothing to worry about, though, because in a few minutes we'd be coming up on the Channel.

"And then out of nowhere comes this German fighter. He's heading for us at full speed in a frontal attack. 'Holy crap,' I thought. 'This time we've really had it. Maybe *Promises* can run away, but we sure as hell cain't.' Only thing I could think of doin' was prayin'—and that's what I done. And I never done it harder.

"Then all of a sudden I'll be damned if I don't hear our little friend's engine roar. About ten seconds later we all felt an explosion. It took me a moment to figure out what happened: *Promises* done rammed that German fighter. *Promises*' pilot done sacrificed his own life to save ours. I suddenly realized that our Red Tail really was an angel.

"Right then and there I started to weep like a baby. Me and the others in *Sluggo* was living because that angel done died for us.

"And I never thought our angel could be black. Never even crossed my mind.

"A couple weeks later back at our base in England Lieutenant Danny tells us our angel ain't dead, that he's hurt real bad and that he's in the hospital. He tells us we's gonna visit him and asks if we wanted to bring some flowers or something. I'll say we did!

"So me and another crew member, Stanley Hope, goes out and buys the biggest bunch of flowers we can find. We puts them in a vase so big we both gotta carry it. At the hospital we both lugs that vase into the room. And who's there: Mrs. R. and two Negro officers, two people I hates. One's in bed and the other's standing. My head starts a-spinnin' when I learns that our angel's a Negro! A black man. Someone I should be stonin'. I starts trying to pick up smells, because they all stink. But there ain't no bad smells. Only smells is from them flowers.

"Now Mrs. R. comes over. Tells me our angel's in that bed and his name is Major Washburn. The one standin' is Colonel Donald, the Red Tails' CO.

"Suddenly I'm losin' my balance. I cain't understand what's going on. Two Negro angels? Cain't be. I remember grabbing hold of a bed pan because I'm not sure if I'm gonna puke or pass out.

"And then Mrs. R. explains to me that we's all God's children, that the only difference is skin color. She asks me if I'd hate Major Washburn if he was a redhead or if he had blue eyes. I says 'No.' 'Then why,' Mrs. R. asks me, 'would I hate Negroes just 'cuz their skin's a different color?'

"And that's when I realizes I cain't hate 'em no more 'cuz they's people. Real people, jes' like you and me.

"I guess from then on I decides to become a preacher so's I can tell everyone how wrong I was; so's I can atone for what I done when I stoned the Jeffersons; so's no more little white boxes will ever be sold; so's I can make sure Negro children is treated the same as white children; so's I can erase racism for good.

"And that's what I've been doin' since I got out of the Army. And that's what I'm doin' tonight. And that's why I wants that letter torn up into little pieces! *Because if it ain't, you all will be allowin' your children to dance that damn lynchin' waltz!*" Chauncey paused again to catch his breath.

"We's gonna play some music for you all written by the Jeffersons. Listen to it, and think about losing them two to racism. What a sad terrible loss that is!"

Chauncey nodded to his wife, and she depressed a switch on their record player. As if by magic, Amelia Polk saw the apparition of a piano appear on stage and there she was seated between Harlan and Zachary Jefferson, their hands once again dancing across the keyboard sending forth the most magnificent ragtime ever composed. In her mind's eye she saw the two men throw their heads back and look up at the ceiling—or were they gazing at the heavens above? Chauncey was right: it was a sad terrible loss. How she missed those two! How she despised her mother! And how puzzled she still was that her father had done nothing to stop the killings. Deep down she knew that the Jeffersons and their murders would never leave her no matter what name she used, no matter where she lived, no matter what she did with her life. She was trapped. There was no escape. She too was a victim of racism—just like the Jeffersons and that young boy who took his own life.

Unable to bear Chauncey, the people in the audience, or the auditorium any longer, she realized she must leave. Slowly, deliberately, she got up from her seat and made her way to the exit. And her letter? She had completely forgotten about it—perhaps because Fortnightly no longer mattered to her.

Glencoe's Small Beginning

Chapter 18

Christopher Wallace had chaired many a meeting in his day—dealing with a variety of audiences, some friendly, some difficult. Yet the audience before him was different. It seemed to him that it was in a state of shock, paralyzed by what it had heard, perhaps understanding for the first time the appalling consequences of racism.

Thus, in deference to his audience, he decided to wait while they listened to the mesmerizing ragtime of Harlan and Zachary Jefferson. And after the music ended, he would begin the perfunctory tasks necessary to conclude the meeting. While he waited, he thought of the press: Would they report what had transpired this evening? He hoped so, for then Glencoe would have made a small beginning, a beginning which might even spread throughout the country.

Finally it was time. He approached the microphones. "I don't believe anyone else will be addressing us tonight," he said, "so I think it's time we vote."

3:30 p.m., Thursday, August 7, 1969
Central School Auditorium
Glencoe, Illinois

"What happened, Grandpa? How did the vote turn out?"

"Hundred percent in favor of cancelin' Fortnightly. But wouldn't'a mattered all that much because that Miss Post, or Miss Polk, just plain disappeared. Nobody heard from her after that. But what did matter was what the press put out—and they had a field day! Your grandmother's saved all the newspaper articles and she'll show them to you back at our house; and the article in Life Magazine was more than we could have hoped for. I'd say that little Glencoe made much more than a small beginnin', particularly when you consider everythin' that followed."

Junior and Jamie Washburn were standing in an aisle of the auditorium awaiting the arrival of Mildred Gold, now a woman up in years but still with a mind as sharp as a tack. They heard one of the auditorium doors open and saw her approaching.

"Hello, there, Judge Washburn. You're looking surprisingly fit for someone your age!" She laughed. "And is this your grandson, the boy you've been lecturing to about our Post Letter meeting?"

"It is. Even showed him the ballroom upstairs where the dancin' classes were held.

"Mildred, I'd like you to meet Jamie Washburn, my travelin' companion for the past couple of weeks."

Then turning to Jamie, he said. "Jamie, this is the famous Mildred Gold I've told you about—the lady with a finger in every pie around here."

"Not so much anymore, Junior. These days I've taken to needlepoint and left all the community service work to the youngsters." Mildred smiled.

"So Jamie, did your grandfather tell you what took

335

place after that Post Letter meeting—the good it spawned and some of the bad that unfortunately followed?"

"No, ma'am."

"Well, then I will.

"About ten months after the meeting, your grandfather was appointed the first Negro federal judge in the country. That was in mid-1948. And about the same time President Truman signed an executive order desegregating the military. And that was only for starters.

"Next came the Brown v. Board of Education decision in 1954 in which the Supreme Court did away with the old 'separate but equal' doctrine ruling that separate educational facilities were inherently unequal. And do you have any idea who argued that case for the plaintiffs?"

"No, ma'am."

"None other than your grandfather's friend, Trenton Richards, a black lawyer and one of the finest legal minds of this century.

"Then about a year and a half later a feisty black woman by the name of Rosa Parks refused an order to give up her bus seat to a white person in Montgomery, Alabama. When they put her in jail, the black community reacted by boycotting the city's bus system. And that led to the city's bus segregation ordinance eventually being declared unconstitutional.

"And almost two years later President Eisenhower got involved when he sent federal troops into Little Rock to allow a group of nine black students to attend the high school there.

"And do you remember James Meredith?"

Jamie shook his head.

"Well, in 1962 President Kennedy used federal and state troops, along with federal officials, to allow Mr. Meredith to enroll at the University of Mississippi.

"And then, unfortunately, the violence seemed to escalate: First, in 1963, Medgar Evers was gunned down

336

in Jackson, Mississippi, and a church in Birmingham, Alabama, was bombed. And in 1964, the year the Civil Rights Act finally became law, three young civil rights workers were murdered in Mississippi.

"That was only the beginning. In 1965 Malcolm X was murdered only a few months before we had another new law, the Voting Rights Act. That, by the way, was just two years before your grandfather's close friend, Trenton Richards, was appointed to the Supreme Court. I suppose you know that he was the first black on the court?"

"I do, Mrs. Gold."

Mildred Gold nodded approvingly. "And then, Jamie, came the saddest day of all, April 4th of last year, when the greatest man of our time, Dr. Martin Luther King Jr., was shot and killed by an assassin. I'm sure you know all about that, don't you?"

Jamie nodded. "The day after Dr. King died we had a special assembly at Central School. Miss Carlton spoke to us about Dr. King and the wonderful dreams he had for our country. We all wept, even Miss Carlton and Mr. Stern."

"Well, then, Jamie, I suppose you now understand that despite the violence, we've made some real progress since the Post Meeting. I believe it spawned some wonderful things even though the times that followed were challenging."

Mildred noticed that Jamie was once again busily writing in his notebook. Then he paused.

"Mrs. Gold, I've got another question: Do you permit dancing to be discussed in your home? Because in my grandparents' home and in my own home I'm not allowed to talk about it or even watch it on TV? I like dancing. I don't understand."

Mildred turned to Junior Washburn. "You want to answer that, or should I?"

"You go 'head, Mildred."

337

"To answer your question, Jamie: Like many other Glencoe homes, including yours and your grandparents, dancing is a forbidden subject in my home. And now that you've learned something about the history of our little village, I think you'll understand why.

"On your way in here, did you happen to notice the name of this auditorium?"

"No."

"Well, c'mon. Let's go take a look."

The three left the auditorium proper and walked outside onto its entry steps. There, above them, in the marble crossbeam they saw the building's name engraved on it:

PERRY ALDEN MEMORIAL AUDITORIUM

"Like that library in Greenville, Mississippi, huh, Grandpa?"

"Yep, seems wherever racism leaves its mark, a memorial's created as an apology. Wished it didn't have to happen that way, boy. But almost always does."

"So why is there no talk of dancing in so many Glencoe homes, Mrs. Gold?"

"It's an unwritten tradition here in Glencoe, Jamie. In honor of Perry Alden. Not much reason for it, except we all knew and admired him. Maybe in years to come younger people will do away with that tradition because to them Perry will be a stranger. But not for a while—not so long as we're around."

"Does that mean that all the dancing classes ended after that meeting?"

"That's exactly what happened. You haven't heard of any around here since then, have you?"

"No."

"Well, Jamie, now you know a little about Glencoe's small beginning. But what you probably don't

338

know is that racism still thrives. Here are some things you might want to look into:

"All those fine Japanese Americans from the West Coast interned for no good reason during World War II. They lost everything. A shameful episode in our nation's history.

"And I suppose in school you've learned about the mistreatment of the true natives of our country, the American Indians—how they were robbed of their lands and forced to live on tiny reservations? That's still going on.

"And the Latinos—the frightful way they've been exploited by the farming interests.

"We've still got a long way to go, Jamie. But I think we're getting there. Don't you, Junior?"

"I think we've made progress, Mildred. But I agree—there's still more to do."

Jamie continued to write in his notebook.

"I have another question, Mrs. Gold: Whatever happened to Mr. Cliver?"

"He went to jail. Served nine months and paid a fine. Then he left Glencoe, and we haven't heard from him since—thank goodness!

"Any more questions, young man?"

"No, ma'am. And thank you for coming."

"You're most welcome. And now, Junior, I've got to run. A meeting of the GWC board."

"Lord, Mildred, I thought you said you've taken up needlepoint?"

"I have. I find I can do that and participate in meetings at the same time."

Mildred Gold smiled, and then walked briskly down the steps of the auditorium to her car.

———

"Gosh, Grandpa, that lady's sure busy."

"She's always been, boy. And speakin' of 'busy,' I think I'd better get you home. Your parents are waitin' for you. And your mother's been busy packin' your bag."

"Busy packing my bag? I thought my travels were over."

"Never said that, Jamie. I said our travels would be over. Your mother's arranged a little more travelin' for you, and I've had nothin' to do with that."

"My mother?"

"Yep. She's taken over the reins from me. She arranged one last trip for you this summer—a little surprise excursion before you start back to school. And your grandmother and I, and your father, well, we'll just be taggin' along."

"I don't understand. I thought …"

"Better talk to your mother."

"How long have you known about this, Grandpa?"

"For just about as long as we've been gone. Every so often your mother and I would discuss this in our nightly phone calls."

"Nightly phone calls? You mean my mother knew all about our travels?"

"All about 'em, Jamie. Do you think for a moment she didn't know exactly where you were and what you were learnin'? And in several of those phone calls she mentioned to me what she had planned for you once we got back to Glencoe. And by the way, your father's plenty upset about it."

"But …"

"No 'buts,' Jamie. C'mon, we gotta get on over to your house. We're late."

Excerpt from Jamie's Notebook, Page 194

Now I really do understand what that dancing thing is all about. Strange, there are Aldens at Central School, but nobody ever told me about Perry Alden.

I guess what impressed me the most was the way the people in Glencoe came together and voted to cancel Fortnightly. I think I'll always be proud of them for doing that. And maybe as Mildred Gold said, it started some really important things.

Something else: I don't blame Amelia Polk. Thanks to my Grandpa, I probably know more about her than just about anybody else. If other people knew what her mother did to her and to the Jeffersons, they couldn't hate her. Too bad her father's weakness prevented him from protecting her.

Epilogue

Chapter 1

4:14 p.m., Tuesday, August 12, 1969
In Traffic on Cicero Avenue
Chicago, Illinois

The traffic heading south on Cicero Avenue was fairly light. Still, to the five occupants packed tightly together in the 1940 Plymouth sedan, the lack of traffic did little to alleviate their discomfort—discomfort caused not only by the car's unusually small interior, but also by the tension which reigned within. The driver, all six feet four inches of him, hadn't said a word since departing his home in Glencoe; and only to add to the unpleasantness, as was his custom he had pushed the two-person bench front seat as far back as he could in order to accommodate his long legs. This resulted in further discomfort to the three occupants in the back seat. Now the driver was staring straight ahead, refusing to acknowledge their presence. Added to this, the look on his face told of his extreme displeasure.

"James," his wife said, "for God's sake, let me drive. At least I'll be able to move the seat forward. Then Jamie can come up front with me and you can sit in back. That will give your parents more leg room!"

But her husband didn't reply.

"All right, James," the driver's father said. "Stop the car and let Dee drive. You're acting like a spoilsport. Jamie's travels with me were all about the Washburn side of the family. Now it's Dee's turn. In all the years you two have been married you've never allowed him to know anythin' about her family. I know, I know. But Jamie's old enough now, and I think you've succeeded in drumming your values into him."

James had had enough. He pulled over to the curb and turned off the ignition. Still not saying a word and continuing to sulk, he got out of the car allowing his wife to drive and Jamie to sit up front next to her.

Jamie had been taking all this in. He began to understand that wherever they were going he would be meeting his mother's family for the first time. In a way this surprised him because at some point he had gotten the impression that she had no family. But if she did, why hadn't he met them before?

"Where do we turn?" Dee asked.

"63rd Street. And then from there you know the way. I don't," her husband replied.

There was something that Jamie noticed that was strange about his mother: the light blue suit she was wearing; and that gold pin attached to her suit coat. He'd seen it only once before. Why now?

One other thing: her hair. She had let it down and he thought it looked particularly beautiful. In fact, to him his mother looked more beautiful than ever—and, despite his father's grouchiness, happier than ever.

"We'll be there shortly, Jamie. And then you can have dinner. Start thinking about what'd you'd like. Anything, dear."

"I don't understand, Mom. What do you mean, 'anything'?"

"Just what I said, Jamie: Anything. And, James, you too start thinking about dinner. Maybe that will bring you out of your funk."

"I'm not hungry."

"Oh, I think you will be."

"And Mom and Dad," Dee continued, addressing her in-laws, "how about you? What would you like for dinner?"

"Anything that's easy," her mother-in-law replied. *"Junior and I will take whatever they have that's ready to be served."*

———

James Washburn was still sulking as they turned west onto 63rd Street. And then, several minutes later, his wife drove the car into a large hangar housing only one aircraft, a three-engine Boeing 727. When they stopped, Jamie saw several people cleaning its windows and a mechanic checking its tires. The jet was painted the same blue color as his mother's suit and bore gold-colored logos on its nose, tail and sides which matched the pin attached to her suit coat.

"Mom," Jamie asked, "are you a stewardess or something? And what's that pin you're wearing? It matches those logos on the plane."

"I'll tell you all about it a little later, dear."

As his mother was getting out of the car, an elderly woman wearing a maid's black dress with a white lace apron over it ran up to her.

"Oh, ma'am, it's been so long! You're still so beautiful—and we've missed you so. Oh, ma'am!" And with that, the elderly woman embraced her.

"And Colonel James, congratulations! Dee wrote to me about your promotion. How are you, sir?"

"Just fine, Amantha. And how are you?"

"Oh, I'm fine, sir. A bit tired from the flight over. But I'll sleep tonight."

Then, looking at Jamie, she asked, "Is this your son, ma'am? Why he's almost a man."

"Jamie," Dee said, "I'd like you to meet Amantha. She took care of me when I was young. We haven't seen each other in some years."

"Nice to meet you," Jamie replied, holding out his hand—but now totally confused.

347

"*And Judge and Mrs. Washburn, so nice to meet you too. Dee has often written to me about you.*"

"*Our pleasure, Amantha,*" Junior Washburn replied.

"*Well, leave your things in the car. I'll have them carried aboard. Inside there's a notepad. Just jot down what you'd like for dinner and for breakfast tomorrow. The beds are already made up, and the pilot tells me we've got enough water for showers.*" Amantha paused. "*And, sir, the pilot also tells me you can park your car here in the hangar while you're gone.*"

"*Dee,*" Amantha whispered, "*Colonel James' special guest arrived. He's waiting inside the plane.*"

Epilogue

Chapter 2

As James Washburn stepped aboard the aircraft, he was greeted by his former commanding officer, Benton B. Donald Jr.

"Nice to see you, James. If my memory serves me, your preference is scotch and soda. Right?"

"Yes, sir," James replied, surprised and pleased to see Ben Donald.

"I also seem to remember that we played a whole lot of cribbage down at Tuskegee Institute. So happens I brought a board and some cards along. Shall we?"

"Sounds great, Ben," James replied. "But can I ask how you happen to be here?"

"Special invitation from your wife. And once we're airborne the pilot has told me he'll take a break and allow us to fly her for a few hours—that is, if you're up to it. We can switch between pilot and co-pilot."

"I might be a little gun-shy. I haven't flown an airplane since I got dunked in the Channel. I was hoping the air force would put me back in a cockpit in Vietnam, but that didn't happen. All I did was fly the light mahogany desk. And I've never been at the controls of a jet which I assume is nothing like flying a propeller-driven P-51."

"Not to worry. It's about the same as driving a later model car. I'll help you along."

Epilogue

Chapter 3

"Mom," Jamie asked after they'd finished dinner aloft, "where are we going? And does it have anything to do with that pin?"

"Later, dear. I think it's time for bed—for both of us. You've had a long day. In fact, many of them while you were traveling with your grandfather. You'll discover that you'll sleep like a baby while we're up in the air. Everybody seems to."

"Can you at least tell me where we're heading, Mom?"

"Over the Atlantic, dear. Tomorrow we'll be in a different time zone. So you'd better get some sleep."

———

"You were right, Ben. She flies like a bird. Easier to handle than a P-51. And, you know, I never realized how much I missed flying."

"I suspected as much. Remember what we discovered many years ago: once Skip Taylor sinks his talons in you, you're hooked."

"I remember. And in some ways I miss those days."

"I think we all do. And I particularly miss Mrs. R. now that she's gone. Somehow, she seemed to make everything happen. What a lady! But nothing lasts forever, James. So I guess we should enjoy while we can."

Epilogue

Chapter 4

"How did you sleep, dear?"

"Fine, Mom."

"Well the pilot tells me we'll be landing in two hours so I think it's time for you to get up. I've ordered orange juice, ham and eggs and milk for your breakfast. If you want anything else, just let Amantha know."

"Can you at least tell me where we're going?"

"To Kendal, England, dear."

"Where's that?"

"Ask Amantha. She'll show you on a map. I'm going to the main cabin and join your father and General Donald for breakfast. Your father flew the plane last night for several hours and I think he's rediscovered his love of flying. At least that's what General Donald tells me."

"And what about Grandpa and Grandma?"

"They're fine. There's a newspaper on board, and you know your grandfather and newspapers. And the last I saw of your grandmother, she was engrossed in a novel."

Epilogue

Chapter 5

Two hours later the 727 touched down at Kendal Airport, coming to a full stop a short distance from the terminal. A tall man in livery greeted them, nodding to General Donald, James, Junior Washburn and Sarah Washburn, and then bowing deeply to Dee Washburn and Jamie.

"So good to see you again, Madam. And is this Master Jamie?"

"It's wonderful to see you too, Lloyd. And, yes, this is Jamie. I think you'll confuse him if you call him 'Master.' "

"Never again, Madam. I promise. But please, follow me. I've brought four hansoms. We'll be taking the back roads. And the younger ones are going mad with anticipation. For their sake, I'd like to start off as quickly as possible."

———

One of the carriages held their luggage; the other three carried a driver and passengers, with Ben Donald and James in one; Junior and his wife in another; and Jamie and his mother in the third.

———

"Jamie," his mother said, "I think now's as good a time as any to tell you where we're going.

"We're off to my family home, where my brothers and sisters and I grew up.

"My parents, Jamie, were foreign born. When they were in their early twenties they immigrated to England where my father became a chartered accountant and later made a fortune trading commodities.

352

"And that I think is what concerns your father most: my family's extraordinary wealth. Your father is fearful that once you find out about it all your goals and ambitions will vanish—for why strive to do something or be somebody when everything is there for the taking? To your father, being a taker is not the Washburn way. Your father has no respect for people who go through life doing nothing on their own and living off the wherewithal of others. He considers it a waste, and in a way so do I. That's why up until now he's insisted that I insulate you from my family.

"Understand something, Jamie: what your father and I want for you is what other Washburns have had: success—and those special feelings of accomplishment that go along with it. And most of all, we don't want my family's wealth taking that from you.

"When I suggested this trip, your father was deeply concerned. He felt that when you learned about my family you might lose all interest in achieving anything on your own. I disagreed—and so did your grandfather. I felt, and I still feel, that you're mature enough and wise enough not to be taken in by my family's millions. Interestingly, not one of my siblings failed to accomplish something of importance—and without the help of our family's resources. Each is self-sufficient and successful and not in the least pretentious or lazy. But, still, your father wasn't convinced—and that's why he was so upset in the car on the way to the airport. I don't often go against his wishes, but in this case I had no choice. Otherwise, you might never know my side of the family.

"Jamie, do you understand at least a little what I'm talking about?"

"I really do, Mom. And I understand why Dad was so upset. But neither of you should worry. My trip with Grandpa this summer taught me that I can do important things. I can be like Bruno Steiner who became a friend of Glencoe's children; or like Christopher Wallace who

353

fought all his life to end racism; or like Dad who saved those lives and became an outstanding attorney; or like Grandpa who became the first black federal judge; or even like my great-great-grandfather, Isaiah, who led a mutiny before he was ten and then brought freedom to thousands. And, Mom, doing something important is what I want to do—and it has nothing to do with your family's wealth and everything to do with something I learned from Grandpa: determination."

Dee Washburn was silent for a moment, deeply impressed by her son who seemed to have grown so much taller—both physically and figuratively—while traveling with his grandfather.

"Jamie," she asked, "are you trying to tell me something?"

"Later, Mom, when we're all together."

Epilogue

Chapter 6

Shortly thereafter the four carriages turned onto a gravel driveway. At its end—some three hundred yards distant—Jamie saw a large chateau-like building. Although he had told his mother his life wouldn't change because of her family's wealth, he was astounded by what he saw.

"Mom!"

"I told you, dear. And this is what bothered your father so. He was afraid it would be more than you could handle."

"But what's this place we're coming to? Where are we? And what about that pin you're wearing?"

———

"I suppose it's about time you knew, Jamie.

"Do you remember your grandfather telling you about Bruno Steiner?"

Jamie nodded.

"And do you remember where Bruno was living at the time of his wife's death?"

"Some manor, I think?"

"That's right. Addis Manor owned by the Nadow family. And that's where we're at."

"But ...?"

"And, dear, I'm a Nadow and so are you. This pin I'm wearing is our family crest.

"And just before Bruno left for Chicago did your grandfather tell you what Bruno's father-in-law told him he and his wife were going to try to do?"

"That they were going to try to have another child?"

"*Exactly. And the Lord blessed them with a healthy baby girl. They named her Delia.*"

"*And that's you, Mom?*"

"*That's who I am, Jamie. The youngest of my generation of Nadows.*"

"*Then if Bruno were alive today he'd be my uncle?*"

"*That's right, dear. And Odile would be your aunt.*"

"*Before I was born, Mom, was Bruno a part of your family? I mean, did he ever come by the house, have Christmas dinner with you and Dad, join you on Thanksgiving—things like that?*"

"*Unfortunately, no. We never told him who I was. Tucker McConnell, the lawyer who handled his affairs, thought it would be a bad idea for him to know that I was a Nadow. You see, his heart was broken after Odile and their infant child died, and I'm told I closely resemble Odile—so Tucker felt it would only rekindle Bruno's sadness if he learned that his sister-in-law was living in Glencoe. That's also why I hardly ever wore my pin. I was afraid Bruno would recognize it.*

"*But Tucker did his best to make Bruno a part of his family. In fact, Bruno had dinner at the McConnells at least once a week and on holidays up until the time he died.*"

Dee was silent. It seemed to Jamie that she was engulfed in sadness—at least for the moment.

"*Bruno was a fine man, Jamie—good to my parents and my brothers and sisters. And a true friend of Glencoe's children. I wish things had been different. But at least we all knew him from a distance—which was better than not knowing him at all.*"

———

356

As the hansom in which Jamie and his mother rode drew near to the manor's main entrance, Jamie saw a line of his mother's brothers and sisters and their offspring waving.

"How many cousins do I have, Mom?"

"Quite a few. You'll meet them shortly."

———

It took Jamie several days to come to terms with the enormity of Addis Manor and the many members of the Nadow family. Just finding his way to the suite of rooms which he and his parents occupied was a chore. And learning the names of his five aunts and two uncles was difficult. He did, however, learn the name of the family patriarch, his Uncle Gnesh, who was in his eighties and confined to a wheelchair. But learning the names of his many cousins was next to impossible, at least on this first visit to Addis.

After he had been at Addis for a week, his mother approached him: "Jamie, I'd like to take you down to the lake in one of our wagons. I don't think you've ever driven a wagon pulled by horses, have you?"

"No, Mom. Do you think I'll be able to do it?"

"Certainly, dear. I'll send word to the stables and they'll bring one up. This time I'd like your father and your grandparents to join us. I've got something to show all of you."

———

The weather was brisk and the groom who sat next to Jamie up front had provided blankets for everyone. Jamie's grandparents had thrown a blanket over their legs, while his parents didn't seem to mind the slight chill in the air. Finally the lake's edge appeared.

"Over there," Jamie's mother pointed. "Let's go to the center."

In assent, the groom raised his hand to his hat. And then, just a few minutes later, the wagon stopped at the entrance to the "Odile and Bruno Steiner Community Center."

"Pretty impressive, Mom."

"Come, let's all go in. It's an interesting facility. For the most part, conceived by your Uncle Bruno."

———

"Well, Jamie, now that we're all here, is this a good time to discuss what you described as 'doing something important'? Because if it is, we're all willing to listen.

"And dear, although sometimes Washburn men appear to be harsh, their love for you is just as strong as the love we Washburn women have for you. And what you're about to say now certainly isn't final. People do— and you may—change your mind as often as you like.

"And something else, Jamie: your mission in life is not to please any of us. Your mission is to follow your dreams, but in a mature, serious, and determined way.

"Am I right, James?"

"I'd say so, Dee."

"Junior?"

"I agree with you both."

"Well, Jamie? Is now a good time?"

"Dad," Jamie said, "I know the Washburns have always been lawyers, starting with my great-great-grandfather, Isaiah. I also know that before the war began Skip Taylor sunk his talons in you and you fell in love with flying. And, Grandpa, you didn't much like that, did you?"

"Guess I didn't, Jamie."

"Well, Grandpa, during our travels this summer you had me taking notes wherever we went. That got me thinking about why I was taking them. Then you told me about Christopher Wallace. And when we were at Northwestern I got a copy of the article he wrote about

Bucky. Pretty powerful and, I suppose, if the times had been right he would have succeeded in getting Bucky on a professional baseball team. But the times weren't right. Still, I loved what Christopher Wallace wrote.

"And I thought to myself that that's what I want to be, a writer. Maybe I could use my notes to write a book about my travels this summer. Today a book like that might get people thinking about the horrors of racism. It might even help them fight it—something like what happened to Shorty Miller after he met Mrs. Roosevelt and then became a preacher.

"So that's what I want to do: become a writer. I know I'm young and I've got a lot to learn. But I've also got a lot to say. And I think what I have to say is important."

Jamie looked up at his father and his grandfather waiting for the sky to fall.

"I think I recall a famous quote about the pen bein' mightier than the sword," Junior Washburn said, trying to add a modicum of levity to what he knew was a difficult moment for James.

"Jamie," James Washburn said, his voice softer than usual, "you know, I've always wanted you to be an attorney?"

"I know, Dad. But that's not what I want, at least not for now." Jamie surprised himself. For once his father hadn't intimidated him.

"Writing isn't easy, Jamie; it's not a game. It's a serious undertaking. Have you really thought this through?"

"I have. In fact, I've already started the book. I've written five chapters."

"Five chapters. Is that so?" James smiled. His son, only twelve years old and plagued by asthma, had done that!

"And do you have a title?"

"*Because of what Reverend Shorty Miller said, I'm thinking of calling it 'The Lynching Waltz.' *"

James Washburn looked over at his father who for once was silent.   He turned to his wife and his mother. They too didn't say a word. Then he thought about his son who at times surprised him. Maybe by being so precocious he was in some small way compensating for his disabling lung condition.

"*Well, I can't speak for the others, Jamie, but I'm proud of you. I'm captivated by your title and excited about your book. Have at it, son. I'm sure your mother and your grandparents are as anxious as I am to read the manuscript.*"

Final Entry in Jamie's Notebook, Pages 226-228

Well, Grandpa's at it again. Yesterday, after I told everyone about the book, he cornered me, and, as best as I can remember, it went something like this:

"You and I gotta talk, boy."

[Uh-oh. Now where was he heading?]

"You got any thoughts about our travels next summer?"

"No," I replied. ["Travels next summer?" Where did he come up with that?]

"Well I do. Name 'Manzanar' mean anythin' to you?"

"No."

"How 'bout 'Chizu Fujimora'?"

"No," I replied again.

[Now I knew Grandpa was about to shift into high gear.]

"Well, we're gonna learn all about Manzanar and Chizu on our travels next summer."

"Does this have anything to do with dancing, Grandpa?" [Knowing Grandpa, I figured he was on one of his dancing kicks again.]

"Maybe. But I'll tell you one thing. It's got somethin' to do with your daddy."

"Dad?"

"Yep. But we'll get into all that next summer."

"But who's Manzanar?"

"Not who, boy. What. Manzanar's a place, a nasty one. A despicable one. Although people there made the best of it. Played a lotta baseball when they could. Even had a makeshift fishin' club when they could get away with it. Produced some heroes too."

[Now I'm really confused!]

"Grandpa, stop! I've got a book to write and you're getting me all mixed up."

"What I want, boy. Maybe even grab your interest. And I've picked a name for your second book."

[Second book? What's he talking about?]

"But I haven't finished the first one!"

"We'll call it 'One of Ten.' "

" 'One of Ten'? I don't understand."

"Manzanar was just one of those places. There were nine others. But you go 'head and write that Lynchin' Waltz book of yours. We'll wait on Chizu, Manzanar and 'One of Ten' until next summer."

———

Well, Grandpa did it again. Got my head spinning. I still think he gets a charge out of doing that.

Somehow, though, I don't mind. Seems as if I keep on learning whenever Grandpa confuses me. And maybe next summer I'll even learn enough to start a second book ... which I might just call "One of Ten."

Additional Comments by Author

Even though I've fictionalized the actions and dialogue of all of my characters, I couldn't have written *The Lynching Waltz* without the psychological backing of those real persons (sadly, all are now gone) who either became characters in this book or who inspired the creation of so many of its characters. Some of these real persons I've already described in my Lists of Characters. But there are others who deserve mentioning:

Christopher Wallace is modeled—at least to a minor extent—after a famous advertising man and Glencoe resident, Arthur Tatham;

Mildred Slotkin Gold is my fictional remake of Hannah Gordon, a Glencoe community activist;

Bruno Steiner is my version of "Otto," a Village of Glencoe employee and a friend to all of Glencoe's children;

Amy Post/Amelia Polk is my fictional depiction of the racist lady who ran Glencoe's dancing program in 1947 at the time Fortnightly was canceled;

The inspiration for General Benton B. Donald Jr. is General Benjamin O. Davis Jr., the Tuskegees first commanding officer and one of my heroes;

Charles "Skip" Taylor is my fictional rendition of Charles Alfred "Chief" Anderson of the Tuskegee Institute who taught so many of its students to fly;

Ex-Flying Tiger Lieutenant Colonel Phillip Cochran is the inspiration for Lieutenant Colonel Phillip Kelsey;

Gerrit Smith and Harriet Tubman were real persons and renowned abolitionists;

Senator Henry Clay was a real person and political leader of his time;

Beloved Central School teachers Margaret Carlson and John Sternig inspired the creation of characters Margaret Carlton and John Stern;

Allan Pinkerton was a real person and head of the Union Intelligence Service during a portion of the Civil War;

Justice Thurgood Marshall was of course the model for my character Trenton Richards; and

Dr. Warren Richman is my fictional reincarnation of Louis A. Richburg, MD, the revered Glencoe physician of my youth (who, while driving on a wintry day in my second grade year, skidded into me—luckily, only a few feet from his office).

Finally, another of my heroes, the late Eleanor Roosevelt (whose appearances, dialogue and actions portrayed in this book have been largely fictionalized), was a committed fighter for racial equality which she equated with freedom. For this reason, and for many others, I've dedicated this book to her.